QUALITY CONTROL: We strive to produce error-free books, but even with all the eyes that see the story during the production process, slips get by. So please, if you find a typo or any formatting issues, please let us know at marie@marietuhart.com so that we may correct it.

Thank you!

Decoding Emma

Marie Tuhart

Hot Blooded Press

Contents

Blurbs

♥

Asher

After my ex-wife's betrayal, trust isn't just hard, it's dangerous. At Fantasies, Inc., I keep things controlled and professional. Until Emma walks in. Brilliant, beautiful, and impossible to ignore. She's supposed to strengthen our software. Instead, she's breaking down every wall I've built.

Emma

Men have always my family name or my sister. Never me. I stopped believing in a real connection a long time ago. Working with Asher is…different. Beneath his annoying control, meant to keep everyone at arm's length, is a man as wounded as I am. And the closer we get, the harder it is to pretend we're not falling for each other.

Our past traumas define us, or so we thought. We never set out to save each other, yet here we are.

Note to Readers

♥

There is some tech speak in this book and they are not misspellings.

FI = Fantasies, Inc.

Chapter One

♥

E^{mma}

I sat in my small car in the warm spring air, trying to convince myself to get out. Why was I so nervous?

My boss, Alex Manning, called me right around sunrise and told me Fantasies, Inc. had hired Tri-O-Tech to streamline and expand the existing corporate mainframe and facilitate seamless integration of domestic and international operations. I needed to be at their facility by nine.

I'd handled projects like this before, so this would be a breeze. Or so I thought until he told me I'd be working on site. When I asked why I couldn't work from the lab at Tri-O-Tech as I'd done in the past, apparently the guy in charge of the technology department was a control freak with a dash of paranoia who insisted all work be done inhouse because they didn't want to permit the degree of access required for a project of this scope to an outsider. End of.

Which landed me, an introvert, a loner, in a place I'd never been to, working with a company I'd never heard of, in an unfamiliar environment, about to start a project on a network I knew nothing about and whose architecture I hadn't been allowed to study. And the cherry on the top of this sundae? I'd be doing this while people I didn't know were looking over my shoulder.

And one more thing: Alex hinted, no, actually insinuated that doing this job would help me get the promotion I craved.

No pressure. Sure…

I sighed.

"Come on, Emma, get your ass out of the car," I muttered as I squared my shoulders and gathered my determination. After I retrieved my backpack and hoisted the strap over my shoulder, I closed my eyes and allowed myself a moment to enjoy the warmth of the springtime sunshine.

Okay, it's now or never.

I had a flash (pun intended) of regret that I hadn't worn sunglasses when the sun reflecting off the mirrored windows of the Fantasies, Inc. building nearly fried my retinas. I could almost make out the company logo—a red heart with devil's horns—in the afterimage flashing on the inside of my eyelids. My sight finally recovered, and I started the short walk to the entrance.

I live outside of Seattle, which meant driving right into West Seattle and dealing with all the traffic. Luckily, I made it with more than enough time to gather my courage.

I stepped off to the side of the automatic doors so as not to block others from walking into the building. Some of them glanced at me and smiled, then continued on their way. They all seemed very relaxed and comfortable.

I glanced down at my black slacks and purple blouse. Yes, I was wearing sneakers, but I wanted to be comfortable. I fit right in.

Well, let's do this.

Taking a deep breath, I stepped through the revolving door.

The coolness of the building's AC wafted over my skin. The lobby was nicely decorated in neutral shades with sofas and chairs arranged in groupings around low tables. There were a few people waiting, probably meeting someone.

The large reception desk was backed by a mahogany paneled wall with the company name and logo in brushed steel mounted at its center. At the desk, a tall man in perfectly tailored slacks and what was obviously an expensive button-down shirt said something to the receptionist who smiled, said something back, and they both laughed.

Another deep breath and I made my way over to the desk. The receptionist glanced at me and made the slightest gesture, and the man turned. When our gazes locked, I stopped breathing. His green eyes were assessing, and I couldn't help feeling like I lacked something he was searching for. I adjusted my backpack and forced a smile.

"You must be Emma Palmer," the man said and extended his hand. "I'm Asher Donahue, head of Technology here at Fantasies, Inc."

"Mr. Donahue." I shook his hand and heat invaded my veins. I took in his short dark hair and the slight scruff on his face. A shaft of awareness slid through my body.

"Call me Asher."

"Emma." I pulled my hand away from his, but my gaze stayed on him. Why did he look familiar? He shouldn't.

"Our first stop is HR so we can get you set up." He gestured toward the elevators with a smile, and damned if my pulse didn't skip a beat or two. "See you later, Jessica." He started for the elevators, and I followed, assessing his broad shoulders and perfect ass, which didn't do much to calm my heart down.

I fought to keep my attention on where we were going, not how he made me feel. He scanned his badge and then pushed the button for the elevator. When it arrived, we stepped in and Asher scanned his badge again, then pressed the button for the sixth floor.

"Access to all the floors is badge-controlled." He paused. "I should've shown you the Savory café and Daily Perks, the coffee shop on the first floor."

"No worries." I kept my gaze on the elevator doors. "The company seems very security conscious." A lot of companies had tight security, but this was next level. I liked it.

"We are."

I barely stopped myself from tapping my toes as the elevator moved. I could smell Asher's cologne. A nice sandalwood and cedar scent that pleased my senses. I gasped.

"Are you okay?" he asked.

"Yes, sorry. I just remembered something I need to do." A white lie, but his question and the tone in his voice made me remember where I'd seen him before. It was at a party I attended several months ago with the douchebag who ditched me the minute we got there.

I ended up hiding in a corner, trying to figure out how to escape the party and make my way home when a couple of women nearby started talking. It didn't take long for their conversation to morph into the typical mean girl sniping. I intended to ignore it—really I did—until I heard douchebag's name and where did he find such a drabu-lous, ordinary plus one. This led to an in-depth analysis of my wardrobe. They were sure I bought my outfit at some second-rate thrift shop. But, hey, thrifting could be great if I had any fashion sense. No, in their opinion, I was completely lacking. Then came the hair critique. The stylist who did my cut and color was incompetent at best, not even worth one star on Yelp. And last but never least... Who taught me how to use makeup, and I definitely didn't take care of my skin because I looked like I was a hundred years old. Yeah, the douchebag was probably just looking to get laid.

Well, thank you very much. Not.

The only truth in their review? Douchenozzle very like-ly was looking to just get laid. What else was new? Another guy out for what he thought he was owed after dinner and a date. I was an object rather than a person.

After the plastics left in search of other victims, I pulled out my phone and tapped the rideshare app. I was paying more attention to my phone rather than where I was walk-ing and hit what turned out to be a wall of pecs and abs that belonged to a drop-dead handsome man.

Asher.

His hands on my shoulders kept me from landing on my butt, his touch firm and gentle at the same time. His head was canted just off center, and his brow creased with concern as he asked if I was okay. His voice was a perfect match to his looks—a little rough, deep, and all kinds of warm, like brandy on a cold day.

I managed to convince him I was fine, and just my luck, before either of us could say anything more, a woman sidled up to him, whispered something in his ear, and drew him away. I never figured out if it took a second or minutes before my phone vibrated in my hand to let me know my ride had arrived.

I returned to the real world when the elevator doors opened to a tastefully decorated reception area. This was definitely not the usual stark, cold utilitarian office décor. Soft carpeting, windows for natural light, yet kept the heat out. Some open area in the center and separate offices along two of the outside walls.

"Good morning, Mr. Donahue," the blonde woman behind the desk said.

"Good morning, Sarah. Miles is expecting us."

"He is." She flashed a wide smile. "Please go right in."

Asher nodded and turned to me. "Right this way." He gestured for me to proceed him. At the end of what was a short hallway, there was a door with the name Miles Holt, Director of Human Resources, on it.

Heat flashed over my skin as Asher brushed my arm to knock on the door. He didn't wait for an invitation before he opened it.

"Morning, Miles." Asher guided me into the office. "This is Emma Palmer. She'll be working with me to integrate domestic and international operations."

The man sitting behind the desk stood. Tailored slacks, open neck of his button-down shirt, both in neutral colors. So business casual seemed to be the style here. His brown hair was cut short; his green eyes twinkled, and his smile reached his eyes as he extended his hand.

"Ms. Palmer, we're glad you're here." We shook hands.

Warm handshake and a feeling of genuine welcome.

"Mr. Holt."

"Please, Miles. Let's sit down." He gestured to what appeared to be a cherry conference table big enough to seat at least ten people. That's when I realized his office was huge. Two sofas and a center coffee table with an arrangement of what looked like fresh flowers, end tables at both sofas, brass lamps, all in all, understated elegance. If I had to guess, the whole room ran at least one-third the length of the entire floor. Miles grabbed an envelope and file folder off his desk, cherry in the style that matched the conference table.

The men waited until I sat before they took their seats. I was used to the other coders in my office treating me like one of the guys. I wasn't sure how I felt about being given this special attention.

"Water, coffee?" Miles asked.

"I'm fine." Was I? My skin felt tight, and my heart didn't seem to want to work right. I took a deep breath. The last thing I needed was to have a panic attack, especially when there was no reason to have one. The last thing I wanted right then was for Asher to figure out I was the torn apart girl he'd almost rescued all those months ago. Thankfully, he didn't seem to recognize me, and it was better that way.

"All right. I have an NDA for you to sign before you can start work." Miles opened the file folder and pulled out a sheet of paper.

"NDA?" Of course. They wanted to protect any information I learned about them. So why was I surprised?

Asher shifted next to me, and my attention focused on him.

"Because of the scope of this project and in the interest of expediency and to avoid any roadblocks, you'll have sysadmin permissions globally. You will have access to private employee information as well as privileged research and development information. We're aware that there is very little likelihood it will be necessary for you to access such information, even so, we require the NDA." Asher crossed his arms over his chest.

He was right to be cautious. Any leak of proprietary information could destroy a company.

"Actually," Asher said. "We also have some special app requests, which, we're given to understand, is another of your strengths. We're hoping you'll be willing to work on that as well. It was part of the agreement with Tri-O-Tech but strictly subject to your acceptance."

"I can do that." It would've been nice for Alex to tell me this.

Miles leaned forward and laced his fingers over the folder in front of him. "I'm assuming you researched us before coming here?"

"I wasn't given time. My boss called me around six-thirty this morning and told me to be here by nine." I glanced at Asher and back to Miles. "I was told the project was network streamlining and integration of domestic and international operations." What had Alex gotten me into? I thought back to the name: Fantasies, Inc. I'd assumed they were a gaming company.

Miles sat back in his chair and glanced at Asher. By his expression, I was pretty sure some silent message had passed between them.

Asher turned his chair toward me, one arm on the table, the other on the chair arm, his posture exuding an air of casual arrogance. "If you don't want to sign, you can leave. And thank you for taking the time to meet with us."

Excuse me?

I stiffened, and my eyes widened. What was his problem? "May I see the NDA and contract, please?" Good. My tone was as cold as the brick in my stomach. I held my hand out, relieved to see it wasn't shaking.

Miles handed it to me, and I began reading. Pretty standard NDA and contract. I wouldn't discuss in any detail what I was doing with anyone outside the company. I wouldn't disclose the inner workings of Fantasies, Inc. I would be an independent contractor with Fantasies, Inc., and they would be paying me directly, not through my employer.

Which immediately raised the question: What was Tri-O-Tech getting out of this? The job was expected to last a month but could be extended if needed. Oh, here was the kicker. I would be working with the head of IT, which meant Asher, almost exclusively.

I blew out a breath and signed the NDA, then initialed each page of the contract, signed it, and pushed both documents across the desk to Miles.

"Thank you." He slid them into the file folder and emptied the contents of the envelope that had been under the folder onto the table. "I want to make you aware that your pay is the same, and Tri-O-Tech is being paid a stipend for you being on loan to us."

I nodded and stared at the items on the desk. A key card with my most recent picture from Tri-O-Tech—but how did they get it—what looked like a credit card, and a lanyard.

"This is your key card. It will open the parking gates for you. The parking garage next door is for employees. It will also work in the elevators and if you need to come into the building or get out of the building outside of business hours."

Oh yes, they were very security conscious, not unusual with companies, but this was a new level. What the heck did Fantasies, Inc. do?

"This card allows you to get food in the café or the coffee shop. It's a perk of working here. Both are on the ground floor, and there's an employee lounge on the second floor."

"I'll take you on the grand tour when we get done here," Asher commented.

I took the cards from Miles. "I'm assuming you got this picture from my boss?"

"Yes, he sent it to me shortly after we called him." He pushed the lanyard across the desk. "This is for the cards. Most employees find it easier than trying to search for them."

Miles gathered the paperwork and dropped it on his desk.

"I'm glad you're staying," Asher whispered.

"Why?" What was it about him that got to me so easily? Even the night of the party, I'd been drawn to him.

"Because I can't wait to work with you."

His expression was a mixture of interest and excitement. Okay, maybe this wouldn't be so bad after all.

Chapter Two

♥

Asher

Why the hell was I flirting with Emma? I couldn't seem to help myself, and there was no company rule about dating another employee. Hell, look at Marcus and Cassie. But this was new for me. We would be working together, and she reported to me, but we both reported to the president, John Boyd.

Her dark hair was gathered and pinned up, and I wondered what would happen if I plucked those uncomfortable looking clips from her hair and let it fall down her back. I'd probably get slapped and lose any chance of any kind of relationship with her, not to mention Miles and John would probably have my family jewels in a vise if Emma walked away.

Whoa. Mind out of the gutter, at least for now. I just met the woman, and today was the first time I'd spoken more than four words to her. Well, that's not exactly true. I met her at some party a few months ago.

Did she remember? She ran into me, literally. With that deer in the headlights look on her face, I had asked her if she was okay, but I got pulled away before I got anything more than a nod. I felt the same invisible pull to her then as I did now. It was more than her looks. Yes, she was a beautiful woman, but she was also very quiet—some would say shy. Is that what drew me to her? It did surprise me she hadn't researched Fantasies, Inc. I wondered what type of company she thought we were. She was going to have a rude awakening when we worked on the project together.

Together. My gut clenched. Like any developer, I hated having anyone else mess with my work. I wasn't super happy at first with having someone else here, but I was coming around to it. I wanted to know why I couldn't get her app to work with mine. It should have been an easy job. But after a few weeks of trying to get the new software and my bridge app to handshake with no results, I had to admit defeat.

Not a good feeling.

Miles put the employment contract in front of Emma. I'd read the contract; it was pretty standard. I watched her as she read it over. Every so often, she'd hesitate, then continue, turning each page face down and placing it on the table, her expression neutral, controlled. Then her brow furrowed just the slightest, and when she glanced at me I knew she'd reached the part that specified she would be working with me exclusively.

As she read the last two pages, the NDA, her hazel eyes widened and she tilted her head as she apparently read and reread the first page, then read the last lines on the second page. The momentary surprise gave way to the neutral expression as she picked up the pages, initialed each one, signed both documents in the appropriate places, then neatly stacked the pages and handed them to Miles.

"Thank you." He quickly signed as a witness and placed the contract and NDA in the folder. "If you have no questions, we're all set," Miles said. "If you have any issues with any employee"—Miles glanced at me—"come see me, and I'll take care of it."

"Thank you."

I pushed back my chair and stood.

Emma followed suit.

"Shall I show you to your new work area?"

"That's fine."

"Asher, a minute please," Miles said.

"I'll wait outside." Emma slipped out the door, and I turned to Miles.

"What's up?"

"Do I need to remind you to keep your head on straight?"

What the...

"How..." I clamped my mouth shut.

"I can see the way you're watching her. Like a nice juicy steak on Friday nights at Whistle Stop when you've been eating chicken all week."

I laughed. "I promise. I'm all about consent."

"Keep the lust out of the office."

"Sure. Like Cassie and Marcus did?"

"Please." Miles threw his hand up. "We all knew those two would eventually end up together. But Emma is a contractor and not technically an employee of Fantasies, Inc."

"Consent and, if need be, a contract written up between us." How would Emma take to a contract about a relationship between us? Why was Miles already going there? Emma and I didn't even know each other...yet.

"Good." Miles shook his head and moved back to his desk.

I left the room and found Emma standing at the window looking out at the Puget Sound. That was another nice thing about the building, the panorama of the Sound. "Enjoying the view?"

Emma jumped. "It's nice."

"Your workspace has a nice grouping of windows to look out." I gestured for her to precede me to the elevator. I had a feeling she'd enjoy her new workspace. I would, too, but for the view of her.

Slow down, dude. You're getting way ahead of yourself.

"We're on the eleventh floor." I tapped my card and pressed the button. "Or do you want the grand tour first?"

"Why don't you tell me about the other floors?"

I regarded her for a moment, then started in. "Floor two is the employee lounge area, floors three and four are storage. Five is Customer Service. Six is HR. Seven through nine R&D. Ten and eleven Technology. Twelve and fourteen Finance. Fifteen and sixteen Operations. The C-suite seventeen."

"That's a lot."

"That's just this building. We own the two buildings across the street as well." The doors opened, and when I tapped Emma's shoulder, she jumped. I took a half step away to give her some space. Did I startle her? Or was it something else? I needed to be more careful. The last thing I wanted was for her to be uneasy.

"This way."

This part of the office was pretty much an open air set-up. Most of the people here liked it that way. It was easier for them to collaborate.

I gestured to the right and down to the end of the hall. "This is where we'll be working." I scanned my badge and opened the door.

She took a step inside and stopped. "Oh goodness."

My lips twitched. I had this office space especially configured for the two of us with three long tables each with three large monitors and a docking station for laptops, and a large conference table to the side.

In the corner opposite the work area, there were a couple of sofas, tables, each with four chairs, and a small fridge and microwave. I wanted us to be as comfortable as possible.

"The servers and routers are in the next room. We're completely wireless, by the way."

She looked like she'd found some kind of hidden treasure. "So much room. I was expecting a small office. Will there be more people in the room?"

"Not usually. I like to spread out when I'm working, and because parts of this project will require modifying code, it'll be nice to have more than one screen to work on, and sometimes, two or three computers are required if we have to run complex debuggers."

"True." She moved farther into the room.

"Let's sit down, and we can discuss how we want to work together."

I gestured to the round conference table.

She moved to a chair and sat, placing her backpack next to her on the floor. I took the seat across from her so I could see her face. Her gaze darted around the room, everywhere but at me.

"Let's start with working hours."

"Don't tell me you keep normal hours?" There was humor in her voice.

"Most of the time." I kept my gaze on her face. "My usual working hours are seven to four-thirty most days. Will that work for you?"

Finally, her gaze met mine, her expression serious. "I guess."

"Guess?"

She shrugged. "I don't really have set hours at Tri-O Tech. Sometimes, I work during the day; other times, I work into the night and start late the next day. It depends on the project."

"I see." I understood. Sometimes, I'd stay late, but not a lot. "It's important to have firm working hours. The company prefers it that way."

Another shrug. "I can work with those hours."

I nodded. "Your keycard has twenty-four-seven access, but you should be aware that HR gets a weekly report. If it's shown you're in the building more than nine hours a day, they'll want an explanation."

"How would they...oh, the elevators?"

"Yes, and for security reasons. That's why you need to scan."

"As you know, the café on the first floor has a seating area if you want to sit there to eat. It's open nine until three. The coffee shop is open six to six. And the other card is the way you get your food."

"Miles said that. I've never had a company pay for food."

I grinned. "John Boyd, our president, feels employees work better when they don't have to worry about paying for food and drinks. It's a perk a lot of us like." I put my hand on the table. "That's not to say staff don't visit local restaurants as well."

Emma nodded, her gaze apparently focused on my hand. The urge to reach out, to touch her, startled me. I was reacting to Emma in a way that surprised me. Right now, I wanted to make her comfortable with me. We had a job to do, first and foremost.

"I mentioned the second floor is the employee lounge area.

"The entire floor?"

"Yes. There are sitting areas, some vending machines, plus lots of games to play."

"Games?"

"Foosball, a pool table, puzzles, and lots of table games."

"Interesting."

"It helps with productivity. We also don't have set lunch times. Sometimes, taking extra time playing games can help stimulate ideas." I paused. "Did you drive in today?" I was curious how far her place was from the office.

"Yes. I live in Memorial. Not much in the way of public transportation."

"True. I live in Zenith, just a little bit south of you." Maybe once she was more comfortable, I'd ask her to commute with me. It would be nice to have company and save on gas. Right. That's the reason. Wanting to get to know her better had nothing to do with it.

"That's a nice area."

I nodded. It was almost ten-thirty. "Did you park in the garage?" They had temporary parking spots for vendors and visitors.

"Yes, in visitor parking. Do I need to move?"

"You'll be fine for today, but tomorrow, park on one of the other floors. Be sure to pick up your parking pass before you leave today." I stood. Perfect time for a pause and coffee, and maybe a chance to talk about things other than work. "I don't know about you, but I could use some coffee and a snack. Why don't we go downstairs, and I can show you the café and coffee shop area."

Emma didn't answer for a moment, and I thought she was about to decline and insist we get to work.

"Sounds good." *Yes!* No way was I going to reveal any reaction other than calm and professional.

She slipped the lanyard with her keycards over her head and stood. "I could use some food. I was a little rushed this morning."

"Let's do it."

In the elevator, I risked a couple of glances at Emma. She kept her gaze locked on the elevator doors. Her hands were in her pants pockets, and her shoulders weren't as hunched and tight as when she first arrived. Progress.

When the doors slid open at the first floor, there were more people in the main area than had been earlier. Even with the number of people in the area, the sound of conversation was muted as staff and visitors made their way to elevators, the café and coffee shop, or to the various meeting areas.

"It's a busy place," Emma commented.

"Yes. Since it's on the first floor, it's open to the public, plus employees from our other two buildings come over here." As I guided her toward Daily Perks, I noticed that she seemed to shrink into herself, just as she had when I first saw her at the party all those months ago. Did crowds bug her?

We got in line, and when we arrived at the front, Amelia smiled. "Hi, and welcome to Daily Perks. Asher, your usual?"

"Yes, please. Emma, what would you like?"

She looked startled that I'd asked her. There it was again, now maybe more evident. That look of discomfort, like she wasn't used to being noticed.

"A vanilla latte and a blueberry muffin, please." Her voice was soft.

"You got it." Amelia glanced between me and Emma.

I almost laughed at Amelia's inquisitive glance. "Amelia, this is Emma; she's on contract here. Emma, Amelia. She runs Daily Perks."

"Cute name," Emma said.

"I like it. Welcome to the company, Emma." Amelia said, placed my black coffee on the counter in front of us and then a blueberry muffin, a chocolate donut, and a vanilla scone.

I scanned my card as Emma's latte was set on the counter.

"Should I scan mine?" Emma asked quietly.

"I've got it."

She smiled, and I smiled back as I handed her the latte and food, then picked up mine. "Do you want to sit down here or go up to the employee lounge?"

"Which is quieter?" She wasn't anxious exactly, but she definitely wasn't comfortable being around this large group of people.

"This time of day? The lounge."

"There, please."

"Okay." What was with Emma? She seemed nervous and out of sorts, a mystery I was becoming more and more determined to solve. Once on the second floor, I guided her down the hall to one of the quieter areas. As soon as the door to the employee lounge closed, her—was it anxiety or just shyness?—disappeared as she sat in one of the chairs at a small table.

I sat and put my drink, food, and napkins on the table. Emma tore open the paper bag holding her muffin, her demeanor now a bit more relaxed.

Had she been like this at the party? It definitely seemed that way. Did she remember me? She gave no indication that she did.

I've thought about that night quite a bit in the months since. I'd been invited by a friend and had only intended to make an appearance and leave until I saw Emma standing alone, looking a little lost and more than a little uncomfortable. Not unusual, especially at parties where they didn't know anyone.

She'd radiated quiet elegance and style, even within the frenetic atmosphere created by a group of high intensity professionals letting off steam. I made my way over to talk to her, and as I got closer, she turned and bumped into me before I could get a word out. I barely had a chance to make sure she was okay when a friend tugged me away.

By the time I managed to detach myself from my friend, Emma was gone. I was disappointed, but that short encounter stayed with me. Now I understood better why she bolted.

In Daily Perks, she'd had the same look on her face as the night of the party: faraway and closed off, even anxious. As we sat in the quiet of the lounge, drank our coffee, and ate our pastries, her body appeared relaxed, but her gaze remained fixed on the table.

This woman was intriguing. Classy, elegant, shy, intelligent, a puzzle. And I never could resist solving a puzzle.

Chapter Three

♥

Emma

I stared at the table, trying to calm my nerves. I would need to get used to being around so many people. I'd managed to keep my anxiety under control at Tri-O-Tech, but it wasn't as big as Fantasies, Inc. Even with the tricks I used to keep from freezing up in large groups, I could feel myself beginning to shut down as we made our way from the elevator to Daily Perks. By the time we got the pastries and coffee, I must've looked like a deer in the headlights when Asher suggested we head to the employee lounge. As soon as the door closed, the relief was almost instantaneous. A couple of deep breaths, and I could feel myself begin to decompress.

The pastries and coffee were delicious, but then, as I finished the last bits, I realized Asher had been unusually quiet.

I'm so used to being alone, I'd almost forgotten I was with anyone. I glanced up to find him watching me. I could feel the heat from the blush move from my chest to my cheeks. I blinked several times as I tried to recover from the embarrassment.

"Sorry, I was lost in thought. You know, onboarding, the software issues…"

"It's fine. Actually, it's refreshing to be with someone who doesn't have to fill the silence with chatter." He flashed a grin.

I couldn't help but smile back. Okay, maybe this wasn't as bad as my mind had made it out to be. The muffin was long gone, and my latte was almost empty. "Shall we get to work?"

"Sure." He stood, grabbed his food wrapper and cup. I did the same, and after disposing of them, we made our way back to the eleventh floor.

As soon as we exited the elevator, I saw my opportunity. "I'll be right there," I said, motioning to the ladies' room.

Asher nodded and continued down the hall. I ducked inside and stopped just inside the door. This was the bathroom? Marble, brass, scrolled tilework. There was a separate area with a vanity where baskets had been stuffed with tissues, napkins, and lotions. The brightly lit mirror over the vanity was perfect for detailed repair of makeup and hair. Elegant upholstered chairs finished off the space.

I turned and made my way into the main part. Six sinks and eight stalls, more marble, and brass, and each stall was designed for maximum privacy. I walked up to the closest sink and washed my hands while staring at my reflection in the mirror.

My eyes were set a little too wide, my features too closed off. I closed my eyes and did some deep breathing exercises that helped ease the feeling of being trapped, powerless, but the tension continued flowing through my body.

I needed to get used to being around a lot of people for this job. Any future promotion depended on that. Maybe it was time to see a therapist about my anxiety.

I shuddered at the memory. I'd tried therapists. Two of them. I hadn't been able to open up to either of them. Instead, I worked alone more and more. I wasn't kidding when I told Asher I worked late. It meant fewer people to interact with, less chance of betrayal.

Would I ever be normal? That was a question I asked myself every day. My trust had been broken too often, and I didn't know how to overcome that.

Ugh. I shook my head and dried my hands. Take it one day at a time; that's all I could do.

Break's over, Emma. Time to jump into the deep end of the pool.

Deep breath in and brushing off an invisible crumb from my slacks, I left the ladies' room and made my way down the hall to the office that was my new place of work.

Office? I chuckled. More like several offices combined. I walked into the room, and Asher glanced up from the computer screen.

"The docking station is for your laptop if you want to connect it."

"Thank you." I grabbed my backpack and slipped into the chair.

"Here are your login credentials. There are two. One is the secure guest login to use for your laptop. The username for your laptop has access to the internet, but no access to the intranet, our internal network. The second is for your workstation here. As I said before, you will have full access from your workstation." He slid a sheet of paper over to me.

"Thanks." After pulling out my laptop, coffee cup, lined pad, and two stress fidgets and arranging everything on the table, I logged on to the guest network. It didn't take long to confirm what Asher had told me. Just for fun, I tried to access the company network from the internet access on the laptop. Nope. I risked a glance at Asher.

"Everybody tries it at least once, Emma." A quick glance and a wink.

Busted, but I had to try.

I connected my laptop to one of my screens then woke my workstation.

Now up and running, I took some time to familiarize myself with how Fantasies, Inc. was set up. I also made a mental note to do some research on exactly what Fantasies, Inc. was about.

Asher had set me up on the message app and assigned me an email. No messages yet, and I decided to deal with my email later.

There was nothing complicated about the subnets. I located various departments, then the programs, folders and files for each one. Each subnet had a locked permissions folder. My creds opened it. There were two documents. The first listed individual and group permissions for read, write, and execute functions, the required conditions for access spelled out in exacting detail. The second document was a list of everyone in that department and which permissions they had. No guesswork here.

I had no idea how long I'd been exploring until I flexed my neck and checked the clock on the monitor. Neither of us had spoken since we sat down. Two hours felt like two minutes. If Asher wasn't going to break the silence...

"I like having the extra monitors. High def?"

Asher grinned. "8k resolution, 32 inch. I aim to please." He didn't look away from his screen.

"I've been taking a walk around the network. Great setup. That's going to make the streamlining a lot easier."

"I'm glad you approve."

Oooookaaaaay...

"Any chance you've diagramed the architecture, or have you kept it locked in your head?" I could play the game too. I turned, folded my hands in my lap, and stayed silent. I even managed to keep my feet still.

He looked up from some notes, tapped the trackpad, then rolled his chair closer and leaned forward, elbows on his knees.

"Until recently, the various departments of Fantasies Inc. have functioned with a convoluted web of different programs. But the company has grown exponentially, and the increasing incidence of compatibility issues is slowing everything down. We've spent the last year redesigning each department's systems and giving them dedicated space on the mainframe, the subnets. Now we need to overlay the project with a really good bridge that connects them seamlessly but also allows them autonomy. Streamlining and integration. I discovered you're an expert at designing specialized apps, and we've had some requests that could utilize that expertise."

"In addition to the—now quoting from the tasking section in the contract—'expansion and streamlining of the network to merge the domestic and international operations and facilitate the integration', what else are you trying to accomplish?" Asher's attitude aside, I was starting to feel like I was in my element.

"First and foremost, obviously, we need seamless communication. But can we do it with the current configuration?"

"I can better answer that question once I've familiarized myself with"—I raised my hand and twirled it in a circular motion—"all of this, everything. First I need to look at the maps of your architecture."

"As you wish." He turned back to his keyboard, opened a command line, and paused. "Watch your center monitor." Then he typed a couple of commands and slid his finger across the trackpad. "In the upper right hand corner."

"Thanks. I do have one more question that's sort of off topic."

He raised his eyebrows along with a quick tilt of his head.

"The company motto. *Make your dreams a reality*?"

"Oh, yeah. I forgot you don't know anything about the company. Maybe I should explain what we do first."

"I'd like that." I turned my chair toward him, and our knees bumped. A jolt went through my body at the touch. What was wrong with me?

Asher looked unaffected and totally relaxed. The mischief in his gaze gave him away. "Fantasies, Inc. is a company that…just like the name says, fulfills people's fantasies."

"Fantasies? Like wanting to be a vampire or werewolf?" He laughed.

"I like paranormal fiction."

"What I mean is sensual fantasies."

"Oh." I felt a flush creeping up my neck to my face. Sexual fantasies. That was new.

"Nothing illegal."

"I hope not."

Does Tri-O-Tech have any idea what this company is about?

I glanced at Asher, and he was watching me, curious with just a hint of concern.

"Let's start with the customer service department. Cassie Adams is in charge of it. She and her team work with focus groups, compliments, suggestions, and any complaints."

"You get complaints?" *Really?*

"Occasionally, if something doesn't go as the client expects or if something isn't quite right. The complaints are few and far between, which is a good thing."

I tilted my head. Made sense. "What are you trying to accomplish with the program?"

"As much automation as we can. Right now, Cassie and her team do manual reports, and I want to automate them."

"I'm surprised things aren't more automated."

"Well, the company kind of took off before we could get a lot in place." Asher shifted in his seat. "There were only three of us when we started this gig." He was justifiably proud.

"How long ago was that?"

"Five years ago. Most of us have been here since the company started."

I thought back to five years ago. So many things had been happening in the world at that time. Government upheaval, political crisis, new laws. "The Sexual Freedom Act," I whispered.

"Yep. With the passage of that act, companies like ours became legal."

"The company is regulated, isn't it?"

"Yes, we do have regulations—a lot of them—that we have to follow. Inspections once a year, and regular reports we have to submit. So far, we've had no issues."

"Sounds like you're expecting something to go wrong?"

A company built on facilitating sexual fantasies. This project was going to be a lot more than interesting. My dry spell had been going on for a while. I wonder...

He rubbed his forehead. "No. Getting the reports together takes more and more time each year. I want to cut it in half or more."

"I can do that."

"*We* can do that."

I couldn't suppress a smile. Developers were so protective of their work. Helicopter parents had nothing on us. When integration or modification of applications, especially those I'd built, was necessary to achieve or enhance compatibility, I wanted to be the one to do it.

"What is the next department?"

"Research and Development, aka R&D. Marcus DeLuca's domain."

"I'm almost afraid to ask." I wasn't really, but my imagination was going wild.

Asher's laughter sent shivers of anticipation up and down my spine.

"You name it, Marcus will try to make it happen. He and his group develop all the things in the name of pleasure."

My curiosity was getting the better of me. "What else could there be besides sex toys?"

"So much more." Asher slid his chair back. "Let's go on a little tour."

"Tour?"

"Yes. It's easier to show you what R&D does rather than try to tell you."

He picked up the phone. I couldn't miss his sense of anticipation. "Hey, Marcus. I'm going to bring the developer I'm working with down and show her what you do...The one on loan for the mainframe project." Asher nodded. "Thanks." He glanced at me. Was that a twinkle in his eyes? "All set, let's go."

I stood. What could I say? In order to make a project of this scope run smoothly, I really needed to understand how each department functioned. Compatibility across platforms could be achieved only if we had a thorough understanding of each department's requirements individually and those requirements' impact on the functionality of the whole. Obvious on the surface, complex throughout.

As I pushed my chair under the desk, I had a thought that stopped me cold.

Four weeks to complete this project? Not likely.

As I'd done with every previous project, I refused to think about the time frame set by the bean counters then glanced at my laptop and told my internal nanny to go take a break elsewhere.

"The door automatically locks when we leave. Only your keycard, mine, my second in command Ben, and security are allowed in. R&D takes up three floors."

I nodded. At least I didn't have to pack up. He pressed the call button. "We'll start on the seventh floor. Marcus is going to meet us there."

"Okay." My skin tingled with… Excitement? Apprehension? Anticipation? All three?

As the elevator doors opened on the seventh floor, a man stood there. Was this Marcus? His green eyes sparkled; his grin was infectious, and his black hair was slicked back. I stepped out of the elevator, and Asher followed.

"Emma, this is Marcus DeLuca, head of R&D." *Question answered.* "Marcus, Emma Palmer, on loan from Tri-O-Tech for the mainframe project and to help solve any integration issues"

I noticed Asher was a little bit taller than Marcus. I wasn't short, but these men had several inches on me.

"Welcome to R&D, Emma," he said, extending his hand.

I shook his hand and managed to maintain eye contact even as my first instinct was to look away. "Thank you, Mr. DeLuca."

"Marcus."

"You'll find we're pretty informal," Asher said.

I nodded.

"Shall we?" Marcus swept his hand out, indicating a door secured with an electronic lock across from the elevators.

"How long have you been in charge of R&D?"

"A year and a half." Marcus reached around me to swipe his badge and hold open the door. "R&D is a fairly new department."

I considered myself an informed person, but when I stepped into the room... I tried to keep my expression neutral, professional. I was pretty sure I wasn't exactly bug-eyed, and I managed to keep my mouth closed, but I'd never seen anything like this. There were tables covered with various toys, definitely of the adult variety. I recognized a few, but I had no idea what a lot of other items were.

"You look shocked," Marcus said. *That about covers it.*

"Emma didn't know what kind of company we were until a few minutes ago," Asher said. He put his hand on my arm. "Are you okay?"

"I'm...fine." The words came out softly. I'd never seen so many sex items in my life. I wasn't a prude, but this was... I kept coming back to the phrase 'unlike anything I'd ever seen'. Was it over the top? Probably not, considering what the company did. I took a deep breath, willing myself not to blush.

"This is our demo room. By that, I mean we have one of everything currently being tested available for use." Marcus extended his arm in a gesture indicating the entire room. "Many of our employees are more than willing to beta test for us."

I felt heat bloom from my center throughout my entire body at Marcus's words. Did I want to be one of those employees?

"Shall we check it out?" Asher tightened his hold on my arm.

"Sure. Why not?" I took a deep breath, trying to steady my heart.

We stopped at the first row of tables.

"Massage oils?" That was a little surprising to me. What did oils typically used for massage have to do with sex?

"Lots of different ones," Marcus commented. A woman with curly red hair motioned for Marcus. "Be right back," he said, then walked over to talk to her.

"Think about coming home after a long day at the computer, and your lover is waiting, candles lit, the massage table waiting for you," Asher said. "Soft music is playing. Your lover undresses you and helps you onto the massage table and has you lay on your stomach."

At some point, he had released my arm and now maintained a respectful distance, making me feel safe even as his words swathed me in sensations. I inhaled a shaky breath.

"I start at your temples. Stroking in a curricular motion, clockwise and then counter clockwise, until I see some of the tension leaving your body." Asher's voice was a husky whisper.

I fought against squirming. My body was already reacting to his words. My skin heated, my pussy throbbed.

"I move my hands to your neck, working my thumbs from the base of your neck down your spine. Up and down, over your neck and head. The tension slowly drains out of you."

His words ratcheted up my tension in other ways.

"Next, while keeping one hand on your perfect skin, I pick up the warmed bottle of vanilla oil." He opened the bottle and leaned in to hold it under my nose. "I pour a small amount onto the curve of your back."

The sweet, rich, and syrupy smell hit my senses. I wanted to sink into the scent.

"I dip my fingers into the oil and spread it over your back as I begin to massage your shoulders, working out all the knots, then I work out from your spine. With each movement of my hands, your body sinks more and more into the table."

I had to remind myself to breathe. My mind felt like it was shorting out; I could barely think. If I didn't stop this fantasy, I'd end up a puddle on the floor at his feet.

"I get it. You don't have to continue." I tried to keep my voice steady and cool, but my skin was on fire, and my body felt more alive than it had ever been.

Professional, Emma. Pull yourself together.

Asher chuckled. "See how massage oils can be fantasy-fulfilling?"

Oh, boy, did I.

Was he trying to arouse me?

My body's reaction to his 'fantasy' felt almost like some sort of betrayal. My ire rose in response to my lack of control, but I pushed it away. There was no reason to get into it with him now. But if something similar happened again, we'd have to talk about boundaries.

The ringing of a phone made me jump.

"Sorry." Marcus, thank goodness, was at the other end of the table and probably hadn't heard Asher's words.

Marcus pulled out his cell phone as I moved on to the next table.

"Asher, can you continue the tour? I have an issue in the lab."

"Sure. Go ahead."

"It was great to meet you, Emma."

Before I could say anything, Marcus left. I took a deep breath. "I never knew there were so many dildos."

"That's one word. We use insertables." He waved his hand at the first table. "Here we have ones that will work for men and women."

I looked the table over. There were ribbed devices, metal ones, glass ones, ones with small hand pumps. I moved to the next table.

"This one is for women," Asher commented.

Goodness. How sheltered was I? I had a vibrator, but that was about it. There were round balls you could insert, a massage wand with attachments, nipple clamps, and a bunch of other items.

Mind. Blown.

My body felt too tight. "I think I've had enough," I whispered. I needed a cold shower—or at least a cold drink.

"Are you sure? There's a lot more to explore." His eyes twinkled, and his eyebrows rose.

Cut the innocent act, buddy. You know exactly what you're doing to me.

"I'm sure." I spun around and headed for the door.

Chapter Four

♥

A sher

I watched Emma walk toward the door. Her color had been high since the minute we walked into the room. It became even higher as I described using the massage oil on her. I couldn't help myself and didn't even try.

She hadn't looked uncomfortable, but she wasn't relaxed either. As I talked to her, her breathing became choppy, and I didn't miss the way she shifted from foot to foot. Oh, she tried to hide it.

Once back in our office, she went directly to her computer. "I'm sorry if I embarrassed you. I wanted you to understand that everyone has fantasies, and that's not a bad thing. We help people relax and live their genuine lives. That's a good thing." I took the chair next to her. I didn't want her to feel shy around me.

"You didn't." She wouldn't look at me.

"Emma, there is one thing you should know. A basic tenet at Fantasies, Inc. is consent. It's a hard line none of us will cross, me included. So, if anything I say or do bothers you, tell me, and I'll stop."

Her head turned. She glanced at me before dropping her gaze to the floor. "I'm fine. This gives me enough to get started." She turned back to her computer.

I let out a breath.

Don't push.

This was only her first day, and she needed time. I had to admit the massage thing turned me on, and I wanted to show Emma how pleasurable it could be. There were so many things I wanted to show her.

Patience was going to become my new motto.

Chapter Five

♥

E^{mma}

I walked into my small home that night, more tired than after pulling an all-nighter to fix a coding issue. "I need a shower," I mumbled. A cold one. My skin felt tight, and I was all worked up. After dropping my backpack by the front door, I locked up and made my way into the bedroom.

In the bathroom, I turned the water on, then stripped. I shivered at the coolness of the water until it warmed up, then let the water flow over me while I tried to make sense of my day.

Note to self: Do not go to R&D with Asher.

I'd spent the afternoon trying to work on merging code, but I could barely concentrate with Asher in the same room. Not just in the same room, but no more than three feet away.

All I heard was Asher's voice as he talked about giving a massage. My fingers trailed down between my breasts to my mound. I parted my labia and teased my clit. A sigh escaped my lips.

I lifted my leg onto the small ledge in the shower and allowed my fingers to slide from my clit and into my pussy. I turned my face up to the spray as I moved my fingers.

In my mind, I heard Asher's voice telling me how he'd caress my skin. "Oh yes," I whispered. "More Asher." It was his fingers caressing my pussy, bringing me to climax.

"Asher," I cried out his name.

I took a shaky step back. Oh, damn that was good, but not good to be fantasizing about the man I'm working with. I lowered my leg and my head, breathing hard and praying I'd relieved some of the sexual frustration. I turned off the water and stepped out.

My nerves tingled as I dried off and slipped on a lounging outfit. I stared at myself in the mirror.

Was that me? My eyes were bright, my skin glowing. I quickly brushed my hair, before making my way to the kitchen. I needed a glass of wine.

The delicious scent of beef filled my senses. Thank goodness I'd put beef stew in the slow cooker before I went to work. Grabbing the bottle of wine out of my fridge, I poured a glass and took a seat in the family room.

My mind went right back to Asher. What was I going to do about him?

His emphasis on consent echoed in my mind. I would give him consent to do just about anything. I shook my head. What was I thinking? I was there to do a job, and I needed to remember that.

I didn't need a relationship with any man, let alone one like Asher. Besides, men were always out for themselves. Was Asher any different? It seemed like it. I watched him today. He didn't hover when I was working or ask me what I was doing. I also noticed that, when people stopped him on our way to the café, he was more than willing to help or chat. I didn't know many in my office who would do that.

Asher was an extrovert. I shivered. I was an introvert, more comfortable being alone. I'd been that way since I was a child. My parents trying to force me into situations I wasn't comfortable in hadn't changed that.

All their misguided—albeit likely well-intentioned—efforts had done was push me further into myself and make me avoid being around people or going to parties. I escaped into books and my own little world as often as possible. Sometimes, it made things worse with my parents, and at other times, they didn't seem to care.

I pushed those thoughts away as I sipped my wine and picked up the book I was reading. Time to live through imaginary characters. Yes, it was a fantasy book, but there was quite a bit of romance in it. Spicy romance at that.

Snuggling down, I began to read, trying hard to forget Asher and my childhood.

Chapter Six

♥

Asher

"Tell us about this software developer helping you," Marcus said after I sat down at the table with him, Cassie, Lucas, and Miles at the local watering hole after work.

"Emma? What's there to say?" Emma had been very distracted this afternoon; so was I, and her honeysuckle fragrance still tickled my senses.

"Evasion," Miles said.

"You met her; what'd you think?" Lucas asked Miles.

"Nice lady. Kind of shy. She had no idea what kind of company Fantasies, Inc. is."

"What?" Marcus's voice rose, and he leaned forward. "And you—" He lowered his voice and waved his hand at me. "—brought her to R&D first?"

Okay, that might not have been the best idea.

I shrugged. "It seemed like the logical choice." Actually, it had given me some valuable insight into Emma. I was attracted to her, but it seemed to be more than a simple attraction. I liked the way her eyes widened at the array of toys, how her skin flushed when I told her how I'd use the massage oil. Maybe I liked her a little too much. Taking her to R&D gave me a chance to see how she would react to the company and what we did.

Oh, some might argue with me about it, but she'd been aroused from my words. And I noticed how her skin flushed, and how she'd shifted from one foot to the other and wouldn't raise her gaze to meet mine.

"Logical?" Miles stared at him. "You'll be lucky if you don't get an HR complaint against you."

"We were talking about what was needed, and she asked me about R&D. I decided to show her what they did. In order for the IT expansion and reconfiguration to go smoothly, she needs to understand what FI does from the inside out." Sure, I could've started gradually with Cassie's department or even Lucas in finance.

Marcus shook his head. "We're lucky she didn't run screaming out of the room."

"Emma is made of sterner stuff." My gut told me she was tougher than she wanted anyone to know, and she didn't seem to shy away when we walked into the room.

"Bring her up to my department tomorrow," Lucas commented. "Finance would be a good place to start. We're getting buried in paperwork right now."

"I can do that."

Dinner conversation was enthusiastic, sometimes pointed, and covered everything from the weather to sports to vacation plans to the latest movies. A great way to let off steam. We were all driving, so the alcohol was limited, but the coffee flowed freely.

The party broke up some three hours after it started. On the drive home, I kept going back to the massage oil fantasy I'd described to Emma. I couldn't shake my attraction to her. She'd intrigued me when I first encountered her at the party, but now... Yeah, there was something more going on here.

I arrived home, and after parking the car in the garage, I sat for a moment to decompress and enjoy the silence. Once inside the house, I locked the door and kicked off my shoes, then stopped at the bar in the great room and poured two fingers of Macallan 25 into a crystal tumbler. An expensive, rare indulgence.

The drapes were still open on the picture windows overlooking Puget Sound. I took another sip of the exquisitely smooth bourbon, enjoying the warmth as it slid down my throat and warmed my center.

I needed some ocean time. Maybe this weekend.

My house in Moclips is right on the beach. The property became available four years ago. I happened to be in the right place at the right time and snatched it up. Getting oceanfront property was difficult. The place needed work, and refurbishing it had been therapeutic for me.

I closed on the property right after my divorce was finalized. The end of the marriage was a nightmare, but thanks to the prenup, at least the distribution of the assets and the settlement had been cut and dried. Once free from my ex, my life was my own again.

I spent guilt-free weekends at the beach house stripping, painting, remodeling, restoring, basically living the DIY dream. The real life *This Old House* odyssey had soothed my soul and helped me recover from the matrimonial disaster and, yep, my ex.

My thoughts wandered. What would Emma think of my beach house?

We could sit out on the deck, watch the waves roll in, and soak in the tranquility. Emma had a quiet personality. She might enjoy some peace and quiet.

Turning away from the moonlit beauty of the small white capped waves on the Sound, I finished the last of the Macallan and left the tumbler on the bar on my way into my home office. I booted up my computer, curious to see how much progress she'd made today.

The logs showed Emma had reviewed the network architecture and the mainframe configuration and set up a file for her notes. Not bad for an afternoon's work.

After shutting down my computer, I wandered into the kitchen, grabbed a beer, twisted the cap off, and padded into the family room. I found the remote under one of the throw pillows and flipped on the 70-inch flat screen TV.

The baseball game was still on. I settled into the recliner, took a long pull of the beer, and felt the tension of the day finally leave my neck and shoulders.

I'd see Emma tomorrow. She fascinated me, and my heart raced as I made a promise to myself.

I would discover all of her secrets.

Chapter Seven

♥

Asher

I glanced at the time on my computer monitor. Where had the day gone? Heck, the week. Emma sat at her desk, frowning as she studied her screen. As of today, we'd worked together for a week, and I still knew very little about her.

She wasn't a chatter box, but she rarely initiated conversation. I wondered about that. What or who had caused her reticence. Throughout the week, I'd seen glimpses of the person I was sure was the 'real' Emma. Like Monday, when we were in R&D, and Emma's increasingly friendly reactions to Amelia at the coffee shop. Emma had even gone down to see Cassie on her own to discuss Cassie's department's needs in the new system.

My frustration, however, was trending high. Emma had begun analyzing the software infrastructure, making notes about necessary changes, and, in some cases, making adjustments to facilitate compatibility in apps I'd developed and/or built. Her changes to the code, mine and hers, were silver bullet level. She was good at her job, a ninja. Even so, I hated allowing anyone to mess with my work.

"You're frowning."

"Yeah." She didn't even glance up from her screen.

I slid my chair over. "What's wrong?"

"Cassie would like an automated survey to go out, but for some reason, when I try to modify existing code to use tools already in place, I can't get my code to mesh with yours."

I studied the screen. "I think I see the problem. You're using version ten of the OS and I'm using version nine."

"Why nine?"

"Ten had too many bugs in it."

"Puh-leeeeeze." She drew the word out. "Any coder worth their salt can fix those bugs easily."

"Oh." Was she challenging me?

I kept my gaze fixed on her face as her eyes moved over the screen, then she tapped the keyboard. I had to force myself to look at the screen. What the...? I watched as she inserted new information.

I was good at my job, but this was a whole other level.

"Emma..." *What the f—*

"I won't break anything."

I was riveted—as in couldn't look away even if I'd wanted to—as she tweaked my code. My code! Damn, this woman was good.

"Try it now." She pushed the keyboard toward me.

I pulled in a deep breath and entered the command to run the preliminary program for operations. The one I could never get to work right. The information scrolled along the screen, then stopped, and an error code appeared.

"See." *Vindicated. Validated. I was right.* Mental fist pump.

Emma wrinkled her nose. "That's different," she whispered and began scrolling through the code. "I need to study this." She was speaking more to herself than to me.

"Not tonight." I pulled the keyboard away from her.

"Asher." She was squinting when she gave me the evil side-eye.

"It's quitting time. You've worked hard all week. We both have. It's time for the weekend."

She stuck her tongue out but didn't argue as she saved the changes and shut down her workstation. I made quick work of shutting mine down because I didn't want her leaving without me.

"Would you like to get a drink and maybe a bite to eat?" Maybe in a relaxed setting, I could find out more about her.

She hesitated. "I don't know if that's a good idea."

"Please. I'd like to learn more about you outside the job, if that's okay." I wasn't going to push her.

I could see her mulling over everything in her head before she said, "Yes, I'd like that."

I thought for sure she was going to say no. Elation filled me at her yes.

Reveal nothing, Asher. Keep cool.

She grabbed her backpack.

"You can leave that here."

Emma stared at me. "I need this over the weekend."

"You can pick it up before you go home. The room is locked, and you, me, Ben, and security are the only ones with access."

She still hesitated.

"Emma?"

"Sorry. You're right." She pulled her wallet out, grabbed some cash and a credit card, and what looked like her driver's license, then stuffed them in the pocket of her jeans. "I'm ready."

"Let's go." I gestured for her to walk ahead of me. And yes, it gave me a chance to admire her swaying hips as she walked to the elevators. Emma fascinated me. We were both silent in the elevator, but it was a relaxed, companionable silence. In the lobby, I waved to the security guard, and we walked outside.

We were getting some nice late spring weather for the Seattle area, as in very little rain, and no lingering clouds to hide the sunset. "The Whistle Stop Pub is two blocks down. Up for a walk?" I gestured to the right.

"Definitely, after all that sitting. At least it's nice out," Emma commented as we started to walk.

"Yes. So, how do you feel your first week went?" I wanted to know what she thought about everything. She'd been quiet all week.

"Not bad. This entire project is proving to be a challenge, but now I understand why. It might take some extra adjustment."

I stopped walking and gently caught Emma's hand and turned her to face me. "You're a badass wizard. Between you and me, we *will* make it work."

We arrived at the pub, and I grabbed the door and pulled it open for her.

"Thank you," she whispered.

After being out in the waning sunlight, it still took a minute for my eyes to adjust to the dim interior of the pub. I glanced at Emma. Her gaze darted around the room.

I didn't blame her. The first time a group of us came here, we were surprised by the décor. Long glossy wooden bar with barstools, leather booths, and rustic tables.

"Hey, Asher, over here," a voice called.

I turned my head to see Marcus waving at me. "This way." Cupping Emma's elbow, I guided her over to the table where Marcus and Cassie sat.

"Emma, great to see you again." Marcus stood and held out a chair for her.

"Good to see you." Emma sat down. "Cassie."

"I'm so glad you came tonight," Cassie said. "I hate being the only woman."

"I didn't realize anyone else would be here," Emma said, glancing at me.

"My bad." I hadn't told her for a reason. I wanted her to learn to relax around at least the department heads and my friends. For reasons I wasn't quite ready to delve too deeply into, this was important to me.

"Who else will be here?" she asked.

I could already see Emma retreating behind her wall. "It depends on what the others have going on."

"Josh and Dean are going to the Mariners game," Marcus said.

"Miles?" I asked.

"Not sure. He said a late issue came up in HR, and he might not make it."

Emma's shoulders relaxed, and I sat back in my chair.

"Here's your beer." The waitress set glasses in front of Marcus and Cassie. "What can I get for you two?"

"On tap beer is fine," Emma said. "Light or amber over dark or stout.

"Same." I was surprised she ordered a beer. Was it because that's what the others had ordered?

"How are you settling in, Emma?" Cassie asked.

"Pretty good." She rubbed her forehead and settled back in her chair. "Expansion and integration at the levels we're working on are a challenge, but we'll get there. Except the boss here might have just derailed my week's work."

I stiffened. "Now wait a second…"

"I'm semi-kidding," Emma said quickly.

"Only semi?" Cassie prompted.

"Yeah, what I'm using is much more functional." A smile played around Emma's lips.

Little tease, but it did make me happy. "We'll discuss it more."

"Did seeing R&D help?" Marcus asked, changing the subject.

Emma's cheeks pinked, and I grinned.

Cassie looked from Marcus to Emma's flushed face then back to Marcus. "You left her alone with Asher in your R&D display room?" Cassie hit him in the arm, trying—and failing—to deliver a charley horse, then turned to Emma. I coughed to cover a chuckle. "Don't let them scare you away."

Emma smiled at Cassie. "It was eye opening, especially since I didn't realize what kind of company Fantasies, Inc. was."

"Men." Cassie shook her head in mock frustration and leaned closer to Marcus, who took advantage of the opportunity and gently kissed her forehead.

Emma watched the couple, and I caught the flash of a wistful expression.

Cassie stroked Marcus's cheek and then straightened. "I hoped you weren't too shell shocked?"

"A little, but I got over it."

Now that was interesting; her reaction seemed like more than 'a little', and she hadn't talked much about R&D since the visit. Was it shock or just surprise? That definitely warranted a future conversation.

But not tonight.

"I will say your questions about customer service were right on track with what I wanted," Cassie said.

"To me, customer service is customer service, no matter what the business does. It's all about having happy customers."

"And good focus groups," Cassie commented.

The waitress returned with the beers. Cassie ordered first, then the waitress looked at Emma.

"I'm not sure yet." She bit her lower lip. "Please take their orders first."

I glanced at Marcus who shook his head. "We'll wait."

Emma rolled her eyes. "Bacon cheeseburger, no tomatoes."

"Fries?" the waitress asked.

"Yes, please."

"Good girl," I whispered, unable to help myself, and Emma stilled then tilted her head. Her expression changed from confusion to curiosity in the blink of an eye, and this time, she didn't look away.

Marcus ordered and then I did.

"You didn't need to wait until I ordered." Emma's voice was barely above a whisper. She leaned back in her chair, her arm resting on the chair arm closest to me.

I reached over and gently squeezed her hand. "It was the polite thing to do."

Cassie laughed. "Emma, arguing with men like Marcus and Asher is pretty much wasted effort. They'll do what they want."

"And don't you forget it." Marcus placed a kiss on Cassie's cheek.

Chapter Eight

♥

Emma

Cassie's words threw me for a minute. It wasn't as if I hadn't noticed how—I wasn't sure what to call it—bossy, micromanaging, controlling, Asher had been this week. Was Cassie validating the behavior? Or...was Asher dominant? There was a fine line between the two, according to the stories I'd read and information on various websites. Every day, he made sure I took breaks and lunch, even if I wasn't ready to. *Looking out for my wellbeing, okay, maybe dominant.* He would insist, even to the point of turning off the computer monitors so I couldn't work. *Bossy for sure, definitely not dominant, and well into PITA territory.*

While it annoyed me, some part of me liked deferring to Asher. I'd been so careful, so anxious around, well, anyone.

What would it be like to have someone confident at my side?

I didn't have a lot of people in my life who cared about my well-being. My parents had never really been all that involved with or about what I did unless whatever I was doing impacted them directly.

They always hung out with large groups of friends and acquaintances, attended lots of parties. I preferred being alone and hated it when my parents made me go with them. I was nervous, sometimes feeling like I couldn't breathe—especially when people got close while trying to get to my parents, ignoring the little girl standing there.

It also didn't help that, during high school, boys were always trying to date me as a way to get closer to my family, their money, their contacts, and influence. Even some of the men I dated over the years were looking to get ahead by using me as a stepping stone.

"Where are you?"

I blinked at Asher's words. "Sorry." The apology was automatic.

"Are you okay?" He shifted ever so slightly closer to me.

"Fine." I really was. It was nice to sit here with Asher, Marcus, and Cassie. How long had it been since I'd gone out with people I worked with? I also reminded myself that if I had any hope of advancement in my career, I needed to be more interactive with people.

Our food was brought, and as we all dug in, I found myself relaxing even more. The second beer might've had something to do with it, but more likely, it was the company.

Cassie leaned over. "So have you learned anything about the other departments?"

I shook my head. "HR seems pretty standard. I haven't talked with the operations group yet."

"That would be Josh and Dean; they run the department together," Cassie said.

I tilted my head. "Together?" Was that unusual? Maybe not. I'd seen departments with two department heads, but it was the way Cassie said 'together'.

"Yes, they're both nice guys. Miles is HR, but you already met him."

"Miles has some ideas on what he wants for HR. With us having contractors in the building, he's trying to keep everything in line," Asher commented.

"Contractors? Are you talking about the coffee shop?" I loved the little coffee shop next to the café; it made life so much easier.

"The coffee shop and the café," Asher said. "And you. While John has some control over the café because he bankrolls it, the coffee shop is all Amelia's. She does rent the space from us, but that's about it," Asher said.

Things were starting to make more sense. Even though I'd been at the job for a week, I didn't venture outside the company campus much. For breaks, I'd grab coffee and a snack at Daily Perks. Lunch usually meant the café if I was hungry. If not, I'd grab a sandwich to go and eat it later in the day.

"John likes to make sure the employees have options while keeping the company secure," Marcus said.

"It keeps employee turnover low. Contractors are another story," another male voice commented.

Asher looked up as the table went quiet. "Miles." Everyone seemed to perk up when he arrived.

"I finally made it." He snagged a chair from an empty table and pulled it up. "Hi, Emma, everything going good for your first week?"

"Yes. It's been great."

"I'm glad." His blue eyes twinkled.

"Finish up with the problem you were having?" Marcus asked.

Miles frowned. "For the moment." He shook his head and looked at Asher. "By the way, I'd like to talk to you and Emma about streamlining some of the paperwork for onboarding new employees. I feel like I'm buried in documents."

"Set up a meeting with us next week," Asher replied.

The waitress assigned to our table had been attentive without being overbearing. She must've seen Miles join our table because she appeared almost instantly. Miles ordered a drink and dinner. "You were talking about the café and Daily Perks, right?"

"Yes," I chimed in. "I'm wondering how they get paid for what Fantasies, Inc.'s employees buy? I mean everything is on our badges." The café were contractors, but Daily Perks was more like a tenant.

"Easy," Miles said. "Payroll gets a report of what is charged on the employee card every day, and they're paid electronically."

I sat back in my seat. "Sounds like an ideal situation."

"It is." Miles smiled at the waitress as she sat his whiskey down in front of him. "It works for us, and since the services are on the first floor, anyone who comes into the building who isn't an employee pays them directly."

"Are we including them in the software?" I asked Asher.

Asher looked surprised by my question. "I hadn't thought about it."

"That's a great idea," Miles said. "We should include payroll."

"That's part of finance. I forgot about them," Asher said. "Why didn't we think about this before?"

Marcus chuckled. "Because Lucas is a control freak."

Cassie glanced at Marcus and grinned. "Lucas would be devastated at that description." Then she directed her next remark at me. "He's in charge of the finance department, if that isn't clear."

I nodded. "I remember Asher mentioning that." Fantasies, Inc. had a lot of departments, but it seemed like the main ones were in the building I worked in.

"When I talked with Lucas, he said he didn't know what he wanted," Asher commented. "He gave me some basics, but he wanted me to wait to do his department."

"It would be easy enough..." My brain began coming up with ideas at lightspeed. I pulled out my phone and began typing notes. If I didn't do this now, I'd forget exactly what I wanted. Several minutes later, I glanced up to see four pairs of eyes staring at me. "Sorry," I squeaked.

"Don't be," Cassie said.

"That was fascinating," Miles smiled at me. "I've never seen anyone with such fierce concentration in a public setting."

"I've had a lot of practice." The words slipped from my mouth before I could censor them.

"What do you mean?" Asher asked.

My face flamed. How could I put this? "I learned from a young age how to filter the noise." I'd also learned how to hide in plain sight. That was the best I could come up with. I didn't want to talk about my family.

The men frowned at me, while Cassie looked intrigued.

"That could be dangerous," Marcus said. "Anyone could sneak up on you."

"That might be true for some, but I've never had an issue. I'm not ignoring my surroundings; I'm focusing on whatever I'm doing but still aware of what's going on around me." Another skill I'd developed as a kid.

Miles jumped in. "He's right, Emma."

I tensed. Asher slipped his arm over the back of my chair, not touching me, but I knew it was there. Was he supporting me? Or did he agree with them?

I took a deep breath. "I get your point, but it's never happened. And I'm careful."

Asher's arm tensed, and he shook his head. "Just because it hasn't happened doesn't mean it won't. I don't want you to do it again." There was my answer.

"Shit," Cassie said softly.

I had no idea why Cassie was swearing, but I was certain I didn't like Asher's attitude. "Asher…" I started as I turned to face him.

"I mean it, Emma."

Excuse me? Heat rose along the back of my neck and in my cheeks.

"Why don't we discuss this privately?" I didn't want to get into it in front of his co-workers. Technically, mine as well, but I would only be with Fantasies, Inc. for a short period.

"We will discuss it now." His grim tone made the hair on my arms rise.

Don't push me, Asher. Just don't. "No, Asher. We won't."

"Maybe now isn't the best time." Marcus had the right idea. Now if Asher would just listen to him.

Asher glared at Marcus before turning his focus back to me. Miles had the presence of mind to stay quiet.

Okay, buddy you want it, you'll get it.

"Asher, we are not in any form of a personal relationship in or outside the office. As such, you have no say regarding my conduct or what I do in my life." My gaze speared Marcus and Miles. *That goes for you both.* My determination surprised me. In the past, I would've avoided confrontation.

Asher glared at me, but I wasn't going to give an inch.

"I am responsible for you as long as you're working for Fantasies, Inc., so you will do as I say."

Oh HELL no, dude.

I straightened my spine. "Your name is not on the bottom line of my contract. You are a colleague, maybe even a peer, if you're having a good day." I stood and maneuvered so that I was right in his face. "I've been taking care of myself since my teens, all without your help, so don't you *dare* come at me with your *you will do as I say* bullshit."

I felt like I'd added at least five feet to my height, and the heat at the back of my neck had turned into a five alarm fire. I pulled money out of my pocket and dropped some bills on the table then looked from Cassie to Marcus to Miles. "Thank you for a nice dinner. Have a good weekend, and I'll see you in the office on Monday."

Without even a glance at Asher, I turned and walked out of the pub.

"Neanderthals. Can't live with 'em, and it's not worth kicking their butts," I muttered

Chapter Nine

A^{sher}

"My man, you fucked up," Miles said.

"Yep. Royally and then some," Marcus added.

I heard their words but right then, they didn't register.

What the hell just happened?

"Aren't you going to go after her?" Cassie asked.

"What?" And just like that, my brain came back online.

Oh shit. I jumped up, dropped some money on the table,

and took off after Emma. Once outside, I double-timed it

back to the building, but didn't see her anywhere. Damn.

I scanned my badge in the elevator, hoping she was in

the office to get her backpack. It was empty and her bag

was gone.

"Fuck." I pulled my cell out and dialed her number.

Voice mail. Ending the call without leaving a message, I

made my way to the garage.

Why had Emma reacted so strongly to my worrying about her? Everyone at the table had stared at me when she got up and walked out. Miles said I'd fucked up, but how? I was only expressing my concern about her safety. Protecting those I care about is in my DNA.

I tried calling her again when I got home. Again, voice mail. This time, I left a message. "Emma, it's Asher. I get that you're upset with me, and we should talk about why. Call me, please. At least let me know you got home safe."

That was all I could do at the moment. Well, I could get her address and go see if she was okay, but that was a bit stalkerish. All right, a lot. I marched into my kitchen and pulled a beer out of the fridge.

Thirty minutes later, my phone pinged, and I picked it up.

"I'm fine. No need to check up on me. I am an adult."

I read the message three times. When did I say she wasn't an adult? What now? I had no idea. This might not be the time to hash this out. I needed to give her time to think, to calm down. I texted her back: *"I'm glad you're home and okay. See you Monday."*

That was the best I could come up with at the moment. It was going to be a long weekend. Tomorrow I'd chat with Miles and Marcus to figure out what I'd done, because I wanted to fix this situation.

***

I barely slept all night long and finally accepted that sleep was out of reach when my phone vibrated late the next morning. A call from Marcus with an invite for lunch with the guys that afternoon.

The front door was open, and I called out before walking in. Marcus responded and told me to grab a beer from the fridge. They were all out on the patio.

Everyone was already there. Miles, Lucas, Josh, and Dean. Marcus shook my hand, and I raised my beer in an air toast to the other guys around the table. "Where's Cassie?"

"She went into town to do some shopping. Said she needed some girl time."

I nodded. Usually Marcus kept Cassie close. I pulled out a chair and sat down at the table.

"Did you talk to Emma?" Miles asked. No small talk. Get right to the point.

"I left her a voice mail, and she texted me she was home."

"That's all you did?" Lucas shook his head. "You're an idiot."

"What?" I took a long pull of my beer.

"Marcus and Miles told us what happened last night," Josh said.

I should've known. Now the shit was going to come from all sides.

"And Lucas is right; you're an idiot," Dean commented.

So it begins...

"Now, wait a second. Why are you jumping in my face? I was only concerned for Emma's safety."

I looked each man in the eye. Okay, no sympathy here.

"Never tell an independent woman she can't take care of herself," Lucas said. "At least, don't act like a—what did she call you—Neanderthal."

And every one of the traitors raised their beer bottles in agreement.

"What do you know about it?" I took another long drink of my beer.

"I know women." Lucas sat back in his chair, his expression a cross between a smirk and a grin.

I laughed. "We've all been out with multiple women. Emma is..." What? Different? Yes, but in a good way. She didn't hesitate to put me in my place last night, and...what? It was more than her standing up to me. Something I couldn't quite explain.

"Have you ever told any woman you work with or have dated what to do with her life, her personal life, this soon after meeting her? Have you even asked Emma out on a date?" Marcus leaned back. raised his arms and laced his fingers behind his head. "Well?" he prompted when I didn't answer right away. "Have you?"

I sat back in the chair. Shit. I shook my head. Why had I reacted so strongly to Emma last night? Was it because I was attracted to her? Maybe, but I'd been attracted to other women and never told them what to do.

"What was even worse, if that's possible," Miles said, "she wanted to take the conversation private, and you refused."

He was right. I had. *Damn, damn, damn, what the hell was wrong with me?* I knew better than to be confrontational with a woman, but I'd done it with Emma. Fear for what I saw as a lack of situational awareness had overridden my judgment.

"You were damn lucky Emma didn't kick you in the nuts. She looked mad enough," Marcus commented.

Wincing, I took another sip of my beer. "You saw her last night." I looked from Marcus to Miles. "She was a thousand miles away in her thoughts. Anything could have happened to her."

"We've all done that. When a solution to a problem pops into our head, we go for it, but you don't know her well enough yet to know how locked in her mind might've been," Josh said.

"We're men," I replied.

Groans floated around the patio.

"Like we can't be attacked," Dean said, looking around the table. "Should we throw him in the pool to wake him up?"

"What? It's the truth." I had no idea what their problem was. While I agreed men could be attacked, we were built to defend ourselves.

"Listen to yourself, Asher." Marcus raised his hands to mimic air quotes. "We're men. She's a woman. She needs to be taken care of. She should do what I say."

"When you say it like that..." Like what? Marcus was repeating everything I'd said almost verbatim. "That wasn't what I meant. I want to protect Emma." My instincts had been on high alert last night; I could see it now.

"Ah, there it is. The protective male," Miles said.

I stared at Marcus. "You can't tell me you don't safeguard Cassie."

"I do. But I'm subtle about it, and she's agreed to the dynamic. Above all, I don't go around telling her what she can and cannot do."

"What would you do if Cassie told you she was so focused on a problem while in public that she didn't pay attention?" I challenged.

"One, Cassie and I have been together longer than, what, a week? And two, that's not what Emma said," Marcus retorted.

I kept my attention on Marcus as the other guys all sat back in their chairs. "She seems to think just because she hasn't been harmed, it won't happen. She said as much. My sister calls it optimism bias. When you and Miles made the argument that it could happen, Emma countered with, '...but it's never happened. And I'm careful'. Great. She's careful, but wishful thinking doesn't eliminate or mitigate the danger. Hell, that pink haze, pie in the sky shit has gotten people killed." These guys were driving me nuts.

"She's an adult, Asher. You have to trust her."

Trust her? I was very aware I had trust issues, thanks to an ex-wife who cheated on me. That was before I came to work at Fantasies, Inc., but the wound was still there. "I do trust her to do her job."

"There it is," Lucas commented.

"What?" How many times had I asked that today? What was I missing?

"Trust her to know what's best for her," Lucas said. "She's managed to live her entire life without you telling her what she can and can't do. How do you think she's made it this far? You've known her all of a whole week, and you're already trying to clip her wings."

Was I? I sat back in my chair and contemplated their words as my mind replayed last night. I caught Emma's muttered quip as she was leaving. She'd called me a Neanderthal, and after my friends' succinct analysis, she wasn't wrong. "Aww, fuck."

Dean raised a hand and pointed skyward. "And the lightbulb comes on," he said, laughter in his voice.

Every head/desk gif I'd viewed in the past flashed across my memory. How could I be so stupid? I'd called her out in public, in front of Marcus, Cassie, and Miles, who were damn near strangers to her. Hell, *I* was damn near a stranger. I was lucky she didn't quit on the spot or as Marcus had remarked, kicked me in the nuts. If it had been anatomically possible, I would've kicked my own ass. I was better than this; I knew I was.

Emma had gotten under my skin like no one else, not even my ex. And Marcus was right: I had royally screwed up. Now, I had to figure out how to fix this.

"What do I do?"

At least my friends could help me get out of this mess. I hoped.

I looked around the table. One chin propped on a hand. One shaking head. Another shaking head. One skeptical, even to the cocked eyebrow.

Marcus leaned forward, lifted his beer, took a sip, and pointed the bottle in my direction. "I'd start with an apology," he offered.

Miles lifted his chin from his raised hand. "Then explain you were only thinking about her safety and protection," he added.

From Lucas, the first of the shaking head twins. "Also, let her know you believe she can take care of herself in any situation. You were only concerned because you know how stupid men can be," he said with a grin. "Definitely mention how stupid men are. She'll agree with that."

"Case in point: How you acted on Friday," Josh, the second of the shaking head twins, commented, his grin as wide as Lucas's.

"I gotta second the suggestion about mentioning how stupid men are. That move has saved many a man's life." Dean lifted his bottle of beer, reached across the table and clinked my bottle in a toast, then raised the bottle again with a knowing wink.

I nodded, processing their advice. I was going to fix this with Emma, even if it meant going down on my knees. Of course, I'd do that in private. No sense in letting the guys rib me more than they were already doing.

I'd make this up to Emma, because I did believe she was a capable woman. And if I had any chance with her romantically, I needed to fix this.

If she'd let me.

Chapter Ten

♥

E^{mma}

I pulled into the parking lot of Jay's Bar & Grill the next day. I was surprised when Cassie called me and asked me to meet her. I'd made quite the scene last night. I liked Cassie, and I didn't have very many girlfriends. It would be nice to make one.

When I walked inside, I noticed all the wood and brick. The place had a nice cozy feel to it. Different than the pub we were at last night.

"Over here, Emma."

I turned and saw Cassie waving at me. I walked over to the table and sat down. "Hi, Cassie, thanks for calling me."

"I'm just glad I had your number. I hate eating alone."

"Until you called, I'd forgotten I'd given it to you the other day." When I'd talked to Cassie about the customer service department, she couldn't remember one of the items she wanted. I gave her my cell number in case she remembered.

"I'm happy you were able to join me."

We looked up when the waitress arrived at our table. "Good afternoon, ladies." She slid two coasters onto the table. "What can I get you to drink?"

"Iced tea, please," I said.

"That sounds good; I'll have one too."

"Be right back with your drinks."

"Have you been here before?"

"I haven't." I stared at the menu trying to figure out what I was hungry for.

"I want one of everything." Cassie looked at me over the top of the menu. "Want to do a couple of appetizers and share?"

"That sounds great." If I was by myself and ordered more than two appetizers, I'd have leftovers for days. "What were you thinking of getting?"

Cassie gave each of the items a mini review. She was a regular here and had tried them all. "So we agree? Pot stickers, mac & cheese bites, and cheesy fries?"

My mouth watered. "Sounds great."

Cassie rubbed her hands together, then stacked the menus and placed them on the aisle side of the table.

The waitress walked up with our drinks and set them on the table. "Are you ready to order?"

Cassie smiled, her enthusiasm contagious. "Yes, we're going to split some appetizers. The pot stickers, mac & cheese bites, and cheesy fries."

"Great choices."

"I'd also like a house salad with ranch, please." Assuaging the guilt over the fried food. I could hear Mother's whispered, *are you sure you want to eat that,* and I shut that down hard.

"I'll have one, too, please." The waitress nodded to Cassie and retrieved our menus. As soon as she was out of range, Cassie wasted no time on small talk. "I wanted to see how you were doing after last night."

I liked direct. "Me?" I wasn't sure what Cassie was worried about. "I'm fine. No worries."

"I'm glad. I was, not worried exactly, just concerned about the way Asher acted."

My breath caught in my throat. *Stay cool. He's Cassie's friend. You just have to work with him.* "He was a bit of an idiot, but I'm over it." I was. Yes, I was angry last night, but I never stayed that way for long. I'd learned as a teenager that I could put my energy into being angry or use my energy for better things.

"I'm glad. I've known Asher for years, and I've never seen him act like that."

"Oh?" While we'd been in the office together all week, I'd been struck by his tendency to be somewhat bossy, even controlling, but he hadn't acted paternalistic or patronizing like he had last night. "I think I pushed a hot button." That had to be the explanation, but I didn't know what that button was.

"Maybe. You tried to defuse the situation, but he wasn't having it."

"He wasn't. I might have been more hardcore than the situation called for, though." I worried about that all night. After all, I still had to work with the man.

"You weren't. He needed to be called out." Cassie leaned forward, propped her folded arms on the table. "Enough about him. Tell me about you."

"Me?" That surprised me. I wasn't used to talking about myself.

"Yes. Have you always lived in the Seattle area?"

"No. I was raised in San Francisco." I didn't miss city life. Sprawling metropolitan cities got on my nerves, one of the reasons I lived outside of Seattle. Even now, there were times when driving into the city for work nearly obliterated my sense of calm. Too many people, cars, everything.

"San Francisco is a nice place. Why did you leave?"

"After I received my BS in computer science, I wanted to move out of California. I applied for the job with Tri-O-Tech, the company I'm working for now, started at the ground level and slowly worked my way up."

"How long did that take you?" Cassie stopped and smacked her hand over her mouth, eyes wide. "I'm sorry. Am I being too nosy?"

I grinned. "You're not. It's okay. It took me about six years to move up to where I am now." I sipped my tea. "What about you?"

We talked about our lives and careers, and I found myself really enjoying being with Cassie and getting to know her.

I missed working with other women. I loved my career, but computer science and information technology were still very male-dominated professions. Maybe it was time for me to move into another position at work, somewhere there were more women.

***

By the time Cassie and I finished lunch, we were chatting like old friends. I was enjoying this budding friendship with her and wanted to explore it. Maybe being around people wasn't such a bad thing. We parted in the parking lot, agreeing to meet at work early on Monday and have coffee together.

I couldn't shake my concern about how Asher might act when we were back to working in the same office. The confrontation didn't happen at work; it was a social situation. Entirely different environments. During professional interactions, I would act like I did any other day and, as far as I was concerned, the issue was settled. Anything beyond that was on Asher.

When I got home, I flopped down on my sofa, wanting to zone out a while after an exhausting week. I turned on a movie I'd seen several times, and let it play as background noise, then picked up my tablet to read the newest addition to my library.

Oh yes. Spicy, sexy romance. Just what I needed.

Chapter Eleven

♥

A sher Monday morning, I walked into the office I shared with Emma, holding two coffees and one of her favorite pastries from Daily Perks. It wouldn't hurt to enhance my apology with coffee and food.

I pushed the door open. Six forty-five. I had time. Wanting to give her space, I hadn't tried to contact her again after I received her text.

Imagine my surprise, when I found Emma already in the office, typing away at the computer.

"Good morning, Emma."

"Morning," she answered, but I could tell she was distracted.

"You're here early." I set her coffee and pastry down next to her keyboard. She glanced at the food.

"What's this?"

"Coffee and pastry, along with an apology for Friday night."

She kept her gaze on me for a moment. "Thank you, but not necessary. We're fine." Then turned back to the computer screen.

We're fine. Her words bounced around in my head. How could we be fine? I'd acted like an ass as I had been so eloquently told by my friends Saturday.

"I do appreciate the coffee and food." She slid her own mug aside, picked up the cup I'd brought, and took a sip. "Perfect." Her attention remained focused on her computer screen after taking a bite of the danish.

"Why did you come in so early?" I sat down and booted up my own computer.

"I had an idea yesterday, and I can't remote into your system, so I played with it on mine. Now, I'm going to see if I can get your program to accept it. If it works, we might be able to complete the integration faster." Another bite of danish.

The excitement in her voice made me smile. "I'm not telling you what you should do, but weekends should be for you and your pleasure." I didn't like that she worked on her days off.

"It was nothing." Her gaze never wavered from her monitor and the code running on the computer.

"Emma, you don't need to work weekends."

"I know, but sometimes when an idea comes to me, I have to pounce on it. You should know that." A bite of danish and a sip of coffee.

I did. "Like Friday night at the restaurant?"

"That wasn't something I needed to be on the computer to do; taking notes was good enough. For this, I had to go into the code to see if what I was thinking was even possible."

"Make sure you log the time you spent."

"What?" She turned her head suddenly, as though she'd just registered what I'd said. "I'm a contractor."

"An hourly one and I want to make sure you get paid for your time." Was she not aware of why it was so important to log her hours? The last thing any company needed was an IRS audit, and I'm not talking about taxes.

"No worries," she said and waved her hand in dismissal.

"Emma." My voice dropped.

"Damn," she whispered as the scrolling code stopped and the last line flashed red. "It didn't work." Her shoulders slumped. "Maybe if I adjust the values once again." She finished off the food.

I shook my head. "Emma, your attention, please."

"What?" Irritation flashed in her eyes.

"My name may not be on the bottom line of your contract, as you so eloquently pointed out, but this is my department. It's my ass on the line for compliance issues, be those mandates state, federal, corporate, and/or departmental. You will log the time you spent on the code on Sunday, so that you'll get paid for it." I wasn't going to back down.

"It's not a big deal."

"Again, it's my ass on the line, so I'll decide what's a big deal. Your contract is very specific about compliance with all federal and state laws, and corporate regulations." I faced her. "How many hours did you work?"

"I'm not sure." She rubbed her forehead. "Like I said, it doesn't matter."

"As I said, the contract is specific and doesn't leave room for flexibility. You have two choices: Put the time on your time sheet or go home now and don't come back until tomorrow in order to level out the time you worked on Sunday. You weren't in the office, so I can't go back and check the keystroke logs, and there's no time stamp on the program modifications."

Her eyes grew wide. "I have work to do."

"I appreciate that, but my opinion doesn't matter. What matters is company policy, contract terms, and state and federal regulations. All of that aside, Fantasies, Inc.

believes in paying its employees and contractors when they are working, that includes weekends, though we do discourage weekend work, as I've mentioned." Then it clicked. "You did read the employment contract, right?"

"I skimmed it." Her gaze lowered.

I shook my head. "I asked you if you *read* the contract." *I could play hardball too.* I reached over and switched off her monitor. The program was running, but the monitor was dark. The outrage on her face almost made me smile. Maybe I was being heavy handed, but I wasn't going to risk my job because of her tantrum.

She reached out to turn the monitor back on, and I captured her hand in mine. "Leave it. It will still be there in an hour."

"An hour? Asher, I have work to do. Let go." She tugged at her hand.

I wanted to keep her hand in mine, but this was a contest of wills. I let it go. "We're going to go over the employee contract, and you're going to log your hours from yesterday."

Her eyes flashed annoyance. "I'll do it later."

I knew she was trying to get me to let her go ahead and work, but this was a no-go for me. I wouldn't let any of the employees slide like this, and I wasn't about to let Emma get away with this crap. Besides, if the C-suite crew found out she wasn't logging her time, they'd terminate the contract faster than I could snap my fingers, then fire me for cause.

"No, Emma. Now." I stood and waited.

She sighed loudly, stood and followed me to the small conference table where I pulled out a chair for her. She stood there.

"Sit."

"Neanderthal fits." She huffed and sat.

I leaned forward and braced on my open hands so that we were almost nose to nose. "This is business and has nothing whatsoever to do with any personal opinions you may have about me." I retrieved our drinks and food from the workstation and took them over to the table. Then I picked up the phone and called HR. Miles' assistant, Sarah, answered. I asked her to have someone bring me Emma's employment contract.

When I sat down, Emma was glaring at me with her arms folded across her chest. "I don't know what the point of this is."

"The point is that you are a contractor for Fantasies, Inc. We are paying you. Again, your employment contract is very specific."

"Is it really that big of a deal?"

"Yes." A knock on the door brought me out of my chair. I took the contract from Sarah with a thank you, closed the door, and placed the papers in front of Emma.

"Oh my, look at this." I pointed to her initials in the bottom right corner of each page. "This means you read it. Every word. But you just admitted that you"—I raised both hands and gestured air quotes—" skimmed it. Significant difference. Now...Read. It. *All* of it. Word for word." For about two seconds, I actually considered insisting that she read it aloud. *Quit while you're ahead, buddy.*

She sighed and picked up the document.

I watched her as she read. Her hair framed her face, making her look too young for me. Again, what was I thinking? I was drawn to her in a way I'd never been drawn to a woman before, not even my ex. And this jousting—there was no other word for it—between us only made the attraction more intense.

Just thinking about my ex should have put an end to all thoughts of anything with Emma, but it didn't. I wanted to find out more about her. I wanted to find out what she thought, what she felt, and discover whether we were compatible in the bedroom.

Whoa! Cue massive record scratch. Way too early for thoughts like that. She'd only been here a week, and so far, all I'd done was piss her off. More than once.

"This isn't right," she muttered.

Her voice pulled me out of my head. "What isn't?"

"This says if I work more than forty hours in a week, then I get paid overtime, and I'm not allowed to work more than ninety hours in a two-week period without the director's permission. Your permission."

"That's right."

When John Boyd started the company, one of his concerns was avoiding burnout, an extremely widespread problem in the profession. I supported his position wholeheartedly. As a result of his provisions regarding work-life balance, FI had low employee turnover, some of the lowest in the state, and high employee satisfaction stats.

"That doesn't make sense. How does the company function like that?"

"It functions like a well-oiled machine. When employees have a balanced work and home life, they're happier, more productive, and take care of themselves."

She shook her head. "Shouldn't that be up to the employee?"

"It is the employee's decision. No one forces them to leave or stay. Why do you view promoting a good work-life balance as a problem?" I was curious what she was thinking.

"A lot of people are single, without family. Sometimes work is better than sitting at home alone."

I straightened. "What you're describing is using you job as an emotional crutch. You don't have a family?"

"I do, but we're not close." She hesitated, and I wondered about the remark, which now prompted a question I wanted an answer to, but not now.

"They live in California."

"Depending on where they live that's only a little over a two to a three hour plane ride."

Emma shrugged. "Are you close to your family?"

"Yes. I have dinner with my parents at least once a month. While my two siblings have moved out of state, we keep in contact."

"Nice. Were you born in Washington?"

"Yes. What about you?"

"California."

"Any brothers or sisters?" At least she was talking to me.

"Two older sisters."

"I'm a middle kid." I pondered her being the youngest. Was she anything like my younger sister, always vocal to get attention. I didn't think so. Emma seemed quiet and reserved. Or was she?

Friday night she didn't have any issues chatting with Marcus and Cassie or telling me off. She was a complex puzzle I wanted to figure out.

"Back to this contract. How do you enforce it?"

"The managers and directors know their employees, and the employees know the rules. If someone logs in after hours or remotely on a weekend, it's flagged and sent to the employee's boss."

"I told you about my working yesterday. If I hadn't told you, you wouldn't have known."

"True, but that's only because you don't have remote access and didn't come into the office where the keycard logs would have shown when you came in, and the keystroke logs would have revealed what you had done while on the network." I could almost see the wheels turning as everything fell into place. "It's why I wanted you to read your employment contract. We encourage our employees to take time off, and while you might think it's not enforceable, it is."

"The way you describe it sounds like a form of micromanagement. There's no way for you to know when I log onto my laptop at home." She sat back in her chair, looking pleased, no, almost smug.

"You're right." She was, because her laptop belonged to Tri-O-Tech. "And no one is preventing you from working on whatever you like…as long as it is not in connected any way to Fantasies, Inc. I'm trusting you to abide by the terms of the contract as agreed."

Emma rolled her eyes. "Unfair."

I rubbed my upper lip so she wouldn't see my grin. I had a feeling she was a by-the-book type of employee once she was made aware of the rules. "Very fair. Keep reading."

"All right." She flipped the page and continued to read. The rest of the contract was pretty boiler plate, but this way, I could be sure she'd read it. When she finished reading it, she tapped a fingernail on the desk then looked at me. "Can I get HR to change the contract?"

"You can talk with Miles, but I doubt he'll change it."

She sighed. "Fine. No working on weekends unless I feel it's necessary."

"And in accordance with the contract specifications?"

Emma nodded, then seemed to have a second thought and spoke aloud. "Yes, Asher, in accordance with the con- tract specifications."

Success. I relished this small win. Now to figure out a way I could fill her weekends. "I'm glad we've got that out of the way." I glanced at my watch. "Since you got here early, why don't we go to the café and celebrate with a real breakfast. The danish was fine, but I need more than that. You might too."

John had made it clear that it didn't matter to him if employees never used their cards for food or they did it all day long. The food policy and insistence on the work-life balance made for a great environment. Turnover in the company was less than five percent.

For IT, turnover was almost unheard of. I worked with my employees to ensure flexibility in a hybrid environment and encouraged use of all the perks the company offered.

"How did it get to be nine already?"

"It's funny how fast time goes." I stood up and cleaned up the table.

Chapter Twelve

♥

E mma

I couldn't believe what I read in the employment contract. Yes, I read it before I signed it in HR last week. I didn't read every word and, apparently, had missed the section about the working hours.

They don't trust people to find their own balance, so they mandate it in a damned contract?

Going forward, I was going to have to deal with the distraction of keeping track of the total number of hours I worked and stop at some arbitrary limit. I understood people needed a work and home life balance, but I was different. I had no good friends; my family was in another state, and I spent most weekends reading, walking, gaming, developing personal apps, and yes, working my job. That was *my* work-life balance.

I appreciated Asher's misguided concern about my eating habits, but coffee and food kept me awake and focused on the job. His critique at the restaurant, the contract, and his observations about my eating habits, it was like living with my family all over again.

When Asher headed for the café, I stopped him. "I'd rather do Daily Perks." I'd texted Cassie and told her we'd have to skip meeting up this morning since I came in so early.

He frowned at me. "You need more than a snack."

He thinks he's looking out for me. Pick your battles, girl.

"She has breakfast sandwiches; I can get one of those." I really didn't want a sit-down meal. It seemed like a waste of time to me. "Please."

Asher nodded, and I followed him into Daily Perks. There was a line out the door. Not unusual, the place was always busy. The café's coffee was too strong and bitter for me, and I preferred the crafted coffees at Daily Perks.

We reached the front of the line, and I smiled. "Morning, again, Amelia. I'll have a large vanilla latte, one of those delicious chocolate chip muffins, and a breakfast sandwich."

"You got it. I wondered when you'd come down for food." She glanced over my head. "Large vanilla latte, large black coffee," Amelia called out to the barista. "Any food for you, Asher?"

"I'll try one of the breakfast sandwiches too. I didn't realize you had those."

"Trying something new. They're easy to heat up."

Asher tried to nudge me out of the way. "I've got it."

Ha! No, you don't.

I beat him to it and scanned my card for our food and drinks, then stepped aside. The consternation on his face almost made me smile.

Once we had everything, we made our way back up to the office. I understood after the first two days why almost everyone had their keycards on lanyards. The amount of scanning was crazy, but I understood about the security.

I sat down at my computer, making sure my coffee and food were well away from the keyboard. I got back to work, but I could feel Asher's presence next to me. What was it about him?

He was nice looking. Okay, some might say he was a handsome devil. His short black hair would get spiky when he ran his hands through it. His green eyes twinkled at times. And that smile...

My bones almost melted whenever he flashed that wide smile at me. It was flirty and sexy.

And his hands...

Strong hands.

Hands that could take care of a woman. Be it holding her tenderly in his arms or bringing her pleasure. Heat flashed through my body.

No, no, no. Fantasizing about someone I was working with? No. What was wrong with me? Maybe not wrong, but I should *not* be thinking like this in the workplace, especially about a colleague.

This fantasizing was part of the reason I worked yesterday—to get my mind off Asher. I was over his comments from Friday night. And the stuff from this morning? Pf-ffft. Just like the crap my family shoveled.

I typed in the command to run the code changes I'd made, picked up my breakfast sandwich, and bit into it. The taste of bacon, cheese, and egg filled my mouth. De-licious. I continued to eat as the lines of code scrolled on the screen. I didn't want to get ahead of myself, but I was feeling those first signs of excitement that always showed up when the app was working without error.

If I could get customer service up and running with their apps, then I could move on to the other departments. I'd only been here a week, but I was still amazed at how the company's multiple departments worked together almost flawlessly even with the hindrance of the software com-patibility issues.

STEM had never been welcoming for women, and we still hadn't smashed that glass ceiling, but we had the hammers, and there were cracks in the glass. Patriarchy was the rule rather than the exception.

My boss at Tri-O-Tech was a bit better. I suspect that was one of the reasons he sent me on this job, not just because FI would be using my software, but he was also aware no one else could do what I was doing with Asher. This assignment was likely my trial by fire.

I was up for promotion to head Tri-O-Tech's development team. First woman in that position, yada, yada, yada. I'd been with the company since they recruited me right out of undergrad. I'd dealt with the misogyny on the job the same way I dealt with the toxicity in my family. To observers, it slid off me like a waterfall. In my mind, it made me more determined to smash that ceiling. Even today, of the top ten CEOs in tech, only one was a woman.

But from my first day here, Asher's team had accepted me without reservation, And the respect on the job, extended without question, was a welcome change. I'd always loved my work, but the acceptance here made the job fun, even when I had to deal with Asher's bossy side.

Fantasies, Inc. would be a nice place to work, and as soon as the thought filtered into my mind, I pushed it away. I had a job. I was up for a promotion. But I couldn't deny that a part of me liked the excitement here.

As for that glass ceiling, getting that promotion would be one more crack in the glass. Was the possibility of that promotion worth going back into what would likely get worse if I accepted that position?

The computer ping brought me out of my head and back to the monitor. I almost pumped my arm in the air. The app had run perfectly. I couldn't wait for Cassie to try it out.

"Finally," I whispered. I double-checked everything, then reached for my cell phone. "Hey, Cassie, it's Emma. Do you have time this afternoon to do a beta test of the new app?"

"It's ready?"

"I believe so. I want you to test it out first, so if there are still bugs, I can fix them."

"Done. How about after we have lunch together to-day?"

I chuckled. "When did I agree to that?"

"Spur of the moment decision since we didn't get coffee together this morning. Twelve-thirty in the café, then I can test the app."

"Works for me. See you then." I set an alarm on my cell before placing it back on the table, feeling lighter than I had earlier. Possibly one app down, about thirty more to go.

"Sounds like you fixed one of the customer service apps," Asher commented.

"That's what I was working on yesterday, I had some ideas after Cassie and I talked Saturday."

"Saturday?" His eyebrows rose.

"Cassie called me to meet her for lunch. There's nothing against it, right?" *Hmm... Was that the slightest hint of sarcasm in my question?*

"Of course not."

"Good." I turned back and switched over to the other screen to begin working on another part of the R&D apps.

There was so much Marcus wanted. I focused on matching up the list he'd provided outlining the program requisites.

How did one make someone's fantasy come true? The research part was self-explanatory. Surveys, focus groups, even individual interviews. Then begin development. Design, test, examine results, incorporate changes, test again, and if everything gelled just right, set parameters for implementation.

I had fantasies. They weren't particularly elaborate or all that romantic. I dealt more in reality.

Yes, I read a lot, mainly romance. The stories and characters, the men, were the fantasy. Maybe the men in those stories were *my* fantasy. The desire to find a man like those depicted in the novels I read. A kind, caring man who would put me before everyone else. I almost laughed out loud. They didn't exist and wishes and hopes wouldn't change that.

Out of nowhere, I remembered last Monday when Asher took me down to R&D with all those items laid out on the table, then whispering in my ear. My face heated, and a shiver of desire slid down my spine. His voice had been so deep and sexy, I'd nearly melted into a puddle of goo at his feet.

Then there was Friday night when he showed me just how chauvinistic he was. An eye-opener that dumped a bucket of ice water over my libido, big time.

Or had it?

I'd been working in a male-dominated field my entire adult life, but I'd never been attracted to any of the men I'd worked with or encountered outside of work...until Asher. Was that a bad thing? It might actually be worth exploring. For now, I had to give up and focus.

Lots of work to get done in the short time allotted for this project. With the time constraints in that contract,

I'd be hard-pressed to complete it on schedule. Unless my contract was extended.

***

"I can't believe you got my app up and running so quickly." Cassie sipped her iced tea.

I set my sandwich back on the plate. "Apparently, I also broke a company rule."

"What rule?"

"Working overtime."

"Oh. I forgot about that. It happens so rarely. What did you do?"

"I worked from home on Sunday and made the mistake of mentioning it to Asher this morning. I was already in the office when he arrived, and he started asking questions."

Cassie's eyes sparkled. "I wish I could have been a fly on the wall."

"Why?"

"Because after Friday night, I can't believe Asher would risk sticking his foot in it again."

I laughed. "He sure did that on Friday, didn't he?"

Cassie laughed. "Poor guy, he's all topsy turvy right now."

Curiouser and curiouser.

"What do you mean?"

"I mean, he doesn't know what to do or say around you. I've never seen him like this."

"Oh." That was food for thought. "You mean he isn't always so chauvinistic?"

Cassie hesitated. "Not like he was on Friday. Like I said, I think he doesn't understand how to deal with you."

I shook my head. "He doesn't have to *deal* with me. I can take care of myself."

"So true. But men like my Marcus and Asher, heck..." Cassie waved her hands. "Men in general like to think of themselves as dominant, alphas, kings of whichever hill they happen to be standing on. The reality is that the vast majority of men don't understand the difference between control and dominance."

"Maybe they should learn that women can take care of themselves."

Cassie laughed. "How can I explain this?"

"What's the difference? I dislike controlling men."

"They don't mean to be. Take my Marcus." Her gaze softened, and her slight smile reminded me of someone keeping a cherished secret. "We danced around our attraction to each other. Our need for each other." Her smile turned just a bit mischievous. "Until Marcus forced the issue."

"How did he do that?" Cassie and Marcus looked like the perfect couple.

"He kept sending me gifts." Cassie's cheeks flushed. "Of a sensual nature." Her cheeks were even more pink now, and her chuckle had the slightest self-conscious edge. "I went to see him to put an end to it and ended up agreeing to spend a weekend with him without any rules."

I sat back in my chair. Thank goodness I'd finished eating, or I would have choked on my food. "How did you agree to that?"

"I won't go into all the details, but let's just say, I wanted to get Marcus out of my system. Instead, not only did he bring out a side of me I'd kept hidden, but he showed me how much fun a dominant man could be. How loving and tender."

I tilted my head, pondering her words. Dominant and, at the same time, loving and tender? Wasn't that a contradiction? I'd seen plenty of couples throughout the years, some of them loving and tender, but I'd seen others where one partner was controlling, even cruel. What Cassie was saying was very interesting.

"I never thought of it that way." I hadn't. "But Asher is more controlling, even to the point of overbearing, than tender."

Cassie swallowed the last bite of her sandwich and dabbed at the corners of her mouth with her napkin. "Asher is still learning. I think he wasn't expecting you."

"Of course he was. He knew I was coming to work here."

"That's not what I meant. He was probably expecting a male coder, not a beautiful woman." Before I could get a word out, she raised her hand. "I know, I know. Stereotyping, but there's still only about one woman for every four software engineers and—what?—maybe thirty percent overall of women in STEM. "

I couldn't argue with facts, but still my cheeks flushed. "I'm just average." Hell, except for that party disaster, I hadn't dated in the last year.

"One day, you'll see it. I'm going to say give Asher some slack. He's gone into protective mode, and he really can't help it."

I nodded. Cassie had given me a lot to think about. Even so, time to change the subject. "You said hardly anyone works overtime?"

"I did. Excellent pay aside, the policies to promote work-life balance were one of the things that drew me to the company. Strict overtime rules. At my other job, I was working up to sixty hours a week. I was burning out, but the company didn't care. Then I applied here. In my interview, I was told about the overtime rule, and I knew I could be happy here."

"It's an interesting rule." I was a bit confused by it. I'd always thought independent contractors set their work hours.

"Yes. Plus, the other benefits are great."

"They are." I held up my keycard.

"There's more than that, but since you're here as a contractor, the keycard and meals are pretty much your only benefit."

My curiosity was piqued, but my phone pinged. I'd set up an app to monitor the running of my program; my phone would ping when the run was finished. I glanced at the screen. *Fail* flashed across the screen. I sighed.

"Problem?" Cassie asked.

"The app for R&D failed." I rubbed my forehead. "It's a difficult one to get right."

"I understand. There is so much to deal with in that department."

"Yeah. Why don't we go up to your office, so I can show you your app, and you can test it for me."

"I'm excited. It will make things easier."

We bussed our table and then headed to Cassie's office.

Note to self: Concentrate on showing Cassie the app rather than on Asher and what Cassie told me about him.

Chapter Thirteen

♥

A sher

I looked at Emma's computer screen. The code had failed. Not surprising. R&D was going to require a massive app. I'd played with the code for days and still didn't see how this was going to fully work, which surprised me.

Glancing at the time on the computer screen; it was after two. I'd just come back from grabbing some food with Miles. I figured Emma would be back from going over the customer service app with Cassie.

I walked over to the windows and looked out at the Sound. Ever since she'd walked into my life, my head had been messed up. Why was I so drawn to her? It was more than simple, straightforward attraction.

The overtime issue wasn't that big a deal. Yet hearing her say she'd worked Sunday set me off. Had it been any of the others in my department, I would have reminded them of the rules and let it go. But with Emma…I practically went off the rails and overreacted, which was well beyond the scope of supervisor/colleague.

Friday night was sort of the same. I was forceful on Friday, but that was mainly because something inside me wanted to protect Emma, even if she didn't need it. She didn't seem to care about her personal safety, so I was damn sure going to make sure she was safe.

I shook my head. When had I decided she was my responsibility? She wasn't, but I couldn't help myself. We'd only been working together a week and yet this need pulsed inside me.

I was sure I'd figure it out, in the meantime, I needed to be careful. Fantasies, Inc. didn't have any rules about dating other employees, but she was a contractor, and we were clients of her company. This could turn into an ethical quagmire if I didn't tread very carefully. I needed to find a subtle way to get to know Emma better.

Tomorrow, I'd ask her to have lunch with me, and maybe I could learn more about this woman who haunted my dreams.

And that was another thing.

Since meeting Emma, she'd been starring in every one of my dreams, most of them erotic. I wondered if she had any interest in consensual kink. I'd been part of the kink community for a while now, but I was still exploring. I'd often found that the consent discussion could be as hot as the scene itself. If done right, going over what a potential partner and I enjoyed and even our limits could be manipulated into a form of foreplay.

How would Emma feel about being tied up and ravished.

The office door opened, and the object of my musings walked in. "How did the testing with Cassie go?"

"Great." She gave me a wide smile. "Cassie and her assistant, Lisa, are going to test the heck out of the app today and tomorrow and let me know of any issues."

"That's great." I said as she sat down at her desk and frowned at the computer screen. "I noticed it failed."

"Yeah." Emma rubbed her forehead. "I'm wondering if we can make the app simpler."

Her idea wasn't a bad one. "Maybe. What are you thinking?"

"We break it down even further. Right now, we have some pretty big categories. What if we broke down toys into things like vibrators, non-vibrating, specialty?"

"That's a good idea. Marcus would be the best re-source. Why don't I set up a meeting with him for tomor-row?"

"Not today?"

"It's almost three, and we leave at four. Actually, you should leave at three-thirty since you got here at six-thirty."

The enthusiasm in her eyes dimmed to disappointment. "If you insist."

"I do. I believe in the overtime policy."

"I get it. It's something I need to get used to, even if it's only for a short period of time."

There was that, but I wasn't ready to discuss eventual completion of this project and her leaving yet. "How would you feel about going out to dinner tonight?"

Her eyes widened. "Dinner?"

Be cool, Asher. One step at a time.

"Yes. We're going into our second week of working together. I know very little about you."

Emma rested her elbow on the desk and propped her chin in her hand "I could say the same about you."

"That's why I'm proposing dinner. What do you say?"

She considered for a moment, and I almost forgot to breathe. "Sure, but would you mind doing something outside of Seattle?"

"Not at all." I considered some suburban restaurants I was familiar with. "What about Tuscany's?" I hoped it was a good place for her.

"That works. It's on my way home. But I'm leaving before you."

"I think I can sneak out. We were both here early." I'd let Ben, my right-hand man, know I was leaving early.

Emma shrugged and turned back to her computer, making notes on the ever-present notepad next to her keyboard.

I picked up the house phone and called Marcus. After securing a meeting with him at nine tomorrow, I opened a new window and began typing in categories based on Emma's idea. It was a good one.

We were trying to design an app that would incorporate all the services we offered under one umbrella with two subdivisions—corporate and client. I was excited about this prospect. When I mentioned it to Josh and Dean in operations, they said it would make their work easier since it would organize negotiations with clients who wanted their services.

I normally didn't get very involved with that aspect of the business. I was the IT guy. Based on what Josh and Dean said, I made a note that we'd need to incorporate the operations app with the R&D app.

I'd built the program to do that, but with all the changes we were making, it would need to be re-written. I was glad Emma was here. My group of specialists were good and worked hard on the routine IT issues for the company. But Emma was smart and saw things I didn't. Fresh eyes helped. Maybe something to discuss at the next staff meeting? I noted a few more ideas, and before I knew it, it was three-thirty.

"Time to log off," I said.

Emma sighed but did as I said. At least she wasn't fighting me on it. We walked over to the garage together. "What floor are you parked on?" I asked her.

"Second."

"I'm there too." When she headed for the stairs, I followed her. "I didn't expect you to take the stairs."

"I sit all day on the job so I try to do stairs whenever I can. Plus, I do a lot of walking."

"Good for you. I run as often as I can for the same reason." I pushed open the second-floor door. "I'll walk you to your car."

She opened her mouth, then shut it. That was interesting. She wanted to object but held back; I wondered why. She stopped next to a small red car.

"This is me."

"How do you get around in winter?" The little two door car would slip and slide in any snow with the ice built up underneath it; there wasn't enough weight to it.

"I manage. I bet you have a big honking SUV."

"It's not big. It's medium sized and great in winter with four-wheel drive."

She laughed and rolled her eyes. "Men and their big SUVs."

"Don't back out until I pull up behind you. I'll be the dark blue SUV."

"I know where Tuscany's is, you know."

"Humor me."

"I'll take your request under consideration." She gave me a jaunty wave as she unlocked the door and slid behind the wheel of her car.

I jogged to where my vehicle was parked two rows away, only to see Emma pull out and head for the exit. Cheeky woman. Once inside my vehicle, I pulled out. Emma made all the lights, whereas I didn't.

After Friday, I decided not to call her. What would be the point, and I'd already stepped over a line with her. If whatever this might be was going anywhere, I had to put the brakes on my protective instincts. I'd see her at the restaurant. One thing was for sure, with her fierce independence and stubbornness, any relationship we might have would never be boring.

She was waiting already at the door of the restaurant as I pulled into Tuscany's parking lot. She waved at me while rocking a big self-satisfied grin on her face.

I shook my head as I pulled into a parking space. *Okay, Emma. You win this round.* I locked the vehicle and went inside to find her talking with the hostess.

"Here he is," Emma said, looking very proud of herself.

If she were mine...

I felt a flush of anticipation. The Discussion was going to happen; I was absolutely certain of it. And the aftermath would very likely involve restraint, at least one spanking, and heat. Lots and lots of heat. Over and over again. I'd never been this attracted to a woman. I wanted to know her intimately. Inside and out.

Shit. Now I had a raging hard on. Thank goodness my suit jacket was buttoned.

"Perfect. Right this way," the hostess said.

I cleared my throat, reminding myself that I needed to play a long game. Emma might show her sassy side on occasion, but she was a skittish woman, and I was not going to risk doing anything that might send her running for the suburbs. Still, I needed her to understand that nothing was more important than her safety.

I cupped Emma's elbow. "You didn't wait for me."

"No, I didn't."

The hostess stopped at a table. I slipped around the pair and pulled out Emma's chair. Her eyebrows rose, but she sat down, and I took a seat across from her. The hostess smiled. "Your waiter will be here shortly."

Luckily, the restaurant wasn't busy this early in the evening. I waited until the hostess was out of earshot. "Next time, you will wait for me."

"Will I?" Emma picked up her menu.

"Emma…" I lowered my voice.

She lowered the menu enough that I could see her eyes. They danced with mischief. "Quit being an overbearing Neanderthal."

"I'm not a Neanderthal." That word was beginning to annoy me.

"If the shoe fits…" She lifted her menu higher.

All right, maybe I was a little overbearing.

I picked up my menu. Lots of good choices.

"Good afternoon, I'm Marco your waiter. May I get you something to drink? Wine, coffee, soft drink?"

"I'd like an iced tea please," Emma said.

"Of course, do you want lemon with that?"

"No, thank you."

The waiter looked at me. "Peroni, please."

"Good choice. I'll be right back with those drinks and some bread."

I folded my menu and set it down. "What are you thinking about?"

"I really want the halibut fish & chips, but the cannelloni sounds so good."

"How about if we do it family style?"

Emma looked up from her menu, tilted her head, and stared at me. "What do you mean?"

"Trust me?" I was taking a chance here. Emma was already thinking I was taking over too much.

"All right, but just where tonight's food is concerned."

Leave it to her to put conditions on it, but I got it. "Thank you."

The waiter returned with our drinks and a basket of ciabatta bread. "Are you ready to order?"

"Yes. Let's start with an order of toasted ravioli, then two house salads, I'd like ranch dressing." I looked at Emma. "Emma, what kind of dressing?"

"Ranch is fine."

I nodded. "Then an order of halibut fish and chips, cannelloni, and fettuccini. Extra plates, please."

"Yes, sir. I'll have the appetizer and salads out first."

"That's a lot of food," Emma said.

"I'm hungry." I was. But any leftovers would go home with her. "So, tell me more about Emma Palmer."

Her cheeks flushed. "Not much to tell. You already know I'm the youngest of three."

"Right. Born and raised in San Francisco." She nodded. "Where did you get your degree?"

"UC Berkeley, in computer science, of course."

I whistled. "Nice."

"Yeah." She ducked her head. "It wouldn't have been my first choice, but my parents insisted, and since they paid for it..."

I nodded. "I went to MIT."

"I think of MIT for engineering degrees."

"A lot do, but they have a great computer science department."

"Were you born and raised in Seattle?"

"Not in the city, but down in Tacoma." My parents still live in the same house.

"Why MIT then?"

I chuckled. "My father wanted me to attend. He thought it would be good for me to get out on my own at college."

"At eighteen?"

"I'm sure you went to Berkeley when you were..."

"Twenty. I did two years at a community college first."

"I'd already done most of the first two years of college in my last two years of high school."

"Ah, one of those gifted ones." She grinned.

"I never considered myself gifted. I picked up coding easily. One of my high school teachers noticed and helped me get into the right math and science classes. The rest is history."

"How did you fare being so far from home?" She paused. "Sorry, I'm curious."

"You can ask me anything you want." I meant that. I wanted Emma to talk to me. Figuring out what made this woman tick was an interesting prospect and a two-way street. "The first six months were hard. But as I made friends, it became easier."

The waiter walked up to their table, dropped off two baskets of bread, the toasted ravioli, and the salads before walking away.

"This looks good," Emma commented.

"Let's eat." She seemed relaxed, so maybe I could learn more about her as we ate.

Chapter Fourteen

♥

Emma

I took a bite of my salad, thinking about what Asher said. I couldn't see being so far away from home at eighteen. Heck, even going to Berkeley at twenty had been a stretch for me. Not that it lasted long. With my parents always busy, and my sisters enjoying their life without parents, I started to grow away from them, not that we were that close.

Actually, my separation from my family had been happening for years. I just didn't realize it until after my first year in Berkeley. I made a few friends, and at the end of the year, I moved into an apartment with them.

That had been the best thing for me. Being away from my family taught me a lot about myself and how resilient I was. By the time I graduated and got the job up here, I had no qualms about moving away. I was better off on my own.

"What drew you into computers?" he asked.

I contemplated his question. "I'm not sure. Maybe the logic behind programming. I understood how it worked without much thought. I like things to be in order" I took a drink of my tea. "How about you?"

"Computers were a challenge for me."

Interesting, a challenge but IT became his career. "So, how was your first year a challenge?" I asked again.

Asher glanced up as the waiter brought our food. My mouth watered at the smells. The waiter removed the salads, then set plates in front of us and arranged the main dishes in the center of the table.

"Enjoy your dinner."

"This all looks so good." It did. My stomach growled. Even though I'd eaten a breakfast sandwich this morning, lunch had been light, and now I was hungry.

"Let's dig in."

I filled my plate and watched Asher fill his.

"Are you going to tell me about your first year in college?" I asked after a few minutes. Did he not want to answer me?

"I never realized how much my mother did to keep our household running."

I bit my lip. "Cooking, laundry, cleaning."

"All that. Luckily, I didn't have to cook much. I had a meal plan and went to the dining hall for most of my meals. Plus they had food trucks."

"You didn't get bored with the food? I sure did."

He shook his head. "There was a good enough variety, and if we wanted something not available, we just ordered delivery."

"That must have been nice." While my parents paid for everything, I spent as little as I could of their money. Instead, I took a part-time job to pay for all the little extras I wanted. My father hadn't been happy about it, but my mother convinced him it would help me in the real world.

The thing was, I took a job in the library, and while I did have to interact with students, it was mostly quiet, and I loved it.

"I'm sure Berkeley had dining services."

"They did, but I preferred to cook at the apartment I shared with my friends."

"How did you learn to cook?"

"I hung out in the kitchen with our chef from the time I turned fourteen. She taught me a lot of basics. I also learned how to do laundry."

"No pink underwear for you," he said with humor in his voice.

"Nope." I couldn't suppress a chuckle. "Did you really turn your underwear pink?"

"Not pink, but bright red."

I laughed; I really couldn't help myself. We continued to chat as we ate, and I found myself relaxing around Asher more and more. Maybe he wasn't the chauvinistic Neanderthal after all.

"Dessert?" Asher asked.

I glanced at the dishes on the table. Most were still close to half full. "No, thank you. I don't think I could eat another bite."

"They have a killer tiramisu."

I shook my head. "Please, have some if you want."

The waiter arrived. "If you would box up what is left, please. I'll have the tiramisu and..." Asher looked at me.

"Black tea, if you have it."

"Yes, ma'am." The waiter rushed off to box up the food.

"No coffee?" Asher asked.

"I don't like to drink coffee at night." Tea would help my food settle a bit; I didn't normally eat as much as I had tonight.

The waiter brought Asher's dessert and my tea and set the leftovers at the empty place across from me.

I stirred my tea then lifted the cup and blew across the tea to cool it enough to take a sip. I glanced at Asher just as he took a bite of the tiramisu. Almost simultaneously he closed his eyes with an expression of what looked like pure bliss, licked his lips, and moaned.

The sound went straight to my soul.

"Have a bite?" He scooped up a piece on the fork and held it out to me.

I started to shake my head, then changed my mind. Leaning forward, I put my hand over his and guided the fork into my mouth. The sweet of the ladyfingers, the sweet Marsala, the bitter of the espresso and unsweetened cocoa, and the perfect mascarpone nearly melted on my tongue. Such a contrast.

I held the fork in my mouth a bit longer than normal before I allowed Asher to pull it back. The heat in his gaze shot through my body. I sat back. "That is delicious."

Asher cleared his throat. "Yes, it is."

Okay, I was playing with fire, but for once in my life, I wanted to get burned. Asher might act like a caveman, at times, but he was also funny and a hard worker.

We finished our dinner, and after what my mother would have called a 'spirited' discussion regarding the check, Asher walked me to my car. He waited for me to unlock it, then he opened the back door and set the leftovers inside.

"Shouldn't you take them home?" I had surrendered about the check but made it crystal clear I didn't think it was fair for him to pay the whole thing. Just as I thought I'd made my point, his whole demeanor changed. Determination, power, I didn't know what to call it, but the vibe, even as subtle as it was, definitely shut down any argument. There wasn't anything scary about it. In fact, it was the hottest experience I could ever remember. Then, as soon as we stepped out of the restaurant, he gently took hold of my arm and whispered in my ear, "You'll behave yourself or I *will* spank you."

The heat that flowed through my veins when he said he'd spank me was molten level. Was Asher kinky? It was possible. After all, he worked for a company that screamed kink.

"I want you to have them." He shut the door and then turned to me.

His body was close, almost too close. "Thank you," I whispered.

I watched as he lifted his hand and followed the movement until I felt his fingers on my chin, and he gently lifted my face ever so slightly so that his gaze captured mine. "I'm going to kiss you now, Emma. If you don't want this, say no."

I opened my mouth, but nothing came out.

He looked from my eyes to my lips and back to my eyes, tilted his head, and his lips touched mine.

It was a soft, barely there kiss, and I wanted more. I entwined my arms around his neck and pulled him closer.

Instantly, his lips parted, and our tongues tangled. His fingers dropped from my chin as his arms slid around my waist, pulling me even tighter against his body.

Oh yes. The kiss deepened. My body caught fire, and nothing was going to put it out—short of a week in bed.

A wolf whistle interrupted the kiss, and Asher lifted his head. I moaned and tried to follow his lips.

"We're in a parking lot," he whispered.

Yep, the mental bucket of cold water put the fire out. Damn, what was I thinking? One amazing kiss from Asher and I was putty in his arms. This wasn't like me at all.

"Yes." I unwound my arms from his neck and tried to step back, but he kept his arms around my waist. I glanced up at him.

"This isn't the time or place to continue this, but later..." He leaned down and brushed his lips over mine before he whispered in my ear. "The gloves come off."

Chapter Fifteen

♥

Asher

It was Friday, and I, for one, was never so glad for the weekend. After having dinner with Emma Monday evening—and that scorching kiss after—she was all I could think about. Emma, on the other hand, didn't seem to have an issue at all.

She'd breezed in on Tuesday like nothing special had happened the night before. It had been special to me. This woman frustrated the living hell out of me. I got zero time alone with her outside of our concentrated coding time. She'd been having lunch with Cassie all week and spending lots of time in customer service, fine tuning the app.

Wasn't that her job? It was, but I wanted her close. She hadn't been unaffected by that kiss. I'd seen the dreamy look in her eyes, her surprise when I stepped back and allowed her to get into her car.

My body had demanded more action, but I ignored it. Emma wasn't a woman to be rushed, but damned if I wanted to wait this long. Tonight, I'd make another move. Because I wanted Emma.

"Crap," she muttered.

"What's up?" I glanced over at her screen.

"I finally got the toy section of the app for R&D to work, but now the flogger section won't work at all."

Emma and I met with Marcus Tuesday and discussed breaking things up into smaller categories so the app could handle them. Marcus didn't have an issue with it, but the program was still hiccupping.

"Let me see." I scooted over next to her and watched the code run on her screen, then stop. "I don't see anything obvious."

"No shit, Sherlock," she muttered.

I opened my mouth to ask her about the attitude when she said, "I'm sorry. You didn't deserve that."

She was tense; I could see it.

"What's wrong?"

She shrugged. "Nothing big."

I glanced at the clock. "It's almost four. Why don't we wrap this up, and head to Whistle Stop?"

"All right."

I was surprised when she didn't put up a fuss, but then she and Cassie had become friends, and she knew Cassie would be there. We powered down our computers and gathered our belongings. Emma had gotten used to leaving her laptop in the office since it was locked, and except for Ben and the head of security, we were the only two with key codes.

We were the first ones at the Whistle Stop, not surprising. Marcus usually stayed until four-thirty, and Cassie wouldn't leave the office without him. I found a table that would hold eight and held Emma's chair out for her.

"Thank you," she said. I sat as she took a deep breath and released it. "I didn't mean to snap at you in the office."

"It's fine." I waved my hand.

"It's not. I'm usually not short tempered."

"What set you off?" I was curious.

"My parents are coming to town in a couple of weeks and want me to attend some event with them."

"And that's bad because?" From the tone of her voice, she wasn't happy about her parents visit or whatever the event was.

She shook her head as Josh and Dean walked up to the table.

"What a day." Josh sat to Emma's right, and Dean sat next to Josh.

"I need this," Dean said.

"How are you, Emma?" Josh asked.

"Good. Busy day?"

I watched the interaction between Josh, Emma, and Dean. She was friendly with them, but not overly so. I'd noticed that when she chatted with them about what was needed for their app.

By the time Cassie and Marcus joined us, Miles and Lucas had arrived, and there were two pitchers of beer on the table and mugs.

"We're all here," Marcus commented.

"About time," Cassie muttered.

The men laughed. "Sorry, Cassie, some of us don't get to leave the office at four," Lucas said.

I glanced around the table at my friends, and my gaze settled on Emma. She looked a bit uncomfortable. She hadn't been around all of us at once yet.

"Are you okay?" I whispered.

"I'm fine. It's interesting to see all of you together."

"Watch out once the beer starts flowing."

Chapter Sixteen

♥

E mma

I wondered what Asher meant. A few hours later, I found out. The men were on their way to being drunk. I'd never seen men put away so much beer. Even though they ate, the guys were unsteady on their feet.

"Another pitcher," Marcus said.

"Nope." Cassie waved the waitress away. "All of you are getting drunk."

"Aw, Cassie. We're fine," Josh said, his words slightly slurred.

Cassie shook her head. "No, you're not."

"How are they going to get home?" I whispered to Cassie.

"Can you take Asher home? The other four can do a ride share, and of course, I can take Marcus."

"What about their cars?" I wasn't sure how secure they would be.

"The parking structure locks down at night. I'll let security know their cars are going to be there."

"It locks down?" I didn't know that.

"Yes. After nine, the gates come down so the only way to get in or out is with your badge. This way no one can walk into the garage and lurk."

I nodded. Another way that Fantasies, Inc. took care of for their employees. "Thank goodness we've already paid the bill."

"Yes. Prepare for a lot of moaning and groaning." Cassie turned to the men. "All right, Lucas, Miles, Josh, and Dean, up and with me to the front door."

The men glared at her but stood. I watched with amusement as they all walked to the front and out the door like obedient puppies. Cassie knew exactly how to handle these guys.

"I can feel your humor," Asher commented.

"If I didn't know better, I would think Cassie was the Dominant."

"Bite your tongue, woman," Marcus said.

"Hey." Asher glared at Marcus. "Don't call her woman."

Marcus snorted, then looked at me. "Sorry. I didn't mean to offend."

"No offense taken." I'd been called worse. Besides, I knew Marcus was drunk, and in a normal situation, he would never call me that. Funny, I was getting to know Marcus mainly through Cassie. I still didn't know a lot about Asher, beyond where he went to school and his family. I wanted to know more, and that was different for me.

"Okay, those four are off," Cassie said, returning to the table. "Let's go." She put her hand on Marcus's shoulder.

"We should go too," I said to Asher. "I'll give you a ride home."

"Whatever you say, sweetheart."

Asher's voice on the word sweetheart was almost a caress. I helped Asher to his feet. While the pub was only two blocks from the office, getting Asher and Marcus back there took twice the time it should have.

We all piled in the elevator; I pushed the button for the second floor, and Cassie pressed the third.

"Have a good night," Cassie said, as I guided Asher out of the elevator.

"You too." Asher had thrown his arm around my shoulders as I helped him to my car. I pushed him up against the vehicle while I pulled my keys out and unlocked it.

"Okay, big boy, into the car."

"This isn't my vehicle."

"You're in no shape to drive." I pushed the passenger seat as far back as it would go and guided him onto the seat. It was a tight fit, but he made it. I secured the seatbelt over him and shut the door.

I huffed then climbed into the driver's seat. I fastened my seatbelt and started the engine.

"I'm not that drunk."

"Yes, you are." I pulled out of the parking spot. "What is your address?"

He rattled it off. I put the brake back on and input his address into my navigation system then drove out of the structure. Asher was quiet as I drove, and then I heard a soft, small snore.

I glanced at him at the next stoplight. His head was slumped to the side. He was asleep or passed out. A laugh bubbled up. Asher wasn't in control at the moment. Would he even remember this tomorrow morning?

Once I arrived in his neighborhood, I drove slowly when I got closer to his house so I wouldn't miss a turn. This was a nice area. Some of the houses were huge, and others were what I considered normal. When the navigation app announced the house was on my left in a hundred feet, I turned into the driveway and stopped at the gate.

"Asher..." He didn't even stir. Louder. "Asher." I reached over and shook his shoulder. "I'm at your house; I need the gate code."

"Seven, four, eight, two," he mumbled.

I rolled down my window and punched in the code. After the gate opened, I drove through. I blew out a breath when I saw his home. A ranch style painted in white and gray, with outdoor lights on.

I pulled to a stop in front of a three-car garage. After getting out, I opened the passenger door. "Asher." I shook his shoulder again. "You're home. I need your help to get you into the house."

He opened his eyes. "Home?"

"Yes. Come on, big boy." Seatbelt released, I encouraged him to get out of the car. I gripped him around the waist, holding on to the waistband of his pants. With slow steps, we made it to the front door.

Oh boy, another keypad. I should have guessed Asher would have some kind of smart house. "Code for the door."

"One, five, three, seven, four."

I was glad he was coherent enough to give me the codes. I heard the lock click, and I opened the door. A beeping started. "Asher, alarm code."

"Seventeen, twenty, and five."

Punching it in, I was glad the beeping stopped. The last thing we needed was the police showing up.

The foyer was large, but I didn't really look around. "Bedroom?" I asked.

"In the back, down the hallway."

Figures it would be all the way in the back. He was getting heavier by the minute. As we made our way down the hallway, I noticed he had low level track lighting, so I didn't have to worry about bumbling around in the dark.

I was happy when we made it to his bedroom. I froze for a second when I walked into the room. Hell, this was huge.

There was a king-sized bed, and I guided him to it. Asher flopped down on his back. I sighed. As lean as the man looked, he was heavy. He looked uncomfortable with his legs hanging off the bed.

I knelt down and removed his shoes and socks, then swung them up onto the bed. I couldn't help the laugh that bubbled up when I saw him. He was sprawled out now. At least it was a king bed, so he had room.

I grabbed a pillow and carefully put it under his head. Next, water and ibuprofen. He was more than likely going to have a hangover in the morning. I almost felt sorry for him.

When I'd found everything, I put both items on the nightstand next to his bed. While it was almost summer, the nights were still cool. Just in case, there was a blanket at the end of the bed and I pulled it from under his feet, shook it out, and placed it where he could easily reach it. Then I left the room.

I paused. "Should I stay?" I muttered to myself then answered my own question. "Nope. Asher can take care of himself."

I turned out most of the lights, leaving one on in the ensuite bathroom, one in the hallway, and one in the foyer, set the lock, let myself out of the house, and drove home.

Chapter Seventeen

♥

"Fuck," I muttered. There was a marching band playing in my head. I opened my eyes and noticed a glass of water and two tablets on my nightstand. I sat up carefully, grabbed the pain killers and the water, and downed them.

How the hell did I get home last night? The events after Cassie telling us we'd had enough beer were fuzzy. A shower would help. I forced myself to move. My pants pulled around my legs.

Hell. I'd slept in my clothes. I hadn't done that since college. I started to shake my head, but pain flashed through my brain. Okay, so slow and easy. It took me longer than I expected to get into the bathroom.

I turned on the shower, stripped, and stepped into the enclosure. Warm water cascaded over my body. I ducked my head under the shower, which mercifully, started to clear some of the cobwebs.

By the time I was out of the shower, my headache had begun to ease, and the events of last night were becoming clearer.

Emma.

She'd helped me leave the pub, drove me home, and got me into bed. It was more than I deserved. I was hammered last night. That wasn't like me at all. Was it because all of us had been together for the first time in a while? Or because I wanted nothing better than to sweep Emma into my arms and kiss her silly, but I had to take it slow.

The mere thought made me smile. Yeah, I'd briefly thought about pulling her into my arms last night and kissing her, but something held me back. Maybe because I knew I'd had too much to drink and it wouldn't be a good idea.

I walked carefully back into my bedroom and dressed. Food and more water. I made my way down the hallway and stopped when I saw Emma in my kitchen. There was music playing on low volume. The rush from the surprise ratcheted up my headache. I cleared my throat.

Emma turned. "Good morning."

"Not yet. I'll let you know after the marching band in my head stops playing. What are you doing here?" My voice was scratchy.

"I felt really bad about leaving you last night in your condition. I hope you don't mind. I thought you might need some food this morning." She gestured to the pans on the stove. "There's water on the table, and I have coffee, if you want it." The smell of coffee and bacon registered as soon as she mentioned the coffee.

"I don't mind." With any other woman I might have, but not with Emma. I filed that to ponder later. I glanced at the table. A pitcher of water and glass sat there. I made a beeline for the table. I needed that water. I poured a glass and chugged it down. *Nectar of the gods.* I poured another one. *Even better. I might survive the consequences of last night.*

I turned so I could see her. "You didn't have to do this." She seemed completely at ease in the kitchen. That chef had trained her well. She moved effortlessly around as she cooked. There was something pleasurable about having her there. Emma fit in my kitchen as if it had been built for her.

"I wanted to."

The aromas of bacon and coffee made me realize I actually felt hungry, even as my growling stomach reminded me.

And there it was—embarrassment and more than a dash of guilt. "Sorry about last night." I shook my head.

Emma looked over her shoulder from where she stood at the stove. "For what? Having too much to drink?"

"That and falling asleep on you." I'd finally remembered I passed out in her car.

"No worries." She waved the spatula in the air and turned back to the pans on the stove. "I will say I was glad when you woke up enough to get from the car to your bed. You're heavy."

"I'm a man in his prime." I mentally smacked my forehead. *Damned ego.*

"I didn't say you weren't, but you're still heavy." She flipped the bacon out of the pan onto the waiting paper towels. "I'm doing scrambled eggs or would you prefer them some other way."

"Anything you cook will be fine." I drank more water. "You mentioned coffee?"

"There sure is." She spun from the stove, took a mug from the cabinet, poured the coffee, and brought it over to me.

"I didn't mean for you to serve me."

"Not a big deal, but only for today. I snooped around to find everything I needed for this feast. I know it was intrusive, and I'm sorry."

I sipped my coffee and moaned as the rich brew slid down my throat. "You can snoop all you want. If you cook half as good as this coffee is, I'm set."

Emma laughed and went back to the stove. Within a few minutes, eggs, bacon, and toast were set in front of me on plates I very rarely used. I usually grabbed take-out on my way home from work because I wasn't much of a cook.

I picked up my fork and took a bite of the eggs. Delicious. Light and fluffy. Bacon crisp and the toast...perfection.

Emma surprised me at every turn. "Where did you learn to cook?"

"Remember? I told you I spent time in the kitchen with the family chef. She taught me very well, and I experimented a lot when I got out on my own."

I nodded. She had told me that. "Do you like to cook?" There were a few things I could cook, but I preferred not to.

"Sometimes, but it's hard to cook for one."

I'd heard people say that something tasted so good, they practically licked the plate. I enjoyed a good meal, but that licking the plate thing never made sense. Until this morning.

"Emma, this was delicious. Thank you." I stood and picked up my plate, then gestured to her plate. "Are you finished?"

"I am. I can clean up."

"You cooked. I'll clean up." I grabbed her empty plate and carried both to the sink and rinsed them.

Emma picked up our mugs. "More coffee?"

"Yes, please." I loaded our dirty breakfast plates and utensils into the dishwasher as she refilled the coffee cups.

I'd only brought a few women here, but none fit like Emma did. I was amazed at how comfortable I was with her in my home.

"Let's sit in the family room," I said as she walked toward the table.

"Okay."

I was proud of the family room. It had an L-shaped sectional along with cup holders and several side tables. I watched Emma pull a coaster from the holder and place it on the side table before setting her coffee cup down. I did the same.

We sat at opposite ends of the sectional, but that was okay.

"I hope I didn't act inappropriately last night." I didn't think I had but wanted to be sure.

"You didn't. Do you drink like that often?"

I shook my head. "No. I'm usually pretty good at cutting myself off."

"That makes sense. You don't strike me as the kind of guy who loses control often."

Silence filled the air. Emma picked up her coffee cup and toyed with it. Was she nervous because she'd let herself into my home? She had no reason to be.

Without saying anything, I walked over to her, took the mug from her hands, placed it on the table, and knelt down in front of her. She didn't look away, didn't even blink.

"Emma." I placed my hands on the inside of her knees. A little pressure and they parted. "I want to kiss you again."

She swallowed as her eyes widened, and her lips parted.

"Would you like me to kiss you?"

She nodded.

"Words, Emma. I need your words."

"Please kiss me, Asher."

I pushed between her legs and leaned forward. I brushed my lips over hers. Soft and easy. She parted her lips with a sigh.

That was my clue, and I captured her lips with just enough intensity to show her I wanted her. Her tongue darted out and touched mine then retreated.

Oh, my playful Emma.

I eased my tongue into her mouth and tasted the rich flavor of coffee and Emma. I didn't know what else to call it. She scooted forward on the sofa, and I lifted my hands up and placed them on her shoulders. Mainly to hold her in place. I didn't want to move too fast.

Our kiss continued, tongues tasting, dueling, and playing. I pulled back first and gazed down at her serene face.

"More, please," she whispered.

"Let's get more comfortable." I shifted and then rose to my feet. Taking Emma's hand, I pulled her up, then I reclined on the other end of the sofa and patted my chest. "Will you be comfortable if you straddle me?"

I could see her pondering the question. I wanted us to both be comfortable, but I also didn't want to loom over her. She needed time to get used to me and what I wanted. This way she could have some control.

"I can do that." Her voice was soft.

I placed one foot on the floor, and she knelt, bracketing my thighs, one of her arms braced against the back of the sofa, the other against the arm. She lowered herself, and I almost groaned when her breasts brushed against my chest.

Damn, we were both dressed, and I was losing it. How had Emma tied me up in knots so quickly?

I didn't know the answer to my question. Since she'd walked into Fantasies, Inc. I wanted her. Hell, when I saw her at the party that night, I wanted her, but I was pulled away, and she disappeared. Was that it? Had I built her up in my mind because I couldn't find her?

No, that didn't make sense. I shook myself mentally back to the task at hand. I lifted my hand and placed it behind her neck, urging her down. "I won't break."

"I know, but..." She bit her lip.

"But what?" Was she thinking she was too heavy for me? "Emma, I can handle you sitting on me."

"I'm not exactly dainty."

Fuck. Who messed with her self-esteem? "You're perfect." I raised my other arm and curved it around her waist. She finally lowered herself completely.

"You feel delicious against me."

"I'm not too heavy?"

"You're not. I don't know who told you that, but they were a fool." I applied very gentle pressure to her neck, and she lowered her head.

Our lips met again, and I relaxed. She wasn't running. She'd kissed me back and accepted what I said. Good. One step at a time. My body wanted more. Hell, my dick had already reacted, but it would have to wait. It was more important that Emma felt comfortable with me.

She broke the kiss, breathing hard, then she buried her face in my chest. "What are we doing?" Her words were muffled.

"Kissing." I stroked the back of her head, enjoying the feel of her silky hair.

I felt the vibrations of her giggle against my chest. "I know that, silly. But we barely know each other."

"I think we know more about each other than you think." I continued to stroke her hair and kissed the top of her head. "I know you're a hard worker, enjoy your job, must have coffee in the morning, and snack a lot."

Emma turned her head so that her cheek now rested on my shoulder. My heart warmed. "Food fuels my brain."

I chuckled. "All those cookies and chips."

She stiffened against me. "Are you laughing at me?"

"No. I'm laughing *with* you because I do the same thing. There is something about junk food that fuels us when we're in the zone."

Emma relaxed against me once again.

"I think we have a lot in common."

"Maybe." Her breath warmed my neck.

"I like having you in my arms." I kept my tone soft. She was quiet for a minute.

"I like being in your arms. It's been a long time since I've been held like this."

"That's a shame." She deserved to be held and taken care of. I closed my eyes. My protective tendency emerged. I couldn't help it. I'd watched how my father treated my mother, supportive, encouraging her to do whatever made her happy. I wanted that for Emma. I wanted her to be happy.

"Why haven't you had someone to hold you?" The direction of this conversation had made Emma uncomfortable. I could feel the tension in her body. I stroked her back as she rested on my chest to try and soothe her.

Tread carefully, Asher. This is one of those make or break moments.

I felt her deep breath. "I have terrible taste in men," she whispered.

That definitely didn't fit the image I had of her. "Oh? What makes you say that?"

"Because all the men I've been out with were party guys, and I'd rather have a nice dinner and spend the night watching a movie while cuddling."

"That's my kind of date."

"Don't you all from Fantasies, Inc. meet up every Friday night?"

"We try to. It was something we started doing right after we joined the company, and over the years, it's become a regular thing."

"What about Cassie?"

"She usually declined. Mainly, it was just the guys."

"But she was there last night and the week before."

"Yes. Since she and Marcus got together, she's joined our Friday group."

"What about the other women at Fantasies, Inc.?"

"I've never thought about it. We don't make it a secret we're at the Whistle Spot."

"But do you invite other people?"

"I invited you."

She tilted her head. "Yes, you did." Emma started to sit up. "And now, I really should get home."

When she was upright, I took her hands in mine. "Stay."

Her expression softened. "Don't tempt me," she whispered as she pushed against the back of the recliner until she had her balance and placed her other foot on the floor. "I have things to do."

I nodded and sat up as she got to her feet, then I stood. "Thank you for coming to check on me and feed me breakfast."

Emma straightened her clothes, a move that seemed more to collect herself since she didn't look mussed. In fact, she looked perfect, her cheeks pink and one corner of her mouth turned up in a kind of half-smile. "I enjoyed myself."

I followed her to the front door. She gathered her purse and keys from the table in the foyer.

"I really did like having you here, Emma." I wanted her to stay, but I also had to respect her time. She slipped on her shoes and then reached for the doorknob. I captured her hand. "Safe drive home." And kissed the back of her hand.

That half-smile turned into a smile that went all the way to her eyes. "Thanks."

I let go of her hand and opened the door, then watched her as she walked to her car, got in, and drove off. I missed her already, and that had never happened before with any woman I'd had in my home.

As I lost sight of her car, the ringing of my cell yanked me back into the here and now, and I reluctantly shut the door.

Chapter Eighteen

♥

Emma

I couldn't believe how relaxed I was as I drove home. It was because Asher didn't seem to expect anything from me. I lifted my fingers and touched my lips. He kissed me. That was something I hadn't expected.

He'd even asked if it was okay before he did it. Consent. How many guys had I dated that just hauled me into their arms and kissed me. They never asked or anything. Just expected me to comply.

My last date found out really fast that I wasn't going to tolerate him trying to kiss me all night long. That's why I was alone at that party. Did Asher remember? I wasn't sure; he hadn't said anything so far, and neither had I.

When I got home last night, I was tired. It wasn't like Asher lived that far from me, about thirty minutes, but after a full day, two beers, and a full dinner, my body only wanted my bed.

Clothes and stuff were still strewn all over my bedroom. While I cleaned up, I kept thinking about Asher's body beneath mine. He was hard where I was soft. But it was more than that. I always worried that I was too heavy, but he didn't care. Just pulled me over him.

But all of this made me realize that there were old tapes still playing in my head. Especially when it came to my size and what I ate. Over the years, I'd gone to therapy about my relationship with my parents and the things that had happened as a child. Until today, I thought I'd dealt with them. I shook my head. I'd finally become comfortable with my body; I'm who I am meant to be, not some artificial person. But when Asher commented on what I ate at work, I got nervous. When he admitted he liked junk food as well, I began to relax.

Okay, so therapy didn't completely get rid of my self-critical demons. I'm a work in progress.

I tossed a load of laundry into the washer and made my way into the kitchen. Asher admitted he didn't cook much, so maybe I could whip up a few things for him to put in his freezer. My hand froze as I reached for my cookbook.

What was I thinking? Asher could take care of himself. He didn't need me to do it for him. My arm dropped. We're co-workers, nothing more. Although that kiss made me feel like there was more.

Get a grip, Emma. One kiss, well, okay, maybe two, but that was it. I didn't need a relationship with Asher.

But I wanted one.

I was at Fantasies, Inc. to do a job, not make out with the head of IT, no matter how much I might want to do that.

Marching out of the kitchen, I flopped down on the sofa and turned on the TV. I needed to re-build my walls. The last thing I needed was a man in my life.

Chapter Nineteen

♥

A sher

When Emma walked into the office on Monday, I could tell she had shut down. Damn, I had hoped she was now comfortable enough to get past at least some of her defenses. I had my work cut out for me, if there was any chance for us.

"Good morning, Emma."

"Morning, Asher." She put her bag in the desk drawer and took her seat.

I took mine next to her. "I'd like us to go to R&D today and have them start testing the app."

She nodded and blushed. "Can't they test it without us there?"

"Yes, but there's a focus group coming in this afternoon, and I want to get their feedback as well."

"I'd forgotten the company uses focus groups."

"Yes. It helps R&D decide what toys and implements our clients want. And evaluate some of our new products." I watched her face. She wasn't giving much away, but I could read the confusion in her expression. "Have you never dealt with focus groups?"

"Not me, personally. Some of the companies I've worked for use them."

"You'll see it in action this afternoon."

"Okay. I am glad most of the R&D coding headaches are done with. I'd like to work on the app for finance this morning, while you look over the code for HR."

"That works." The focus group wasn't due until one, and we'd probably be done by three-thirty or four at the latest, based on the last couple of meetings I'd sat in on.

I pulled up the code for HR and started running it. Out of the corner of my eye, I watched Emma.

She seemed intent on what she was doing. The finance app should be one of the easiest. They didn't want a lot, just a way for the employees to clock in and out, schedule vacation or PTO days, and to update what they were working on. There was extensive security, but it should integrate well.

Plus, Lucas wasn't sure what else he needed right now. He was busy trying to find a forensic accountant who could help him figure out what was happening with the company Fantasies, Inc. wanted to acquire. It was going to be a lot of work for him, and I wanted to build something that would help him and his team until he figured everything out.

***

The reminder for lunch popped up on my screen. Three hours felt like three minutes.

"Lunch time," I said.

"What?" Emma frowned at her screen.

"Emma." I patted her shoulder. "Time for lunch."

"It is?" She blinked, then seemed to come back to the present. "What time is it?"

"Eleven-thirty."

"I don't go to lunch until twelve-thirty."

"We have to be in R&D at one. Lunch, now."

She sighed. "All right."

I understood her frustration. I hated the real-life interruptions when I was in the zone.

"You probably don't want your stomach growling during the focus group."

"My stomach? Whose stomach has been gurgling for the last thirty minutes?"

"Point to you." My stomach had been reminding me I'd held off on having my usual junk food snack this morning in preparation for lunch. "Let's go." I stood and held my hand out to her.

"We're going to lunch together?" For a couple of seconds, she looked at my hand like it had six fingers before she took it and stood up.

"That we are." Trust. She was trusting me, holding my hand in front of other people, and I wasn't about to let her down.

We rode the elevator down to the first floor, and I guided her into the café. Wanda saw us and waved.

"Asher, Emma," she said. "I have your table ready."

"Table?" Emma glanced at me.

"Thanks, Wanda." I rested my hand at the curve of her back and led her across the room, following Wanda around a set of wooden room dividers.

I grinned when I saw what she had done. Behind the dividers was a table for two by the windows. "This is perfect, Wanda. Thank you so much." Emma looked confused as I pulled a chair out for her, but she sat down.

"I'll bring your meal over," Wanda said before she walked away.

I took my seat across from Emma. Two waters and two iced teas were already on the table.

"Asher, what is the meaning of this?" Emma waved her hand over the table.

"I wanted to take you to lunch." I pointed to the dividers. "This way we can have a private lunch and chat."

Emma shifted in her chair. "What do we need to have privacy for?"

For a moment, I debated with myself on what I was about to say. I wasn't one to sugarcoat things, and I had a feeling Emma would appreciate me being up front with her. "How about the fact that you've rebuilt a wall between us."

Her gaze dropped to the tabletop. "I don't know what you're talking about."

"You do." She'd worked with me for over two weeks now. "Saturday morning, when you let down that brick wall and finally opened up to me, I saw a different woman. A woman I like."

Emma ran her finger through the condensation on her iced tea glass. "That woman doesn't exist."

"But she does. Tell me why you're hiding her."

She shook her head and still wouldn't look at me. Maybe this wasn't such a good idea. No, I was just second guessing myself. This was the best I could do while we were at work.

I blew out a breath that was a cross between a huff and a sigh then reached across the table and patted her hand. She lifted her head. "Let me tell you what I saw on Saturday. I saw a woman who'd finally relaxed and was happy."

She frowned. "I'm happy."

"Are you?" I was going to keep challenging her. *Gently dude. Don't mess this up.* "You were open and comfortable Saturday. If I overstepped a line Saturday, tell me, and I'll apologize."

She opened her mouth, then closed it and shook her head.

"Words, Emma."

She was focused on the table and the patterns she drew in the water ring from her iced tea. "You didn't overstep." She looked up but didn't raise her head all the way. "I gave you consent."

Progress...sort of.

"And do you take that consent back?"

Now she had raised her head and her eyes widened. "Why would I do that?"

"Are you afraid of me?"

"No."

Now or never...

"Then talk to me." I was going to lay it on the line. "I know we're working together, but I want to see you outside of the office. I want us to go out together."

"Isn't there some fraternization rule?"

I laughed. "No. If there was, Cassie and Marcus broke that rule a long time ago." I waited, but when she didn't say anything, I decided to go ahead and ask. "How do you feel about seeing me?"

Emma bit her lower lip before answering. "I want to."

"But..." I heard the hesitation in her voice.

"There are so many things you don't know about me."

"Then tell me."

"Not here." She glanced around. "I know this is pretty private, but there are some things I don't talk about in public."

Now that was interesting. What made her not want to talk in public?

"I can understand that. What are you willing to talk about?" I was throwing the ball back in her court.

"I've had a handful of relationships."

I stiffened. I hadn't expected her to say that, but it was a good start. "Any serious?"

"No." She glanced up as Wanda came around the screen, pushing a small cart.

"Lunch as ordered." Wanda drew the cart to a stop next to the table. She put two small Caesar salads on the table, then a club sandwich and fries for Emma, and my burger and fries. "Enjoy."

Wanda left, and I glanced over at Emma, her focus now on her food. "Did I get it right?"

"How did you know I don't like tomatoes?"

"I didn't. I've seen you order club sandwiches, but Wanda told me you always get them without tomatoes. Not a tomato fan?"

"Not really. I do use them in recipes but usually cut up so small you get the taste and don't notice the chunks."

"Another thing we have in common."

Her eyebrows rose. "We do?"

"Yep, I don't eat tomatoes either. Not on my burger, not on anything. In a sauce is fine, but not big chunks of tomato." I shivered. "I don't understand people who can eat them whole."

Emma laughed, and my skin tingled at her reaction. The wall was coming down; she was relaxing, and that was good.

I dug into my salad. "I've had one serious relationship." Might as well get it out of the way.

"Your tone has me thinking it wasn't a good one."

"It wasn't." I hated talking about Tiffany, but if I wanted a relationship with Emma, it was necessary. "Tiffany was my wife." Emphasis on the past tense.

"You were married?"

"Unfortunately." And what a disaster that had been. "I found Tiffany in bed with another man."

Emma's fork hovered in midair. "What the…" She carefully placed the utensil back on the plate. "Why would anyone do that?"

I blinked. "Most ask me what I did to make her cheat on me," Asher commented.

"I bet none of your friends here asked that."

"You have some great instincts and insights."

"Go on. Are you okay with telling me what happened?" She picked her fork up again.

"Tiffany told me she cheated on me because I wasn't giving her the satisfaction she needed." I took a bite of my salad.

Emma stared at me and then started laughing. "I wouldn't presume to comment except to say that I can't imagine you not satisfying a woman."

Another reaction I didn't expect. I sipped my iced tea with a prayer that I wouldn't choke. "Why do you say that?" I wanted to know what was going on inside her head.

"Because when you kissed me, you woke feelings I'd never imagine were possible." Her cheeks turned red when she realized what she'd just said.

Satisfaction flowed through my veins at her words. "You enjoyed our kisses?"

She bit her lip and looked down at her plate before raising her head and looking me directly in the eyes. "Yes, I enjoyed them."

Yes! Mental fist bump.

"I'm glad. Because I want to do more of that." I actually managed to sound almost calm.

"Asher." Her voice was low, and she glanced around.

I grinned. "Anyway, I walked away from the marriage."

She nodded and pushed away her empty salad plate. "Men just want to get close to me because of who my parents are."

I opened my mouth to ask who her parents were when she shook her head and said, "Not here."

I nodded. "What do you like to do in your spare time?"

"I take long walks, read, or just binge watch something. What about you?"

"I enjoy watching sports, hanging out with friends, and hanging out by the ocean."

"Your home is close to the water?"

"To Puget Sound yes, but nothing beats the ocean. Listening to the waves, watching the birds and the people hunting sand clams."

"Do you spend a lot of time at the beach?" She took a bite of her sandwich.

"When I can. I have a place out on the coast." I ate one of my fries and watched as she dabbed her lips with her napkin. *Lucky napkin.*

"How nice. I've always wanted to live by the ocean. But that's one heck of a commute."

"Yes. Which is why I live where I do. I can still see the water every day."

We chatted about really mundane stuff as well as the upcoming R&D meeting and finished up our lunch, just in time to make our way to R&D.

***

Marcus met us at the elevator and led us to a room where we could sit and observe the focus group behind a one-way mirror, and he took a seat with us. People walked into the room, Cassie the last one in the room.

"Good mixture of gender and racial diversity." Emma remarked.

"It's more than that. Cassie tries hard to make sure we are inclusive in our focus groups. Gender identity, lifestyle, sexual orientation, disabilities." Marcus said.

Emma sat up straighter. "Interesting, resulting in more accurate findings."

"We make toys, furniture, tools, to accommodate and enhance sexual experience for as broad a base as possible; knowing what works in as many dynamics as possible is important."

"I agree," Emma said. "I didn't mean to be offensive. I honestly never thought about it like that."

"We pride ourselves on inclusivity," I said.

"Good." She tilted her head. "We might need to make a few slight changes to the app, but honestly, I like this."

"I like you," Marcus commented. "You get it."

Emma grinned. I sat back and relaxed. This was going to be...interesting.

Chapter Twenty

♥

Emma

Thank goodness Marcus didn't take my faux pas for ignorance. I knew better than to generalize. I sat back and listened.

"I want all of you to know we have three others listening in today. The R&D department head, the technology department head, and one of his contractors." Cassie raised her hand, palm out. "Before you ask, they're here because we're developing a new app that our focus groups have been asking for."

"That's cool," one woman said.

"This will be fun," a man commented.

"Okay. Let's get started." Cassie held up a toy. "Comments?"

I studied the toy. It looked like a normal vibrator to me.

Comments were detailed and informative about everything from the intensity of the orgasm to the ease of use and even how it fit in the hand. The results were the same for each item, toys, furniture, even clothing.

"That was intense," I said to Asher two hours later. Marcus had left the room to meet up with Cassie.

"It was. Lots of information. And we'll likely use every bit of it in one way or another."

"More than I expected." It was true. The people in the focus group had given us a lot to think about. They had some great points, and I wanted to make sure to take what they said into consideration. "I need to get back to my computer to get out all the thoughts in my head."

"Let's go."

Once back in the office, I sat down at my workstation and started writing. First things first. Diversity. New categories. More user-friendly interface with clear descriptions. I wrote a few more items, then looked at the list.

"Why haven't we discussed the diversity aspect before now?" It should have been automatic for both of us.

"I didn't think about it."

"Asher, it's important." I couldn't believe I hadn't asked about it before today.

"It is, but I'm not sure what you mean in the context of the app."

"I mean…" I stopped and started writing as another thought popped into my head. "Sorry, had to get that down."

"No worries."

I smiled. "Diversity. By that, I mean not only making sure there are things for gender identity and orientation but also for those with disabilities. The app needs to be user friendly with that group as well."

"I'll check with Marcus; I'm sure he has some ideas."

"Good. I'm going to start working on new code. R&D is getting a major upgrade." I turned to my computer and got to work. I was excited to be on the ground floor of this.

***

By Thursday, I wanted to pull my hair out. Not only could I not get the app to run right after the customization for R&D, but my mother had called me yet again. I really didn't want to deal with her, but she'd just keep calling. Luckily, when she called the next time, I was alone in the office after Asher ran up to talk with Lucas.

"Yes, Mother."

"You finally answered. I've left you voice mails."

"I know. I've been busy with work." It was the truth, but also, I'd been ignoring her.

"Your father and I will be hosting a fundraiser Saturday at the Seattle house; we expect you to make an appearance."

I sighed as I lowered my head and rested my forehead on the desk. Not exactly banging my head on the desk to make this stop but close enough. *Damn it! Does this crap never end?* "You know I dislike them." Why couldn't I tell her no? I was an adult. Maybe because she was my mother?

"Just make an appearance with us, then you can leave. An hour tops."

Like I believed that. My parents would drag me around, introducing me to everyone as their successful daughter. They didn't even know what I did for a living.

"One hour, that's all."

"I'll send you the details along with your invitation. You'll need that to get in. Bye."

Great. Another exclusive party. A headache in the making. I put the cellphone back on the desk, screen down. *Better than throwing it across the room.*

"You okay?" Asher asked.

I jumped. "When did you get back?" Damn, how much of the call did he hear?

"A few minutes ago. I didn't want to disturb you since you were on the phone." Asher took his usual seat next to me. "Want to talk about it?"

I'd been avoiding this conversation since Monday. Maybe it was time to have it, especially since we were the only two in the office. I didn't want to do this at work, but it was probably for the best.

"That was my mother."

Asher nodded.

"Remember when I mentioned last Friday that my parents wanted me to attend an event with them?"

"Yes, you said that's why you were in a bad mood."

"Yeah. Well, the event is Saturday night, and I'm expected to attend." *Must not grind teeth, must not grind…*

"You would prefer not to?"

I raised my hand and pointed at Asher. "Ding, ding, ding. We have a winner." Angry and frustrated just about covered my headspace right now. "Let me explain my family to you. First, you might have heard of my parents, Roger and Victoria Palmer."

Asher didn't say anything, but I could tell he was thinking. "The name sounds familiar, but I can't place it."

"Palmer Logistics. Dad's first, best adored child."

Asher blinked, and I watched as the lightbulb came on and his mouth opened. "Palmer Logistics? As in the computer chip manufacturer and applied technologies?"

"Yep." I gave myself a pat on the back for eliminating sarcasm from my tone.

"Why aren't you working for him?"

Seriously? "No way." Work with my father? Hell, no. We had different philosophies on a lot of things, including business. "Trust me, that would end up with one of us murdering the other."

"Go on."

I leaned back in my chair. What was the saying? 'And now for the rest of the story'. Deep breath. "Let's just say growing up meant lots of family events and lots of parties."

"Even if you didn't want to go?"

"Right. I was forced to go. I hated them. My sisters enjoyed them. I used to sneak off and find a quiet corner."

"I don't blame you."

I flashed Asher a grateful grin. "As I got older, boys at school started paying attention to me. Not that I was interested. I enjoyed learning not flirting. Anyway, most of them were more interested in my family than me."

"That's not right."

"Finally, someone who understands." *I covered my mouth. Oh boy, did I let that slip out?* "So, I began to ignore the boys, and while I was still forced to go to parties, I got very good at sneaking off or just staying in my own head."

Asher leaned forward, his head lowered, braced his elbows on his knees, and laced his fingers. When he looked up, his expression left me feeling like he really understood on a gut level. "Is that what you meant when you said you stayed aware even while you concentrated on something?"

"Yes. At parties, it was useful to keep some of the men away from me. At home, my sisters would torment me."

He sat up straight, but his hands remained clasped in his lap. "What men?"

"Long over with." I waved my hand in dismissal. "Let's just say that, even after I left home, people still tried to use me to get to my parents."

"I would never do that." Asher leaned closer to me.

"I know you wouldn't." I did believe him. He hadn't even realized who my parents were, even though Palmer was a pretty common name.

"Does Tri-O-Tech know who your parents are?"

I shook my head. "I don't talk about them. They might've found something when they backgrounded me, but they would've had to go a lot deeper than the typical search. There's never been any clue that they know. I'm pretty good at covering my tracks. I'm only telling you because I told you I would."

"Got it. So guys used you to get to your parents." He unclasped his hands and seemed less tense, now more curious than concerned. "Why did your parents make you go to these parties? Why do they want you at this one?"

And there's the complication. "My parents are pretty self-absorbed, more concerned about how they're being perceived than how their children feel. My sisters love going to these events." I blew out a breath. "Those two wouldn't know how to do anything but style their hair, apply their make-up, and flirt."

"I'm sorry you grew up with shallow sisters. You deserve so much more." His whole demeanor telegraphed genuine empathy and understanding. Something inside me began to warm. Cautious but appreciative.

"You don't have to say those things."

"I do." Asher took my hands in his. "I mean them, Emma. I've watched you since you've been here. You're kind, generous, and everyone enjoys being around you. You don't put on an act, and you're a hard worker."

I ducked my head. I always felt like I wasn't doing enough and that people never saw me. "Thank you." That warmth was spreading, and I liked the feeling.

"So, this event on Saturday. Are you allowed to take someone with you?"

I frowned. "I don't know."

"Find out."

"Why?" Why was he so interested?

"Because I'm going with you. You'll have not only a bodyguard that night, but someone who will make sure no one takes advantage of you, not even your parents."

Heat filled me and caution evaporated. He championed me. "Is it obvious that I'm that weak?" I hated not being able to stand up to my parents, although while some might say I did after I got my degree and moved away, that phone call proved the ties—chains?—still existed.

"Sweetheart, you are not weak." His grip tightened on my hands. "You're strong. You only need to learn how to be assertive."

I laughed. "That's never happened."

"Oh, it has. Remember that drive to the restaurant where I told you to wait, and you didn't? You have no trouble telling me what you think and feel. Now you just have to apply it to your family."

"You don't get it." How could I explain?

"Maybe I don't. But I'm not going to let you walk into the lion's den unsupported."

"You don't have to do that." I did appreciate what Asher was offering.

"I do. Did your mother send you an invitation? I'm assuming such events have invitations."

"Yes."

"Look at it."

"Stop with the damned orders, Asher." His commands were starting to get on my nerves.

He grinned. "There's that assertiveness."

I pulled my hands from his and opened my email. Yep, there was the invitation. *Yuck, another black tie performance.* I looked at the invite. It was addressed to Emma Palmer and guest. "Looks like I can bring a guest." That was different. Usually, it was an invite that said Roger and Victoria Palmer and family. Good. Word was out that I wasn't living at home.

"Good. Let me see." Asher took the phone out of my hand before I could stop him.

"Hey." I went to grab it back, but he held it away from me.

"All right. Saturday, at seven in the Hunt's Point area." He glanced at me, one eyebrow raised, and a knowing smile. "Very exclusive." Asher continued to read the email. "Black tie. No worries there." He handed my phone back to me. "I'll pick you up at six. That should give us enough time to get there." And an unspoken but clear *don't worry, we got this* attitude.

I shook my head. "You don't have to do this." How would I explain Asher's presence? Not that my parents cared.

"I want to do it." Asher rolled his chair back to his workstation. "Now that we have that out of the way, let's discuss what Lucas just asked me for."

I put my phone away and tried to concentrate on what Asher was saying, but I wasn't doing so well with that. All I could think about was Asher being with me on Saturday, keeping me company.

Okay. Looks like I'm going to need a dress.

Chapter Twenty-One

♥

Emma

"Cassie, I need your help." I walked into her office Friday morning. I went through my closet last night. I was right. I didn't have a dress that would work for Saturday.

"What's up?" Cassie gestured to the chair in front of her desk.

I sat down. "I need a dress. Can you help me?"

Cassie leaned forward and braced her elbows on the desk. "What kind of dress?"

"A black-tie party kind." Cassie was the only one I felt comfortable enough to ask about this. Asher wouldn't understand.

"Hmmm." Cassie tapped her lips with her finger. "When do you need it?"

"Tomorrow." This was a lost cause. There was no way I could get a dress that would live up to my mother's standards by tomorrow.

"Give me a second." Cassie picked up the phone and dialed. "Celeste, it's Cassie. Do you by chance have time around eleven thirty for a friend and me? She needs a formal dress for tomorrow night. Yes, I know." Cassie nodded. "Nothing that shows too much skin."

"No leg slits," I whispered. I hated when men ogled my legs.

"No leg slits, I'd say a size..." Cassie prompted me with a look.

"Eighteen." My cheeks heated. I wasn't a small woman.

"Eighteen, maybe smaller. Perfect. Thank you so much, Celeste. I owe you." Cassie hung up the phone. "That's all set. Meet me here at eleven fifteen, and we'll go to the shop."

I nodded and stood. "Thanks, Cassie." I left her office, hoping I could find something modest that worked with my body type.

***

After trying on the fifth dress, I was beginning to lose hope. The dresses were all nice, but nothing worked. My mother's disparaging comments ran through my head on repeat.

Celeste knew couture inside and out. All of the dresses she had picked out were beautiful and definitely flattering, but I couldn't stop Mother's voice in my head.

"Let's try this one."

"Sure." Black was slimming, they said. I took the dress into the changing room and stepped into it. Strapless. The bodice, embroidered with silver thread and accented with silver beading, fit like a half-corset, laced in the back. The floor length skirt was four layers of black chiffon that flowed over my legs and swirled around my ankles as I turned to see the back.

"Cassie, I need some help."

"Come on out."

I blew out a breath and exited the changing room.

"Let me tighten the bodice," Celeste said and stepped behind me. She pulled the laces tight.

After Celeste finished pulling the laces and tied them, I adjusted the bodice and assessed the reflection in the full-length mirror with a critical eye.

"Emma, that's perfect on you." Cassie gushed. Celeste smiled her approval.

I frowned. "Is it?" I stood on tip toe and watched the dress move as I turned to the full-length mirror and blinked several times. That was me? The half-corset showed off my breasts. The chiffon flowed from the bodice to the ground like a waterfall.

"I knew I'd have something," Celeste said. "Twirl, dear."

I did as she said. The dress moved with me and didn't hinder my movements at all.

"This is the one," Cassie said. "You'll knock everyone dead in this."

Tears filled my eyes, and I blinked them away. I felt beautiful for the first time in my life. That was sad, but in another way, very liberating.

"Black peau de soie one-inch heels and a lace shawl will compete the outfit." Celeste flittered around me. "What size shoe?"

"Seven."

"Let me go look, I think I have a pair that will work. I know I have the shawl." Celeste walked away.

I couldn't stop staring at myself.

"What time is this shindig tomorrow?" Cassie asked.

"Seven. Asher is picking me up at six-fifteen." I froze.

"Okay, what do you say I come by at five? I can do your hair and makeup for you and help you with the dress."

I let out a breath. Cassie didn't say anything about Asher going with me. "I can't ask you to do that."

"You didn't; I offered." Celeste bustled back in with shoes in one hand and a shawl in the other. Both worked perfectly. I quickly changed out of the dress and back into my normal clothes.

Celeste was putting the dress into a garment bag along with the shoes in the bottom and the shawl over the hanger. I braced myself for the cost.

"Okay it's going to be three hundred for everything," Celeste said.

"That's it?" I couldn't believe it.

"Yes. I'm giving you the friends and family discount."

I handed Celeste my credit card, thinking I was being undercharged, but had no idea what to do about it. The transaction finished, and I picked up the garment bag.

"Cassie, I expect to be first on the list for the toy trial," Celeste said.

Cassie winked. "You're on top for the next year. Thanks, Celeste." Cassie pulled me out of the shop.

"What was that about?" I asked.

"Celeste loves our toys. I've known her for years. She did me a favor by squeezing us in today, so I'm doing her one."

I shook my head. "Is that why the cost was so little?"

"No." Cassie grinned. "Celeste knows exactly what she's doing; she gave you the lowest price she could because you're my friend. And don't worry about it."

"But…"

Cassie pulled me to a stop. "Believe me, Emma. Celeste won't be out any money by giving you the dress at cost. Her clientele is exclusive, and they pay through the nose for her dresses. She understands us girls."

When we got back to Fantasies, Inc., I laid the dress in the back seat of my car and then headed to the office. I'd taken a little extra time with lunch, but I would make it up this afternoon. Asher wasn't in the office, and I breathed a sigh of relief.

At least he wouldn't question me as to why I took a long lunch.

What would Asher think of the dress? A part of me couldn't wait to find out.

Chapter Twenty-Two

♥

A sher

I looked over at Emma at the pub that night. She was chatting happily with Cassie. For an introvert, she was doing a great job making friends with Cassie.

And right now, I wanted to spend some time alone with Emma. We'd shared a few kisses, but it hadn't gone much further than that. I wanted more.

As if she knew I was thinking about her, Emma turned her head and stared at me. Her eyes went wide for a moment. What did she see? Did my expression give me away? I didn't think so.

"Maybe it's time to get a room for you two," Marcus whispered in my ear.

I turned to look at him. "That obvious?" Hell, I was usually better at keeping my thoughts off my face.

"A little, but she's looking at you with eyes that want to eat you up, so I would say it's mutual."

I digested Marcus's words, then looked over at Emma. She was staring at me. Oh yes, there was hunger in her eyes. I cleared my throat.

Marcus chuckled and stood. "Honey, it's time for us to go home," he said.

"Of course." The women stood and embraced.

I stood up. "We should probably go as well." I'd been very careful tonight to only have one beer. I wasn't about to repeat what happened a last week.

As a group, we walked back to the parking garage. Marcus and Cassie went on their way, and I walked Emma to her vehicle. "I'll see you tomorrow at six-fifteen." I held the door open for her.

"Yes." As I was shutting the door, I noticed a white garment bag lying on her back seat.

"Buy something new?" I asked after she rolled down her window. Her cheeks turned pink.

"I didn't have anything for the event tomorrow."

"I can't wait to see you in it." I brushed a kiss over her lips, then walked to my vehicle. I waited until I saw her pull out before I started my car. Too many things could happen.

I pulled up one of my smooth jazz playlists for the drive home. Traffic was light, and I was enjoying the music and the drive.

Until my cell rang.

I answered, using handsfree. "Hello?"

"Asher, finally." My mother's voice was loud and clear. Her emphasis on 'finally' grabbed my attention.

"Mom, is something wrong?"

"Oh, no, dear. Everything is fine. You never called me back."

The relief was immediate. But messages? "You left me a message?" I hadn't seen any calls, voicemails or texts on my cell. Had there been any, I would've responded right away or as soon as convenient.

"At work."

"Mom, how many times have I told you to call my cell or text me." I couldn't help the flash of frustration in my tone.

"I know, but I forgot. I wanted to remind you that your dad's sixtieth birthday is coming up."

"That's not until fall."

"True, but I wanted you to put in vacation now. I know you; you'll forget or swear that company you work for can't afford to let you leave for a week."

She wasn't wrong. "I've already scheduled the time off." Taking vacation time was almost unheard of for me – even in the face of the company's work-life philosophy. My work is my life.

"Oh, good. Will you be bringing a friend or maybe someone special?"

I shook my head and chuckled. She always asked me if there was someone special in my life. I was tempted to talk to her about Emma. "Maybe."

"Tell me about her. It is a her?"

I laughed. "Yes, Mom, she's a her. Her name is Emma, and we're working together."

"Another person in tech. Well, at least you can talk about whatever it is you do."

It still amazed me that Mom has never understood about my career. Even so, she's supported me doing what made me happy. "Yes. It's a pretty new situation."

"Don't let that ex get into your head. She was never right for you." I could picture her *mother knows best* expression. I'd seen it often enough as a kid.

I rolled my eyes, but I wasn't surprised at her advice. Mom never liked Tiffany. I always thought it was funny how she had a sixth sense about things like this. "I know, Mom. Emma is the total opposite."

"Tell me how she's different."

I paused. How was Emma different? "She doesn't chatter at me all the time, doesn't demand that I take her out, or spend money like I'm a bank or a mint. She doesn't get upset if I have to work late now and again." Although I hadn't worked late as often since Emma arrived, and honestly, if we had to stay late, we never went over an hour or two every week.

"A woman who can take care of herself." I could tell by her tone she was analyzing every word I said.

"Yes. She's beautiful, Mom. Intelligent eyes, curvy figure, doesn't feel the need to be in the latest fashions, and smells like honeysuckle."

Mom's laughter filled my vehicle. "I've never heard you wax so poetically about a woman."

"Like I told you, Mom, Emma's different." As I was telling Mom about her, I was beginning to realize how unique Emma really is. "I'm taking her to some event her parents want her to be at tomorrow."

"Who are her parents?"

"Roger and Victoria Palmer. The family owns a big tech company in California."

"And she working with you in Washington? Why?"

After everything Emma'd told me about her family, I had no problem answering that question. "Probably because she wanted to make it on her own."

"Makes sense."

I pulled into my driveway and tapped the remote to open the garage. "I'm home, Mom. Is there anything else?"

"No, dear. Keep a hold of this young lady. She sounds interesting. Bye."

The call ended, and all I could do was shake my head. Some people would've probably thought Mom was nosey, but I knew her questions were motivated by love. I sat in the car after the garage door came down.

I wondered how Emma would feel about my family. Mom's a traditional homemaker who'd never wanted to work outside the home. My dad is a retired engineer.

My brother's a doctor who enjoys working in the emergency room—something about organized chaos and no boredom, and my sister's a lawyer, a public defender in the AG's office for the Western District of Washington—lives the principle of fair and impartial justice.

Mom and Dad supported all three of us doing what we wanted and never held us back. Maybe that was why I had a hard time understanding Emma's parents. Were they completely blind to what an amazing woman their daughter is? I was going to let my gut make the final call, but I was steadfast in one decision: I would have Emma's back tomorrow night, no matter what

Once inside, I took a quick shower and then went through my closet.

Luckily, I still had a tux. I took it out of the garment bag and laid it on the bed. I checked it over, replaced it in the bag, and hung it up in the doorway. Didn't even need to be pressed. Digging back into the closet, I finally found the black dress shoes and opened the box. They were in perfect condition; a quick brush up and they'd look brand new. Gold monogramed cufflinks (thanks again, Mom) and studs for the shirt, yep, right where I always kept them, the box now all the way in the back of the drawer. No surprise.

When was the last time I really dressed up? It had been a while. And I didn't miss it one bit. But for Emma, yeah, I'd do the penguin suit. I wondered about the garment bag in her back seat. What kind of dress had she bought?

Is that why she took a long lunch? Dress shopping? I couldn't picture Emma in anything too revealing, that wasn't her, but the chance to see her in formal evening clothes was too good to pass up. I would have to wait until tomorrow.

I'd done some preliminary research on the occasion and the venue after she showed me the invitation, so I knew what we were getting into. I also did some research into her family. Not something I would normally do, but after everything Emma told me about her parents and how they'd used her and her sisters as props to give the impression of 'the perfect family', I wanted to know more.

I stood in front of the full length mirror on the closet door and thought through what I'd found out.

The Palmers didn't run with 'regular' people. They hung out with what I called the MGZB crowd. Yeah, *that* crowd. Along with well known, *very* well healed Wall Street types, and the cream of the business and technology fields.

The internet revealed everything, some of it unforgiving. I found pictures of a teenage Emma looking uncomfortable in clothes that didn't fit her. In several family shots, she was leaning away from her family. My heart broke for her.

My rumbling stomach snapped me out of my musings. I'd only had an appetizer at the pub, so I made my way downstairs and called for pizza.

It was time to relax and plan. I wanted to make damn sure Emma had a good time.

Chapter Twenty-Three

♥

Asher

At six the next evening, I pulled up to Emma's place and parked in the short driveway. The cute cottage suited her. I knocked on the door, and it was immediately opened. My mouth dropped open, and I almost forgot to breathe.

"You look…" My mind shorted out. I tried to gather my scattered thoughts. "Fantastic, incredible."

This vision was way, waaaaaay more than that. I was struck stupid.

Emma's brown hair had been styled in what my sister called an up-do and pulled back from her face. The stray soft curls at her neck and around her ears seemed to dance in the draft through the open door. Her diamond studs flashed in the ambient light. The gown. Yeah. Perfection. Silver scrollwork and beading on a bodice that looked more like a corset and framed her full breasts perfectly. The black skirt was made of some kind of fabric that flowed over her curves and moved with her in a way that made my mouth water.

"Thank you. You look very handsome."

"I've been told I clean up well." I couldn't take my eyes off her. Lust, desire, and heat roared through my body. How unfair was that? We were going to an event where her parents would be, and all I wanted to do was strip that dress off and ravish her. I sent up a silent prayer of thanks that I was wearing a double breasted jacket.

"That makes two of us." She reached behind her and picked up a small black purse along with a shawl. "I'm ready." She stepped outside, pulled the door shut, and locked it.

I held my arm out to her. "May I?"

She slipped her arm through mine. "Yes. These heels may not be high, but I'm a little unsteady in them."

As I helped her into the car and watched her gather the skirt and arrange it over her legs, I gave myself a mental pat on the back for choosing the Beemer instead of the SUV. Unsteady? Her movements were fluid, graceful, and her dress accentuated them perfectly. Until tonight, it'd never occurred to me that a woman could make getting into a car look like foreplay.

Well, Ash, now you know.

We hit a little bit of traffic, and it was after seven when we arrived. The uniformed guard at the gate checked our names against what was probably a guest list on his pad, opened the gate and motioned for us to go on. The drive was at least a quarter mile, bordered by a perfectly groomed lawn, old growth hardwood trees, and flowering shrubs.

I didn't see the house until I was almost on it. I pulled into the circular driveway and whistled. With the gate, long drive, and incredible grounds, I probably should've anticipated the house. Mansion? No, mansion didn't quite do it justice. Maybe the only slightly smaller and a little more conservative cousin to The Biltmore. Yep, *The* Biltmore.

"Whoa! This place takes 9-figure real estate to a whole new level."

"Yep." Emma sounded sad.

I reached for her hand, squeezing gently. "I've got you."

A valet—of course—stepped up to the car and opened the door. "Good evening, sir, ma'am. Name please."

"Donahue." I handed the valet the fob as I got out of the car, even more sure I'd made the right choice to use the Beemer.

"Donahue," the valet repeated as he wrote it on a ticket, accepted the fob, and handed me the stub. "Please go on up."

I walked around the car and cupped Emma's elbow. We climbed the elegant granite steps and were met at the top by two people with pads who were dressed like Secret Service agents. I didn't miss the bulge just under each one's left arm. *Umm...yeah...* "Invitation, please."

Emma pulled up her invitation on her phone. "Thank you, Ms. Palmer, and your guest?"

"Asher Donahue," Emma said softly.

The man typed on the device. "Thank you. Please, enjoy."

I guided Emma inside. No metal detectors, but there were two more of the Secret Service types standing on either side of the entryway.

We barely had time to make our way to the middle of the foyer when an older woman rushed over, arms extended. She was wearing an elegant, obviously custom made evening gown, not a single snow-white hair out of place, jewelry that, while minimal—necklace, bracelet and earrings—was definitely of the Harry Winston variety and probably cost more than my house.

In a voice that was as refined as the woman herself, she cupped Emma's shoulders.

"Emelina."

Chapter Twenty-Four

♥

E mma

"Emelina," Mother said as she came up to us. She must have been watching the door. We weren't that late.

"Mother." She pulled me closer and air kissed my cheeks, then looked at Asher.

"And who is this?" Her gaze went over him from head to toe. The Assessment.

"Asher Donahue, meet my mother, Victoria Palmer. Mother, this is Asher."

Asher took her extended hand. "A pleasure to meet you, Mrs. Palmer." Then, in a move like a gentleman of the Old World, with the slightest bow he kissed the back of her gloved hand.

I stood there in shock as my mother fluttered her eyelashes at him, and her cheeks pinkened.

Slickest move I've ever seen in real life, straight out of Jane Austen.

"Mr. Donahue."

"Asher, please."

Mother's gaze turned back to me. "Your father is around here somewhere."

"Right here, dear." My father walked to my mother's side. I made introductions once again while my mother's gaze took in my outfit from head to toe more than once. I steeled myself for her negative comments. It never mattered what I wore; there was always something wrong with it

"Emelina, I'm not sure that dress was a wise choice."

Right on cue. It never failed. It was all I could do not to congratulate her on her consistency and predictability.

"It's really not flattering."

I took a deep breath, but before I could say anything Asher spoke up.

"I hate to disagree with you, Mrs. Palmer, but Emma looks absolutely perfect."

I glanced at Asher with a silent *thank you.*

Asher grinned.

"Maybe, but still, that's a lot of skin on display."

Really? I shook my head.

"It's very modest considering some of the dresses other women are wearing. Yourself included. You have more skin showing that Emma does."

"Her name is Emelina." Mother's voice dripped with disdain.

"That may be her given legal name, but she has said she prefers Emma, and I think it fits her perfectly."

My body twitched at Asher's words. No one, and I mean *no one*, had *ever* defended my choice of clothing or preferred name to my mother. I glanced up at Asher. He was smiling, but his features were tight.

He pulled me closer to his side as if to let me know I wasn't alone. I'd let him know how much I appreciated his support later on. For now, I was interested to see just how far this would go before my mother hung herself. Asher was proving to be a worthy opponent. I'd stopped defending my choices to her years ago.

Someone called my name out in a high pitch voice. "Emelina." I barely restrained my cringe.

"Incoming," I whispered to Asher as my two sisters flounced toward us.

"Magnolia, Seraphina," I said as we exchanged air kisses.

Magnolia openly gawked at Asher. "Hello, handsome," she practically purred. "I'm Magnolia." She held out her hand.

"Ms. Palmer." Asher held it briefly.

"And I'm Seraphina." Not gawking, but definitely an expression that screamed Asher wasn't even as good as the dirt under her shoes.

"Ms. Palmer." Asher was polite, cool, but not quite enough to freeze water. His eyes narrowed as he spoke to my sisters.

Magnolia turned to Seraphina, her mean-girl smile plastered firmly in place. "Why don't I give Asher a tour while you talk with Emelina." She reached for Asher's arm.

Asher took a step back. "While I thank you, I think I'd rather have a tour with Emma." The neutral, completely unemotional, professional businessman.

"But she's never been here," Magnolia commented. She was right; I hadn't been here before tonight. Dad bought this overblown castle after I was out on my own. The thought of showing up here ranked somewhere beyond anathema.

Asher smiled, but I could see it didn't reach his eyes. "All the more fun for us, exploring together. Now, please, excuse us, I'm sure we'll see you later." Asher tightened his arm around my waist and guided me away from my family.

"I spied an escape," he whispered.

Together, we walked through the foyer and main ballroom, out the back door. Several guests were gathered around the bar and buffet set out on the slate patio. Cloth covered tables and slip-covered chairs were set at random distances. The candles in the hurricane lantern centerpieces had been lit.

On the lawn, tents had been set up with more cloth covered tables with fresh flowers and candle centerpieces and chairs. Waiters flowed through the crowd with food and drink. Asher led me down the stairs and to the left, then down another set of steps to where the pool was lit up.

There weren't any people here. He guided me closer to the pool house and then turned to me.

"Emelina?"

I giggled. "You're hung up on my name?" I expected something else. When he stayed silent, I continued. "I really dislike my full name."

He shifted until he was standing in front of me. "Were you trying to test me by not telling me your sister's a predator?"

"No. Why?" Magnolia was acting like she always did. Did he mean my reaction when Magnolia said she'd take him on a tour? Unlike other guys I'd brought home, Asher didn't rise to her bait.

"Because your family is much worse than you told me." He shook his head. "Let's say sharks have nothing on them."

I laughed, pleased with his accurate evaluation. "You have no idea." We sat on two of the lounge chairs on the pool house's covered deck. I toed off my shoes and stretched out on the chair. I was no fan of high heels, and my feet were now much happier.

Asher took off his tux jacket and draped it over the back of a nearby chair, then settled on the chair next to mine and crossed his long legs at the ankles. The shirt he'd worn with the tux framed his torso perfectly. Wide shoulders, narrow waist.

"I'm so glad I didn't let you come alone. Have you always endured that crap?"

I nodded. I didn't know how to explain the elation I felt at his protective diversions. No one stood up to my family, but he did. Maybe because he didn't feel the need to suck up. Asher was secure in who he was and what he did. And he didn't need my parents' approval.

"You do know they're going to corner us again," I said.

"I figured. How long do we have to stay before we can make a polite exit?"

"At least an hour, maybe a little longer." Mother had insisted only an hour tops, but I also knew she didn't mean that.

"Any idea why we're here?" Asher settled against the back of the chair, letting his head fall back on the cushion, and closed his eyes. The perfect relaxed pose.

This gathering was no different than any of the others. I was no fool; no way was I going to lower my guard. "I have my suspicions. Don't be surprised if a photographer suddenly shows up." That was my parents' MO. They wanted family pictures to show everyone the family was intact. After all, one mustn't risk upsetting the stockholders with the implications that might come with family dissention.

"I can deal with it. Why don't we go get some food and try to relax a bit."

"Relaxation at these parties is not an option." Lord only knows what else my parents had planned, especially since they didn't tell me—warn me—my sisters would be here.

Asher stood up, put the tux jacket back on and buttoned it. I had a flashing thought that he looked like he could be the main character in a romance novel. *Don't drool, Emma. And whatever you might feel, be careful.* Of course my mind would pour a five-gallon bucket of ice water over my momentary fantasy. *Thanks a lot. Not.*

I slipped my shoes on and looked up to see Asher's hand extended to help me stand. When I was steady on my feet, he didn't release my hand as he guided me back to the main part of the yard. He found us a table for two, and when he released my hand, I immediately missed the warmth of his grasp. He pulled out a chair with a slight bow and sweep of his hand as an invitation for me to sit.

"I'll bring back nourishment and liquid courage." He winked, and stroked my cheek so gently, I almost didn't feel his touch. I could have sworn my heart turned over, but when I blinked, he was on his way to the buffet, and I was left trying to process the heat, the butterflies, and the desire that had risen from his merest touch.

I had no perception of time until Asher put a full over-sized dinnerplate mounded with various items next to the centerpiece, then two glasses filled with some sort of gold liquid, flatware, two regular size empty plates, and two linen napkins.

"One of the waitstaff helped me appropriate a tray for all this stuff and told me to stash it under the table so I wouldn't have to make a second trip." There was that wink and a smile again. And sure enough, the butterflies took flight in my belly.

I shook out the napkin and spread it in my lap to try to cool the heat in my cheeks and took four items off the plate. Asher did as instructed and slid the tray under the table across from our chairs, sat down, and filled his plate.

"Enjoy. This stuff looks delicious. I'm not sure what half of these things are, but they looked good, so I went for them." Asher set the plate down and immediately took a bite from what looked like a stuffed mushroom and moaned in apparent delight. I sipped my drink to try and suppress a giggle.

"Cider?"

He nodded as he swallowed the bite then sipped his drink. "I figured it would be best if we both kept our wits about us." We clinked glasses.

"Smart man."

We didn't talk while we finished off everything he'd brought from the buffet. And he was right; all of it was delicious. No surprise really. My parents hired only five star caterers.

We'd just emptied our glasses and were leaning back in our seats when my parents glided over with my sisters. My father looked at the table, then flagged a waiter down. He told the waiter they needed more chairs and another table. The waiter gave my father a nod and moved a table and chairs for four next to ours. After he positioned the last chair, he picked up the tray under our table and stacked the plates, glasses, flatware, and napkins on it. He lifted the tray and set one side on his shoulder and braced it on his raised hand. Just as he turned to leave, he winked at Asher. Ah, the tray thief. Asher nodded and smiled as he returned a two-fingered salute to his partner in crime.

My sisters scrambled to see who would sit next to Asher. Magnolia won. I stifled a chuckle at their antics, knowing it wouldn't go over well. I'd learned over the years to keep my head down literally and figuratively. Asher didn't know that.

"Asher, what do you do?" my father asked after he sat down.

"Like Emma, I work in information technology." Asher's hand slipped off the table and rested on my thigh. He squeezed it ever so slightly, and as I moved like I was getting more comfortable in my chair, I quickly stroked his hand to thank him for his support.

"You work in the same place as Emelina?"

"No, sir. Emma is on contract to the company I work for. She's helping me with mainframe expansion and streamlining, along with merging our domestic and international divisions."

"How fascinating," Magnolia purred, leaning closer to Asher. He gave her a pointed look and shifted closer to me.

"I see." Dad nodded. Even though he worked in applied technology and owned one of the largest chip manufacturing companies in the country, I knew he didn't understand a darn thing Asher had just outlined. He'd never understood why I majored in computer science or why I'd chosen my current career path. None of my family did. "And what is your company name?"

I quickly covered Asher's hand with mine and squeezed...hard.

Asher glanced over at me, then lasered on my father and answered in a voice so smooth even James Bond would've been proud. "Fantasies, Inc."

Dad hesitated, then frowned. "I'm not familiar with them."

I took a breath. Good, then there wouldn't be any awkward conversations.

"Oh, I've heard of them," Seraphina said.

Oh shit. This is about to go sideways.

Seraphina looked smug, totally pleased with herself. "It's that company that arranges salacious hook-ups."

"It's not a dating business, Seraphina," I said, earning a dirty look from her. "It's a perfectly respectable company." I may have been a little ignorant when I first walked into Fantasies, Inc., but the organization was good, and there was nothing even slightly salacious about it.

"I doubt that." Mother's lips were pinched together.

Magnolia was examining her manicure, then looked up directly at me, her resting bitch face expression firmly in place. "I heard it's a sex toy company." She laid her hand on Asher's arm in an open invitation.

Oh, to hell with this crap. I rolled my eyes.

Asher shook Magnolia's hand off his arm. "Fantasies, Inc. is not a"—he raised both hands in an air quote gesture—"sex toy company. We respect and understand what our clients want. We recognized a need and filled it."

"A sexual need." Mother made no attempt to hide her disgust.

"It can be," Asher said. "Our clients want a safe space to enjoy all aspects of life, and we ensure they can do just that."

"I can't see how a place like that can make money," Father commented.

"I can't comment on the financial aspects as I'm not privy to the corporation's books. I can say I'm paid higher than my counterparts in other technology companies."

"I don't care what money it makes. Emelina, you will quit this job," Father demanded.

I could see the satisfied grins on my sisters' faces. As if I cared.

"I have a contract."

"Contracts can be broken," he said.

I shook my head. "I'm not going to break it. I like working there."

My mother gasped as if I'd said something totally obscene.

"I may not know all the ins and outs of the adult toys business but working on this project with Asher is fun."

"And the place you work for is okay with his company claiming any technology product you develop?" Dad wasn't going to let this go.

I stiffened. "They are not stealing anything. I'm configuring, expanding, and improving existing systems. Any code I write or apps I develop will be properly licensed." I wanted to say more, but that would only lead to an old argument, and I wasn't going to waste the energy.

"I think it's interesting," Magnolia commented. "Asher, have you used the company's products?"

Asher flinched, and I looked at him and followed his gaze to his lap, and I could see Magnolia's red painted nails. She had her hand in his lap. *Assault. That's fucking assault. Goddamn the bitch!* My entire visual field took on a reddish haze. Every hair on my body was standing up. Asher squeezed my hand, and over the buzzing in my ears, I could've sworn I heard a whisper that sounded like…Asher.

"I've got this, Emma. Relax. I got this."

"Magnolia, if you don't remove your hand from my lap this instant, you will not like my reaction." His tone was hard, and now definitely cold enough to freeze water, even though his expression and body language radiated calm.

Magnolia stiffened, her lips curved in a pout. "I was just trying to show you I'm more fun than my sister."

"That's it. We're done here." Asher didn't raise his voice as he stood, pulling me up with him, but the edge in his tone cut like a razor. Magnolia's hand hovered in the air. He didn't release my hand when he turned to address my father. His expression remained dead calm, but there was something almost scary about his gaze. "Mr. Palmer, Fantasies, Inc. is an ethical business. We do not steal intellectual property of *any* kind. Period."

Then he focused on Magnolia. "What you did when you touched me in that manner without my specific consent is classified as fourth degree assault. I'm not going to press charges at this time because Emma is a friend, and I have enormous respect for her. But if you *ever* pull a stunt like that again, make no mistake, I *will* ensure you are prosecuted to the fullest extent of the law." Magnolia was so pale, if she hadn't been sitting down, I was sure she would've fainted.

Asher wasn't finished. He speared Mother and Seraphina. "Everything Emma said about you people was accurate. In fact, she was generous in her descriptions. None of you deserve that generosity. Your familial issues are yours to deal with, but when I'm with *Emma*"—he looked directly at Mother when he emphasized my preferred name—"you will treat her with courtesy and respect. End of discussion."

There was a moment of paralysis. None of them moved until Dad sputtered and spoke.

"Emelina, you're going to let him talk to all of us like that?" he blustered.

What Asher had said and done left me with the feeling I could conquer anything—even my family. Maybe I didn't have to live under the shadow of my parents' control and their notoriety. Maybe I could—finally—stand up for myself.

"I am. You see, Asher sees *me*. The me you all ignore or belittle because I refuse to fit into your mold. He respects me, too, unlike you. He's a wonderful man who has made me realize I don't need your toxicity in my life." For the first time in my life, I saw, without the constraint of emotion, who these people really are. I had lived every day hoping they would love me for who I am, and today I realized that wasn't going to happen.

I felt Asher squeeze my hand. He had unlocked something in me that had always been there but was dormant. No longer.

I was finally free.

"Goodbye." I didn't let go of his hand, but I also knew if I looked at him, I would dissolve into a trembling mess at his feet. We made our way from the yard, through the house, and down the steps.

Asher gave the valet the ticket, and within a few minutes, his car arrived. He held my door open and helped me in. I watched him from the side mirror until he was behind the car and turned toward the driver's side to see him open the door, get in, fasten his seatbelt, and put the car in gear. He turned to me before he depressed the gas pedal, his expression tender, his smile warm.

"You've crossed your Rubicon, Emma. It only gets better from here." He turned, pressed the gas and, tires throwing gravel, drove away.

The silence in the car was thick. I think he knew I needed the silence to process everything that had happened. It wasn't until we were at the stoplight that Asher turned to me. He tilted his head like he was trying to solve a problem in his head.

"How did you grow up to be so normal with family like that?" He untied his bowtie and unbuttoned the top button of his shirt.

"Ignored them?"

Asher let out a breath and gestured for me to come closer. "Seatbelt," I said.

"It will stretch. This light takes forever. Come over here."

I wiggled out of the chest restraint and let it contract behind me then leaned as close as I could across the console. He cupped my face and brushed a soft kiss across my lips and a firmer one on my forehead.

"I'm sorry," I whispered.

"You have nothing to be sorry for." He rubbed my shoulder. His touch sent rivers of awareness through me. "I..." He took a breath and blew it out. The light turned green, and we started forward. "I can't believe your family. Your sister openly flirting with me and touching me. Does she do that a lot?"

"Every boyfriend I ever brought home or introduced her to. You're the first one who didn't take her up on it. Most of the guys I met didn't seem to care which sister got them into the family."

"Fuck. That's messed up."

"It is."

Once we were merged and up to speed, he caressed my shoulder. I laid my head on his hand and caressed his hand between my cheek and shoulder. I lifted my head, took hold of his hand, and dropped a quick kiss on his palm before lacing my fingers with his and resting our clasped hands on the console.

"Asher..."

He glanced at me and smiled. *I've got to know... My curiosity was going to drive me nuts.*

"What would you have done if Magnolia hadn't removed her hand?"

Asher laughed. "I wondered how long it was going to take before you asked." He chuckled and gave me the side-eye. "I would've grasped her hand and removed it, using just enough force to make her uncomfortable and that was necessary to make my point." He squeezed my hand, then lifted it and dropped a kiss on the inside of my wrist. There were those crazy butterflies again.

It's pretty warm in here...

Then came the cool-down.

"Your father is a real piece of work. I couldn't believe he demanded you quit your job, and then thought you'd just walk out after signing a contract."

"He expected obedience. Did you see his expression when I said no?" It had felt so right.

"He looked like he'd eaten something sour."

I had to laugh. Now that I was away from them and had time to decompress, it really was kind of funny. "It got even worse when you pointed out that Fantasies, Inc. is an ethical, completely legit company."

Asher's demeanor took a serious turn. "Your father's isn't."

"No. I've heard the rumors about his company, and I've witnessed him breaking contracts without a second thought about lawsuits or the impact on the contracted businesses."

"I'm surprised people will still work with him."

"He pays top dollar to those who will do what he says." I sighed. "Thank you for standing up for me."

"Meeting them validates what you told me."

"I'm sorry it went down the way it did. I thought they might be on good behavior. I should have known better."

"Well, they might have some explaining to do."

"Why is that?"

"One of the very major players in the entire country was close enough to overhear our little get-together, and he didn't look pleased at all."

I sort of snort-giggled then slapped my free hand over my mouth. "My family wasn't exactly being quiet."

"It was more than that. In addition to being the CEO of one of the largest hedge funds in the U.S., Gerald Woodall is a friend of Fantasies, Inc.'s president. I met him once at the office."

I straightened. "Are you talking about *the* Gerald Woodall?" *Whoa!* That man had control of more money than God, never mind what he had personally. *Looks like Dad stepped into some very deep sh...*

"Yeah, I don't think your family is going to be welcome in that grand circle again."

"It's going to be worse than that," I said. A part of me felt vindicated, like Karma had finally taken care of business, and then came the guilt for feeling that way. "Remember, my father is in computer chip manufacturing and applied technologies. If word spreads..."

Asher's laughter filled the car. "Serves him right."

I moved our clasped hands into my lap and relaxed against the seat for the rest of the drive. I think I dozed off more than once. When we arrived at my cottage, Asher escorted me to the door. After I opened it and turned on the lights, he drew me into his arms. "Thank you for a fun night."

"That was fun for you?"

"It was." He leaned down and brushed his lips over mine.

I deepened the kiss. I didn't want Asher to leave, but I didn't know how to ask him to stay. Instead, we stood there in the doorway, making out like teenagers. Finally, Asher lifted his head and stroked my cheek.

"Go inside, my Cinderella."

"What if I don't want to?" I was tempting fate, and I didn't care.

"Go." He turned me around until my back was to him and I was facing my front doorway, then he swatted my butt.

Heat spread through my body from the spot where his hand landed. "Again," I said softly.

I heard him gasp, then felt another swat, this one with a bit more force.

"Inside now or I'll forget I'm a gentleman."

Before I could retort, he gently pushed me inside and pulled the door shut. He spoke through the closed door. "Dream of me."

I leaned against the door and slid down it until I was sitting on the floor. *Bank the fire, girl, or you're gonna be a pile of ash on this floor.* I didn't try to get up until I heard his car engine start followed by the sound of him driving away.

I made my way into my bedroom and undressed. Luckily, the ties on the bodice were at the bottom where I could reach them.

Dream of him, he said. He didn't have to know I was already doing that. My skin still tingled from the swats he'd given me. Maybe if I was a good girl next week, I could get him to give me more. A giggle escaped. Was working for Fantasies, Inc. corrupting me?

Nope. I'd wanted to explore the kinkier side of sex for a while now, and I trusted Asher more than any man in my life. Could I get him on the same page?

Chapter Twenty-Five

♥

Asher

My mind had been filled with Emma not wanting to go inside. I'd been tempted to push her inside and find her bedroom, but she wasn't ready yet.

We hadn't had The Talk. I needed to find out how far she was willing to go with me. I grinned. Yes, I had some kinky tastes, and while I was pretty sure Emma could handle what I'd like to do to her, that didn't mean we didn't need to talk about it. That was going to happen sooner rather than later.

It had been a busy week in the office, so Emma and I didn't get to talk much outside of work, and that conversation was not something I wanted to handle over the phone and definitely not in or around the office.

"Time to head out," I said.

"Five minutes," she muttered as she continued typing.

"That's all I'm giving you." If I wasn't careful, she'd stretch those five minutes into an hour or more. When Emma was in the zone, she barely remembered anything else. I found myself making sure she took breaks.

She would get upset with me for interrupting her and making sure she took a walk to get coffee or a snack. She always thanked me for making sure she moved, but there were still times when she pushed.

I gave her eight minutes, and when she didn't come up for air, I pulled her chair back.

"Hey." She leaned back and glared at me.

"You said five minutes; I waited three extra minutes."

Something must have shown on my face, because she didn't even try to argue or get more time. Instead, she stood and shut down her workstation.

"Anyone ever tell you you're a bossy SOB?"

"Rarely. But most people remember to take a break and give their mind a chance to recharge. You, on the other hand..."

It was getting easier to read Emma. I watched her expression as she gave way to necessity. *Don't say I told you so, and for god's sake, Ash, don't look smug.*

"Okay, you're right...again." She raised her hands in mock surrender. "Thanks. I would have stayed at this for several more hours."

"Which is why I insisted."

"Don't you ever get so involved with a task you forget where you are? Or how much time has passed?" She gathered up her things, hoisted her bag onto her shoulder, then as she always did before leaving, turned in a circle to be sure she hadn't forgotten anything.

"I do." She turned out the lights as I set the alarms, and we walked out the door together. "Haven't you noticed my alarm going off."

"Now that you mention it, yes."

"I set one for two hours when I start coding, so I don't get lost." I'd done that for years because, like Emma, I could dig in so deep, the world could end, and I wouldn't know the difference. That wasn't good.

"I probably need to start doing that."

We stepped out of the elevator, and I turned and walked backward to face her. "Nah, that's why you have me." I winked and smiled, then turned to walk beside her. I held her hand as we made our way to the garage and the floor where we parked.

No one could make the usual Friday after work social hour. Opportunity was knocking.

As I was still figuring out how to approach her about dinner at my house so we could talk, she stopped at her car and leaned against the driver's door.

"Night, Asher."

So much for opportunity. "Night." I was parked two slots down. I watched as she opened the door, stashed her stuff, and climbed in. I waited like I always did to make sure she drove away safe and sound.

Nothing happened. Her door opened. "It won't start."

"Be right there." I unlocked my car and tossed my stuff in the back seat. "Pop the hood," I said as I walked back to her. Emma popped the release and stayed in the driver's seat, her chin resting on her crossed arms propped on the steering wheel. Opening the hood, I looked at the battery and checked the connections. One was loose; I tightened it. "Try it now."

I could hear her press the brake, then glanced around the hood as she pushed the ignition button. Nothing except clicking. Car problems were not my forte, but I knew enough that clicking and the engine not starting were definitely not good. Friday night after six, finding a mechanic would be close to impossible. And nothing I could do. Then I remembered Chase. I'd set up the network in his shop, and he told me if I ever needed a mechanic... Problem almost solved.

I looked at Emma. "I think your battery is totally dead, or it's the alternator."

"I guess I need to call for a jump or a tow."

I opened my mouth to tell her I'd give her car a jump, then had what I thought was a better idea. "Why don't we do this. Let me give you a jump, and we can drive it to a mechanic I know for a slow charge overnight. Then I can drive you home. I'll pick you up tomorrow, and we can retrieve your car and decide on next steps." *Chill, Asher. Don't rush her, buddy.*

The next ten seconds felt more like an hour. "All right. But I don't like the idea of you having to drive so far out of your way to my house."

That missed opportunity decided to give me a second chance. I was going to open that door.

"You could stay at my house."

Her eyes widened, but there was nothing in her expression or body language to indicate reluctance. "Let me think about it."

Luckily there was an empty space next to her, so I pulled my vehicle into the spot, then opened the rear hatch.

After I grabbed jumper cables, I hooked them up and had her start her car. It purred to life. Emma grinned at me. I tossed the cables back into my vehicle and grabbed a rag to clean my hands.

"Do you need to go home and grab extra clothes?"

"No. I have a bag in my car."

"You're prepared." I liked that. During winter, I kept a packed gym bag in my car in case winter decided to dump a ton of snow on us. It happened last winter. We spent the night in the office waiting for the snow to clear enough to drive safely. Yes, it was spring now, but it was still early in the season, so I wasn't quite ready to put away the extra clothes.

"Our winter weather can be unpredictable, so I keep a bag with everything I need for an overnight stay if I get stuck and have to check into a hotel."

"I do the same." I paused. "So does that mean you've decided to spend the night at my house?" I leaned on the open door as she settled in her seat and belted in.

Was that a twinkle in her eyes? "Maybe."

I felt a shot of anticipation at her answer and smiled as I closed her door. "Follow me." I fought the urge to fist pump as I walked to car, feeling like a kid on Christmas morning.

I pulled out of the garage and checked the rearview mirror to make sure Emma was following me.

Traffic was light, so we made it to Chase's shop before he closed. I told him what had happened, and he held his hand out for the keys. Emma dropped them into his palm.

"I'll slow charge it overnight and see what happens in the morning."

"Thanks." I shook his hand. "Appreciate the help, man. We'll talk in the morning."

He tapped the bill of his baseball cap, glanced at Emma as she was walking away, and nodded. I cocked an eyebrow and smiled. *You'd better believe she's mine.*

I caught up to Emma just as she was opening the rear door of her car. She sighed. "I guess that's the best I can hope for."

She retrieved a medium size gym bag from her trunk, probably her emergency clothing stash, and I shouldered her backpack on the short walk back to my SUV.

I put her gym bag and backpack in the back seat while she got settled in the passenger seat and I got in. Belt, mirrors, phone in holder. Before I started the car, I glanced at Emma to make sure she was belted and comfortable. Her brow was slightly furrowed, and it looked like she was biting her cheek.

"Hey, it'll be fine." I patted her hand where it rested on her thigh. "You have a place to stay and a driver to take you wherever you want."

She hesitated.

"Emma, there's no pressure. I have a guest bedroom."

Her sigh of relief made me grin. Was she worried I was expecting her to go to bed with me tonight? While it would be ideal, I wasn't going to pressure her into anything if she was the slightest bit reluctant.

I backed out of the parking space and glanced at her as I pulled out onto the street.

"Asher, I don't feel like this is fair to you."

"What d'you mean?"

"I mean, you're doing a lot for me, and I'm just a friend."

I thought about her words for a minute. "I'm glad we're friends. But I would like us to be more."

"You would?"

I turned to her while I waited for the traffic light to turn green and, almost immediately, had to turn my focus back to the road as the car in front of us began to move forward. "Yes. But this isn't a conversation I want to have while I'm driving." Definitely not.

"Agreed."

Emma fell silent, and even though I told her I didn't want to continue on that subject, I missed hearing her voice.

"I don't have much in the way of food to cook. Why don't we stop and pick up something?"

"That's fine."

"What would you like?" I wanted her to feel comfortable in my house.

"Whatever you're in the mood for."

I barely bit back a retort. "Emma, this is a decision we can make together. Tell me some of your favorite foods."

"Pizza, sandwiches, salads, I'm not super picky."

"Pizza it is." There was place I frequented that made the best thick crust pizza. "What do you like on your pizza?"

"You're going to think I'm crazy."

"Never."

"Chicken and pineapple."

I did a double take and then laughed. "I like pineapple on my pizza too."

"Usually, people look at me like I'm nuts and say it ruins pizza."

"Never." Within minutes, we were at the pizza place. I told Emma to relax and went inside to order. They weren't too busy, and we were on our way with a large pizza, salad, and cheese bread.

When we got to my place and parked the car in the garage, I went to grab her bag while holding our food.

"No, Asher. I'll get my backpack and bag. You take care of the food. We can't risk the stuff ending up on the floor just for the sake of chivalry."

I laughed but wasn't offended. Once inside, I plunked the food in the kitchen and guided her to the guest bedroom.

The ball was in her court now.

Chapter Twenty-Six

E mma

I took a deep breath as I placed my bags on the bed in Asher's guest bedroom. My heart rate wouldn't slow down. Not since he suggested I spend the night at his place.

I wiped my hand on my pants. I was nervous, and it wasn't from the car battery problem. All I could think about was spending the night in Asher's bed. We'd shared several kisses, each one more intense. And then there was tonight.

Sleeping together was a natural next step.

I shook my head. I'd never felt such an intense attraction to a man before. I rarely slept with anyone I dated, but with Asher... Should we consider dinners at the pub with others as dates in addition to the two private dinners we had together? And we had lunch together almost every day. I walked out of the bedroom and down the short hall and found Asher in the kitchen.

"Would you like something to drink?" he asked.

I wasn't much of a drinker, but I needed some liquid courage. "Do you have beer?"

"Any respectable man does. I have several different ones." He listed off the brands to me, and I picked one. "Go sit down. The pizza, salads, cheese bread, and plates are already on the coffee table. I'll bring the beer."

Always the gentleman.

I sat down on the sofa, and within a few minutes, Asher brought my beer in a pilsner glass and handed it to me. I noticed he had a glass of water. "You're not having one?"

"No."

I sat my beer on the coaster on the table and looked at him. "Maybe I shouldn't have one either."

"Emma." He said my name softly. "You're fine. My choice is to not have one tonight."

I nodded, took a sip of the drink, then put it back on the table. We ate in silence while the TV played at low volume in the background. Once we were finished, I helped Asher clean up. We said very little, only necessary things. Pass whatever. More bread? Another drink? You wash, and I'll load and dry since I know where everything is. The undercurrent was mostly companionable with only the slightest hint of awkward. There was an elephant in the room, for sure, and when we sat back down, my nerves kicked up.

I couldn't stand it another minute. "I don't know how to start talking about tonight." I was aware he wanted to talk before we made the decision to sleep together. That we didn't talk about it over dinner was no surprise.

Asher turned toward me. "Start however you want. I won't pressure you, Emma. I meant what I said; you can sleep in the guest room, if you want. We can spend the night in my bed. But only if you're absolutely comfortable with it and it's what *you* want. Consent and you being comfortable with the decision are everything."

The tension left my body as I sank against the back of the sofa. "I told you that people liked to get close to me because of my parents."

"Yes, I remember."

"Before anything more happens between us—" I stopped, not knowing what to say.

"Nothing will happen that you don't want."

The outside seam on Asher's slacks and the pattern of the couch upholstery suddenly became worthy of close examination. Better that than having to look directly at him.

"I hate to bring it up, but do you have any questions about my family from last Saturday night? I know it was a lot to take in. I don't want them to come between us." There, I got it out.

"Nope. They have no place in our lives."

He spoke with such finality, it took a minute to sink in. Something inside me broke free. Looking Asher in the eye was easier now. "There is something else I need to tell you."

He placed his hand on my arm and gave it a squeeze. "I'm not going anywhere."

His open acceptance put me even more at ease. Words came easier.

"I've always been good at solving problems. Working with computer programs made sense to me." My stomach clenched. "In high school, I was on a team, and because of my work, we won a special state event." My breathing hiccupped. To this day, the memory brought up a lot of unresolved feelings. "The guys took credit for what I'd done, and everyone believed them, even my family. My father told me that's what I deserved for being so anti-social."

I caught his whispered curse as he scooted closer.

"It wasn't the only time that kind of thing happened. It's one of the reasons I choose to work alone rather than on a team."

"The tech industry in insidious."

"And extremely misogynistic. Alex Manning, my boss at Tri-O-Tech, is a good guy. But again, he's male."

"Is that why you were worried when you came to work at Fantasies, Inc.?"

"Not really. This is the first time I've been asked to work on a project of this scope directly on another company's mainframe, including any required modifications to the entire software infrastructure. The Tri-O-Tech employment terms state specifically that anything developed while employed by the company is the company's property. That includes patent rights. Usually, they take it and do whatever they want."

"That doesn't seem fair."

"I'm generously compensated, way above industry guidelines, so it's good. But developers don't get named author credit on R&D. It's a 'we paid you for it, so we own it' paradigm." I shrugged. "Anyhow, when I was told I'd be working inhouse at Fantasies, Inc., I was reluctant, anxious, worried, call it whatever you choose, about working an office with people I didn't know and meeting their expectations."

"Your work has been outstanding."

"I tried to hide it."

"Can I put your worries to rest about anything you do for Fantasies, Inc.? You will be given full credit and compensation."

"Thank you." My lips twitched. He was doing everything possible to assure me that I would get appropriate credit for my work, something no one had done before. Warmth bloomed in my chest and spread through my body. I didn't want Asher to feel sorry for me—no way—but I couldn't deny it had been a long time since I'd felt my work was genuinely appreciated.

"I know it's long past, but that doesn't change the fact that I want to go kick those now grown idiots' asses and show them how wrong they were to do that to you. Same for those individuals where you work who make you uncomfortable."

Happiness enveloped me like a blanket on a cold day. "You're sweet."

Asher's green eyes flashed, and I leaned into him. The instant I was in his arms, our lips melded. His lips were soft against mine, and I wanted more. I curved my hand around the back of his neck, holding him to me.

He got the message. His tongue felt light as a feather against my lips, and I opened to him. A shiver moved through me as our tongues tangled and dueled with each other. I never wanted this to stop.

Several minutes later, Asher raised his head, his eyes dark with desire. "Before we go any further, we need to make sure we're on the same page."

Kissing seemed like a good start and continuing it would let us take this wherever it was going. Hopefully, to his bed. Oh, yes, that's what I wanted. To be in his bed.

"The bedroom?"

His chuckle tickled my ear.

He was giving me an out, but I didn't want one. I wanted him. With my free hand, I took his and placed it on my breast. "I want this. I want you."

In an instant, his lips covered mine once again, but this wasn't the soft kiss of before. This was one of possession. *Yes.* I wanted this. I kissed him back with all the passion building up in me. I didn't have to be passive with Asher. I could be myself.

Something inside me broke free, like a bird being freed from a cage. I let my hand drop from his neck to his hard chest. His heart was racing, and I smiled against his lips as I unbuttoned his shirt.

Asher hadn't moved his hand where it rested my breast. I wanted so much more. "Touch me."

He lifted his head and stared at me. "You touch me first."

Power surged through me. He was letting me take the lead, do what I wanted. Heat rose with need. Opening his shirt, I placed my palms on his pecs. So hard, so strong. His chest hair tickled my skin, and I wondered how it would feel against my nipples. I trailed my fingers over his hard abdomen.

I was enjoying the feel of his body under my hands and how his abdomen contracted beneath my touch. Surprise and a sense of awe flowed through me that I could affect him like that. Finding his belt, I ran my fingers over the leather, before finding the metal buckle. With precise movements I undid it. Slipping one hand into his slacks, I began to lower the zipper slowly as his cock hardened.

His low moan echoed inside me. "Sweetheart..." His voice was husky. Lifting my head, I stared into his eyes filled with desire. *I did this to him.* Joy, euphoria, and the underlying thread of power filled me. "Maybe we should take this into the bedroom."

"Not yet." I framed his face with my hands. "I...want...this." I punctuated each word with kisses all over his face.

How could I possibly convey what I was feeling?

No one had ever let me set the pace.

Asher saw me. The real me. I wanted to show him how much that meant to me.

Shifting, I straddled him. His cock jumped against my pussy, and igniting a fire in my core. Instantly, my bones melted. I'd done this to Asher. "You feel so good against me." Releasing his face, I played with his nipples and shifted against his hard cock. I couldn't wait to have him inside me.

Patience, Emma. We have all night.

"Emma." Now, his voice was strained.

"I'm right here." I slid my right hand between our bodies and found the opening in his boxers. I had access to his cock. Hard and pulsing, I cradled it in my fingers before lightly tracing from base to tip.

"Do you have any fucking idea what you're doing to me?"

"Making you as crazy for me as I am for you." I'd no idea where these words were coming from, and I didn't care. I had hot steel in my hand. His cock twitched and power surged through me.

I'd done this to him. Me. Little Emma Palmer who everyone wrote off as shy and cautious. The one who never took charge. Empowerment was a heady drug.

"Please, baby."

Asher's voice was strained. I lifted my gaze from his gorgeous cock to his face. His jaw was clenched.

"Am I hurting you?" Should I let him go?

"Hurts so good." He rested his forehead against mine. "I'm loving your touch, your boldness. But honestly, I'm ready to explode."

"That might be a little messy." I bit my lip when he groaned as I stroked him again. Freedom hit me with hurricane force. For the first time in my life I felt truly free. Free to do what *I* wanted, to feel *my* power, and to enjoy myself.

"Bedroom, please." His plea was music to my ears.

"I think it's time." I didn't want to release him, but I did.

"Thank God." The next thing I knew, Asher had me in his arms, my legs wrapped around his waist. He took a step and stopped. "Hold my pants up or we're both going to end up in a pile on the floor."

"I wouldn't mind that. It could be fun." Where was this flirty tone coming from? Stroking his spine, I found the waist band of his slacks and grabbed it. "Some other night we'll test out the floor."

His body shuddered, and his arms tightened around me. "Words like that are not helping me keep control."

"Who said I wanted you in control?"

Asher grumbled under his breath as he walked toward his bedroom. He was so strong, and I felt safe in his embrace. The soft light of the beside lamp filled the room as he carried me to his large bed.

"Tonight you're mine." I captured his lips with mine.

We were going to have so much fun.

This was only the beginning...

Chapter Twenty-Seven

♥

A sher

My control was hanging on by a thread, but I wouldn't break. The shy woman I knew was gone and in her place was a woman full of passion and heat.

And I was here for it.

Grasping her legs, I pulled them away from my waist and slid her soft body against mine until her feet touched the rug.

Her eyes were soft and filled with passion, her lips red and slightly swollen. My dick reacted. I captured her lips, and our tongues tangled with each other. I used mine to mimic what I wanted to do with my cock. I needed her so much. But her satisfaction would come first.

"Asher." Her voice was breathless.

"Beautiful." I ran my fingers over her arms, enjoying the slight shivers that shook her body. She was so sensitive.

"You're the beautiful one." Her palms caressed my chest and unbearable pleasure flowed through me. "Your heart is beating so fast."

"All because of you."

Her breath brushed over my chest, then she kissed my left pec. The kiss shot a shaft of desire straight to my dick. Not enough. I wanted more. I wanted us both naked. "Shirt off." I grabbed the hem of her shirt and pulled it up, forcing her to move her hands.

I tossed her shirt aside and then looked down at her and lost what little breath I had left in my body at her lace covered breasts. Lord, I hoped I wasn't drooling. I gently brushed my finger over the top of one breast before moving to the other. Her skin flushed under my touch.

"More," she whispered, arching toward me.

"Your wish is my command." I would deny her nothing tonight. "Talk to me Emma."

"What do you want me to say?"

"Tell me what you want. How I'm making you feel." I needed to hear from her that I was affecting her as much as she was affecting me.

Her hands left my waist. "Touch me." She guided my palm over her breast.

"I can do that, but let's get this off." Finding the front clasp and released her bra. "Fucking perfection." Her breasts were full and her nipples hard.

Need filled me. Without another word, I closed my mouth over one nipple and was rewarded with a moan. I swear I could taste her honeysuckle scent as I laved her nipple, before I switched to her other breast.

"More, I need more."

Her whispered plea spurred me on. My free hand slipped over her belly and beneath her pants. Heat scorched my palm.

"Asher, I need you."

"As I do you." I paused for a moment trying to work out how we were going to get fully undressed. "Sweetheart, take a step back please."

She raised her head and stared at me.

"We need to undress."

It took a minute for her to process my words. "It will be my pleasure." I pressed my hands against her shoulders until she took a step back. With careful movements, I pushed her pants and underwear down. My dick twitched as her body was revealed.

Patience, Ash. Slow and easy.

I knelt to remove her shoes and socks, and her fingers tangled in my hair and stroked softly. I lost what little breath I had left in my lungs. Fighting my own need, I removed the rest of her clothing, then stood.

"Your turn."

Her eyes gleamed. Emma kept her hands on my chest as she slid down my body. My shoes and socks were the first to go then she put her hands inside my slacks. In an instant, she had the slacks and boxers at my feet.

Emma glanced up at me, and I lost it. I needed this woman. I grasped her arms, pulled her to her feet, and allowed myself the sublime indulgence of taking in her nakedness.

Perfection.

"Teasing time is over."

Her sweet scent filled my senses. I almost buried my face in her pussy and tasted her nectar.

What had I done to deserve her? Whatever it was, I'd do it a thousand times over to keep her with me just like this. Naked, breathless, and all mine.

Her fingers grasping my cock brought me out of my thoughts.

"Easy, sweetheart. I don't know how much longer I can control myself if you keep this up."

"This is all mine," she whispered as she gentled her touch but continued to stroke my shaft.

It took everything I had not to squirm under her hands. No woman had ever made me feel like this. Powerful yet vulnerable. I clenched my jaw as she ran a finger over the head of my dick and spread my seeping precum around.

"Fuck." The word escaped before I could stop it. Enough. I couldn't take it anymore. Squeezing her breast made her moan. A sensual haze came over me. Grasping her waist, I guided her to the bed and gave her a playful push.

She fell back with a gasp. I didn't give her time to recover before I knelt down and braced her legs over my shoulders. Her pussy was rosy and glistening. I couldn't wait to dive in.

Chapter Twenty-Eight

♥

Emma

Asher pushed me onto the bed, and I almost laughed until he knelt down and placed my legs over his shoulders. "Asher."

"Sweet smell. Do you taste like honeysuckle? I'm about to find out."

His lips covered my pussy, and I almost came out of my skin. I wasn't ready for the heat that invaded my body. He licked my pussy, and his tongue teased my clit.

Oh dear god. I never knew a man going down on me could feel so good. With each pass of his tongue my passion grew. "More." I tightened my legs around his head and closed my eyes.

My breathing increased as everything in me was pulled tight. For a moment, I allowed myself to think I was getting ready to orgasm, but that wasn't possible.

Using a vibrator, I could climax but never with a man.

Oh fuck. He'd pushed two fingers into my channel, and his tongue was now playing with my clit. I couldn't breathe. I opened my mouth to tell him to stop when my toes began to tingle.

My fingers curled into the quilt as the tingling spread through my body. Asher didn't stop what he was doing. His fingers pumped in and out of my pussy while his tongue continued to lash my clit.

I couldn't hold on. Did I even want to? With a small cry, I let my body go. He rode out the trembling of my body and my legs tightening even more around his head. He gentled his touch and his pulsing tongue as I rode the wave of completion.

After a minute—or was it five—Asher guided my legs off his shoulders. "You do taste like honeysuckle."

I wanted to answer him, but I couldn't even form a coherent thought. Asher lifted me, and I shivered as my back touched the cool sheets until his heat warmed me.

"So fucking sweet." I didn't open my eyes. I was basking in the afterglow of my orgasm. The first by a man.

What did that mean? I'd analyze it later, right now, I'd enjoy being close to Asher and relish his brand of loving.

***

Being held by Asher was pure bliss, but my man needed attention. Yes, I considered him my man. Shifting in his arms, I curved my fingers around his hard cock and reveled in its heat.

"Emma, don't start something you might not want to finish."

I raised my head and gazed at Asher. His features were tight as if he was in pain. "Am I hurting you?"

"Hell no." Fire blazed in his eyes.

I grinned. "I have no intention of not finishing." Knowing he was more than ready, I deliberately slid slowly down his body until his cock was poised at my lips. I knew the delay was torture, but I was in no hurry. Then, in one deliberately slow movement, I licked the glistening head.

"Fuuuuuck."

Power surged through me as I enveloped his hardness in my mouth. Salty with a hint of sweetness. A taste I could become addicted to very easily. I pulled back slowly until only the head of his cock remained inside my mouth before I licked him again.

"That's it." In an instant he pulled me up over his body. "I can't stand the torture."

"Torture is it?" I grinned.

"Yes." He rolled me onto my back and quickly put on a condom. "Since you want to play..." His cock nudged against my pussy.

Oh, yes. This was what I wanted. Him inside me, taking me to the stars, and filling me with pleasure. "Take me," I whispered.

"I plan to, darling." His lips covered mine as he maneuvered his body between my legs and thrust.

I gasped into his mouth and broke away from the kiss as he filled me. "Oh God, so hard, so good. I can feel the ridges of your cock pulsing against me." My pussy clenched around him. It had been so long, and I needed Asher. I needed relief, more than just physical. I needed someone who believed in me. A partner.

I froze.

Was I getting in too deep with Asher? Maybe. But right now, I didn't want to analyze our relationship. I wanted him to fuck me, and I wasn't going to stop him now.

"You're so tight around me."

"It's been a while."

He eased back and then thrust again.

I lost what little breath I had in my lungs. Without thought I curved my legs around his waist, as my lips found his.

Each time he drove into me, I fell deeper and deeper under his spell. That was all Asher and how he made me feel. Alive. I wasn't ready when my climax began to build, starting with the tingles in my toes as it worked its way up my body.

No. I wanted this to last longer, but my body had different ideas. I'd curved my arms around his back and now pulled him closer as my body shattered into a thousand pieces. I tore my mouth away from his to pull more air into my lungs as my orgasm rolled on and on.

Asher was still inside me, pulsing into his own release. Pleasure bloomed in my chest. This man, this wonderful man had taken me to the stars and back before taking his own pleasure. Again.

All too soon, Asher placed a soft kiss on my lips and rolled onto his side. Passion still blazed in his eyes, and it made me want to pull him right back on top of me. But I hesitated.

"Be right back." He slid off the bed.

I admired his tight naked ass as he walked to the bathroom and sighed. Asher was beginning to mean something to me, and I wasn't sure if that was a good thing or not. My gut clenched in distress, but I wasn't going to worry about it right now.

Asher was the best thing that ever happened to me, and I needed to remember how he made me feel seen and loved. I bit my lip.

How was I going to survive him?

Chapter Twenty-Nine

♥

A sher

I realized I was smiling. Warm. Content. Happy. As the memories replayed, I opened my eyes.

Nope, not a dream. This is real.

Emma was lying on my chest, sound asleep. With the lightest touch so as not to wake her, I moved a stray strand of hair off her face. Damn, this woman had gotten beneath my skin in more ways than one. Last night had been mind-blowing. Real life was better than any dream could ever be.

I wasn't one to wax poetic about women I slept with, but Emma? She was everything I could hope for and more.

She began to stir, turned her head from one side to the other, yawned, moved her arms upward in a half-stretch, then opened her eyes.

"G'morning," she whispered and yawned again, this time with her hand covering her mouth.

"Morning, sweetheart." I leaned down to kiss her, but she shook her head and kept her hand over her mouth.

"Morning breath." Her remark was muffled by her hand.

"I don't care." I reached under her arms, pulled her up my chest, and took her lips in a hard kiss. When I pushed my tongue between her lips, all I tasted was Emma's unique flavor. I broke the kiss when my cell ring. *Damned phone!*

I was going to let it ring, then I remembered Emma's car. "Be right back."

I slid out of bed, found my pants on the floor, and pulled my cell out of the pocket. "Hello." I turned to face Emma, who was leaning on one elbow, the sheet draped over her, showing just the top curve of her breasts. She watched me, a sexy grin on her face.

Temptation and I have to pay attention to this call. Control yourself, Asher.

"Yes, I understand. We'll be over in a couple of hours." I ended the call, turned the phone screen side down on the nightstand, then sat on the bed and memorized every aspect of the woman under the covers. "Keep staring at me like that, and we'll never leave this bedroom."

Her eyes brightened. "Maybe another day. Was that about my battery?"

"Yes. It's dead. Chase is going to install a new one."

Emma pulled the sheet around her as she slid out of bed. "Thank you." She brushed a kiss across my cheek before she made her way out of the bedroom. Then I heard the guest bathroom door shut.

I stood and took a step before I could stop myself. *No.* If I went in there, we'd never get out of this house. I grabbed some clean clothes and went into my bathroom. I turned on the shower then brushed my teeth. Memories from last night kept running in my head, and I was semi-erect when I stepped into the shower. I decreased the hot water and let the water flow over my back as it cooled.

Nope. I will ignore my body and think about a plan.

Okay, yeah. Once her car was fixed, I'd follow her home and convince her to pack more clothes and come back to my house.

Even considering that was another new thing for me. I'd never asked a woman to stay at my house before. I was breaking all of my rules for Emma.

I wanted her with me.

Chapter Thirty

♥

Emma

Monday morning, I drove to the office with a big grin on my face. Asher and I spent the weekend together. Chase installed a new battery, and my vehicle was purring like a contented kitten.

Asher had followed me home, then convinced me to go back to his place.

Not that it took much. I wanted to spend time with him. But I had my conditions. I was taking my car. That way I could leave from his house on Monday and not have to go home or ride with him. He agreed, and I packed enough.

Now it was back to the real world, rather than the little cocoon we'd built over the weekend. Asher was waiting for me when I parked, and we walked into the building together. I stopped at Daily Perks to get my usual coffee and muffin. Asher was checking something on his phone and suddenly headed up to the office in a rush, saying he was needed, so I grabbed his coffee too.

He was on the inhouse phone when I walked into the office. I set his coffee cup next to him and went to my workstation, arranged my coffee and muffin next to my keyboard, and dropped my backpack under the desk. I'd get my laptop out later.

"How the hell did that happen?" Asher bit out.

Oh boy, that didn't sound good. I reached over to switch on my computer.

"Emma, don't." He wasn't yelling, but his voice stopped me cold.

"What?" I straightened and stared at him. I didn't move to sit down.

"Don't turn it on." His tone left no room for questions. He went back to his call. I watched him on the phone, and he actually looked somewhat pale. "I'll get started on this end. ... Yeah, good move on the network. I'll call you as soon as I have anything. You do the same." He slammed the receiver down.

He was furious, and his features were tight.

"What happened?" I pulled out my chair and slowly sat down. I didn't take my eyes off Asher.

He picked up his coffee and took a sip. "Thank you for this."

"You're welcome. Now tell me what's going on."

He grimaced. "There's a high probability there have been multiple unauthorized attempts to access encrypted files on one or more of the servers."

"Why didn't they notify you?" My heart dropped. "How bad?"

"They didn't find it until this morning because the security protocols weren't tripped until about two hours ago. Nothing pinged overnight, and just after the day shift came on, the alarm tripped. Ben immediately pulled up the access logs and the keystroke logs. He's locked down the network so that only he and I can get on right now. Even Boyd can't log on. Luckily he's not here yet. Anyway, Ben sent out a nine-one-one to the team. That's why I had to bolt right after we walked into the building." Asher raked his fingers through his hair. "The team's not sure how bad this is yet; they're still digging into the logs."

"That's why you didn't want me to turn on my computer."

"Yes. We're on our own subnet, and I can access the company mainframe from here. Ben did tell me that none of the firewalls were breached. He wasn't willing to go into more detail. At least not yet."

"I get that." I pulled my laptop from my backpack. "Do you have a back door into the system?"

"Yes, but that's not how they got in. Like I said, there was no breach."

I could almost feel Asher's frustration. There was even an overlay of anxiety. My mind was going full tilt, and I kept coming back to the same conclusion, the only scenario that made any sense at all. But there was no way I was going to reveal even a hint of what I was thinking until I was sure.

"Understood. But I can use a program I developed to go in through the back door to see if it can shed more light on the situation."

"You can do that?" Asher dropped into the chair next to me.

"Can't you?"

"I've never needed anything like that. My side hustle in undergrad and grad school was white hat hacking. Ben, me, and one other person were hired to break *into* networks to find their vulnerabilities. We never thought of developing anything like that."

"Then let me show you." I brought up my program on my laptop and then Asher connected me to the mainframe through the back door. Hopefully, because the app was running on Asher's credentials, the system would allow the program to run without erecting any containment.

While I was setting the sniffer's search parameters, Asher filled Ben in on what we were trying to do. Ben authorized my laptop on the intranet and gave me a couple of lines of code that would allow the program unfettered access to the mainframe, and once the input was complete, I let the program off the chain. If there was any kind of pattern that set off the intrusion alarms, my program would find it.

Three nerve racking hours later...jackpot. "Here." I pointed to the screen. "Look at this. Activity on the R&D server triggered the alarms, and—"

"That much we already know, Emma."

"If you'd let me finish..."

Asher pointed to a notation. "Is this what I think it is?"

"That's what I was trying to tell you. What you see is the initial discovery. But look four lines down. That's the breakdown. Short version... Someone or someones accessed an encrypted partition on the R&D server. I don't know if it was a brute force attack or credentialed. The logs will tell us that. Anyway, once in, they tried to access this file." I tapped on the screen. "Do you have any idea what this is?"

I turned to Asher. He didn't answer right away, then his brow furrowed, and a minute later, he picked up his cellphone, tapped the screen, swiped twice, tapped again, and put the phone to his ear. The person on the other end answered right away.

"Ben, me. Open our text app…Yeah, the encrypted one. I'm going to send you something, and once you identify it, I'll need you to securely delete the text immediately." Asher looked at me and then took a photo of the screen. Swipe, swipe, tap, thumbs tapping the screen, and swoosh.

Almost immediately a soft bell, likely a confirmation that the text had been received. "Are you thinking what I'm thinking? … Yeah, Emma's sniffer found it. I need you to see if there's a pattern." Asher closed his eyes in what was clearly an 'oh, shit' moment. "Access and keystroke. I'll have Emma send you the complete file from the app. How long do you need?" He massaged his forehead. "Got it. Conference room in fifteen. … Yeah, Wall off R&D, then reopen the network. … I know. Marcus is gonna go ballistic when you tell him. … Absolutely tell him why, but don't call him on the house phone; call his cell."

No house phone. Call his cell? Had Asher…

"We'll be able to give everyone more details in the meeting. … Absolutely. I want to keep this as sequestered as possible. … You've got your hands full. I'll make the calls. … See you in in a few. … I'll definitely pass the word."

Asher ended the call and stared at the screen. I wanted to take his hand, squeeze his shoulder, something to let him know I had his back, but it looked like he was trying to gather himself.

I sipped my now-cold coffee and took a bite of my muffin. He'd mentioned to Ben about me sending a file, so I went in and found the sniffer's backup file and compressed it so that it would be ready to go. Just as I finished up, Asher gently grasped my shoulder.

"Thanks for your help, Emma. You probably saved us hours of scouring logs and trying to collate gigabytes of information. Ben said to tell you dinner and the best wine money can buy are on him Friday, anywhere you want to go."

I rubbed his arm, then took his hand. "We'll figure that out later. I have the file ready. Where do you want it sent and how?" While Asher was on the phone, I had more time to study the findings. I was now nearly certain of my original hypothesis, but I decided to wait until the meeting and hearing Ben's information.

Asher leaned forward, picked up his coffee, and drained at least half the contents. He put the cup down and laced his fingers on the desk, studying the desktop like it had all the answers he needed if he could just tease them out.

"I've heard that when you work for a company long enough, your co-workers become like a second family. It wasn't until FI that I understood the truth behind that." When he looked at me, his eyes looked infinitely sad. *He's figured it out. Oh, Asher...*

"When a member of your family betrays you, for whatever reason, the first emotion is probably a mixture of disbelief and sadness, and they say the next emotion is anger. Kind of like the stages of grief in a really fucked up order. I have a feeling this is going to get a lot worse before it's over."

I knew what he was feeling and no longer cared that we were in the office. I stood up and put my arms around him. He embraced me and rested his head at my waist. What could I say? Best to just be there. We held each other until he reached for my arms and took my hands in his. I leaned over and brushed a kiss over his lips then on his forehead.

"We've got this, Asher, and I've got your back. Now where and how do you want me to send this file?"

Chapter Thirty-One

♥

Asher

No sysadmin in their right or deranged mind ever allowed themselves to think that they had an impenetrable firewall, but my team had come pretty damned close to accomplishing exactly that.

Ben, my second-in-command at FI, and I met in our freshman year in high school and bonded over code, games, making it better, run faster, busting industry limitations, DSL, the miracle of broadband, what our parents called 'all things computer'. Then we discovered Tor and thus began our adventures on the darknet.

Ben came up with the idea of dabbling in cybersecurity after we encountered Bjorn Arneson, the insane genius who would become our third cohort and eventual co-founder of Gatekeeper Security, named after his darknet handle. Our primary mission—the skill that paid the bills and tuition—in those early years, break into corporate networks to find vulnerabilities and plug any holes. Do legally what we caught BJ doing before he ended up busted and scooped up by the feds in a deal to avoid prison time.

Ben, BJ, and I met John Boyd in grad school when he approached us about designing a website to sell everything from adult toys to kink furnishings and later to helping clients make sexual fantasies a reality. Graphics and website design were sort of a hobby for me, and when I told Ben and BJ what John wanted, they were onboard before I even blinked. Sex toys, kink, and fantasies? Who could pass that up? In less than a year, that collaboration had given birth to Fantasies, Inc. BJ thought FI was a fantastic idea, and he put up some serious money to help with startup, but he decided to expand Gatekeeper, which was now one the three best and most respected cybersecurity companies in the world.

FI blew up beyond even what our wildest speculation could have come up with, and we recruited Tim Campbell and Will McDonald from Stanford. Ben and I 'met' them in our online gaming group while fighting aliens, zombies, vampires, and other universal threats to help us recharge. Ben and I were impressed with their mad gaming skills, out of the box tactics, and strategy, all of which complemented their professional expertise. We invited them to intern with FI during their undergrad summer breaks sophomore and junior years and onboarded them after graduation. They were now the co-leads of what I considered one of the sharpest IT teams in the business.

Whether it's the deepest classified US Government agencies or John and Jane Q Public with a cellphone or other electronic device connected to the internet, odds are better than seven in ten that some bad actor or actors would be successful in their hacking attempts, be it by brute force or the end user inviting them in through malware.

Fantasies Inc.'s number was up today.

"Tell me what you do know." We'd already been here for an hour, and no one had any concrete answers.

"We're still checking all the firewalls, mainframe and subnets, to find where they got in. It's looking—" Tim said. His red hair was sticking up so that he looked like he'd stuck his finger in an electrical outlet.

Will broke in. "Bossman, right now, everything is preliminary. I don't want to say much more than that because, at best, it'd be speculation. The only sure thing at this moment: There was no breach of any of the firewalls."

Ben looked directly at me. "I don't want to go where that sign is pointing, at least not yet, until we have some concrete findings that give us no other choice."

I waved his apology away. "I trust your work."

"Thanks, but I'm not sure I do, not at the moment," Ben muttered.

Will rubbed his eyes and raked his fingers through his hair. "I haven't been through every line of the logs yet, but I didn't just scan them either. The first review did not show *any* breach of the main firewall or the subnet firewalls. All security updates are current. Scans have not turned up anything. Being able to do this and not leave a trace is thirteen thirty-seven level...or..."

The conference room door opened, but there'd been no knock. I was expecting John Boyd since I'd notified him, but it was Emma, balancing her open laptop on one arm and closing the door with her free hand. She didn't move from in front of the door. Ben nodded a greeting. Will and Tim looked to me and then back to Emma.

"Emma Palmer, meet Tim Campbell, and the ginger next to him is Will McDonald. You've met Ben. Emma's on loan from Tri-O-Tech as project manager for the streamlining and expansion. She's something of a rock star when it comes to development."

Emma's cheeks turned a deep shade of pink as she looked down at her laptop.

"Nice meeting you, Emma."

"Welcome, Emma."

She nodded to Will and Tim and gave Ben a shy smile.

"Hi Emma. I meant what I said about that dinner and wine."

"Thank you." She put her laptop on the table next to me and pointed to the screen. "Sorry, for the interruption, but I thought you might want to have this information," she said softly.

"What did you find?"

"Whoever it was didn't breach the main firewall or the subnets, but you've probably already figured that out."

Ben frowned. "It looks that way."

I gestured for Emma to sit down.

"Do you have a way to project this so everyone can see?" she asked.

"Yes." I woke the ninety-eight inch monitor and pulled it out just enough to read the label on the back. "Here's the mirror address." I read off the alphanumeric code.

"Thank you." Before I was back at my seat, her laptop screen appeared on the monitor.

"All right." Her voice shook a little bit, and I smiled with a half nod. "It took me a bit of digging, but whoever this is, they used valid credentials, which indicates…"

I watched the screen as she pulled up a hasty diagram of how they got in.

"Shit," Ben muttered.

"Exactly," Emma said. "No matter how I dissect this, I keep coming back to the same conclusion." She glanced at me, and I nodded. "At this moment, it's circumstantial at best, but unless we find something more definitive, our intruder is a current or former employee."

And the chorus erupted, "What the f—"

"Quiet. Emma, explain, please."

Emma looked around the table and used the laser pointer to call our attention to the information on the screen. Any shyness was long gone. She was in her element.

"There's been no breach. The sniffer found what is at best a very thin pattern, but it also picked up similar breadcrumbs dropped in a suspicious pattern. No alarms activated until the footprints in the forest, if you will, reached the firewall for an encrypted subnet on the R&D server. This is only preliminary, but the characteristics look like some form of ghostware."

I could see the wheels turning as the team thought it through. Ben and Tim spoke at the same time.

"But we—" Ben didn't take his eyes off the monitor.

"There's no way—" Tim turned to Emma, his expression showing the slightest hint of accusation. If I didn't know him as well as I did, I would've missed it.

I raised a hand. "Hold up. One at a time. Tim, you got the first syllable out. Go ahead."

Tim glanced at me and then focused on Emma. She didn't wait for his comment. "I followed the trail. They started with HR, tried to get into IT, then tried R&D, then back to IT." Emma glanced at me, and I had a sinking feeling about what was coming next. "They got into the main server, but didn't mess with anything—at least as far as I can tell right now. Then"—now she locked on me— "they tried three times to access our subnet. No joy." She used the laser pointer to trace a path on her diagram. "Apparently, they tried one more time on R&D, made it through the server firewall, again, a legit pass. And here's where it gets interesting. They were in for about forty-five seconds, backed out, and then they did manage to access the company email directory, but as soon as they did, the intruder alarm trips, and our intruder hauls ass off the network, but not before the alarm trace routes to Seattle. Our intruder is local."

"Shit," Ben said again, under his breath.

"The good news is they didn't get far."

I breathed a sigh of relief.

"There was no direct breach of services."

"Did they copy the directory?" Not as bad as it could have been, but still a breach. One I intended to make sure didn't happen again.

"Doesn't look like it. Here's the thing, though. Ghostware is so sneaky, even virus protection doesn't catch it until it's too late. All of this activity until the email directory, was executed with legit credentials – at least as far as I can tell right now. However, and it's a big caveat, the reason I think it was some type of ghostware is because, while the credentials never triggered anything, I can't identify who those credentials belong to."

I nodded. "Anything else?" She bit her lip, which told me there was more, but she was reluctant to say. "Emma, anything you say will stay in this room."

She blew out a breath. "I know the servers held, but we need to check every system to make sure they didn't slip a trojan or other virus in."

Tim shook his head. "We have protections against that."

"We had protections to prevent incursions, and look what happened there," Will commented.

"I saw your protections, and they're excellent, but you know how sneaky ghostware can be." Emma said.

"Yep, that's how it got its name.

"I agree." My team was good, but she was right. "Let's get on this right away. It's going to take time. We've got to nail down how it got in, whether it was deliberate or accidental secondary to a malicious website, phishing, whatever. I'll send out the orders for refreshers on internet, email, and text safety. What has me going round in circles is the question: What were they looking for?"

Ben held my gaze. "If the SOB comes back, we will get them." He stood and extended his hand to Emma. "Again, thanks for your help. You saved us a lot of hours. Now we have to confirm your preliminary information."

Emma shook his hand and smiled. "Happy to help."

As Tim was about to pass Emma, he extended a closed fist. "Much respect." Emma inclined her head and gave him a fist bump.

Will stood and held Emma's gaze then put his open hand over his heart and inclined his head. "Thirteen thirty-seven, ninja. Thirteen thirty-seven." Emma blushed and, to my surprise, seemed to glow from the inside out.

"Thank you, Will." Before she closed her laptop, she watched as he left and Ben followed him and closed the door.

Emma picked up her laptop and stared at the closed door. "Wow..." she breathed then turned to me. Her expression made the room seem warmer, the sun through the windows a bit brighter. She cleared her throat.

"We're going to have to go over every log entry to try and find a starting place. I know I said the findings were preliminary, but because of the intruder's behavior, I'm ninety-nine percent certain this is ghostware. One thing I'm absolutely certain of is it was brought in by a current or former employee. I need you to take me through your out-processing procedures."

Emma held her laptop to her chest like protective armor. I cupped her shoulders and held her at arm's length. "You showed some serious game and didn't even flinch. Do you believe me now?"

She lowered her eyes. The blush slowly rose up her neck and into her cheeks. "I was doing what you're paying me for—my job."

I tilted my head and leaned forward just enough to catch her gaze. "Emma, Ben and I have worked with some of the best in our profession, top-tier. Tim and Will don't impress easily if at all." I raised her chin and kept my other hand on her shoulder. "I wasn't exaggerating. You managed to corral an incredible amount of information that would've taken days to collect and analyze, and you did it in"—I glanced at the clock over the door—"under three *hours.*"

"The sniffer did what it was designed to do."

"Yep. *You* built it, tested it, perfected it." I folded my arms across my chest. Emma didn't look away. Did she have any idea how respected she was in the profession, respected by colleagues who'd made their marks, earned their street cred? Had she been so brainwashed by her family and the misogynistic pond scum that were the underbelly of the STEM professions?

I raised her chin and speared her with my gaze. No way was I going to let her minimize her accomplishments both within the project and her assistance with this intrusion. "Do you know what thirteen thirty-seven means?"

She shook her head. I was mildly surprised on the one hand, on the other, not so much. I chuckled. "I didn't think so. How about wizard, guru, rock star?"

She tilted her head, one raised eyebrow and a half smile. "Of course I know what those designations mean. I haven't been living under a rock or in a cave, Asher."

I couldn't suppress a chuckle, but I gave myself one brownie point for trying. "One, three, three, seven, is leetspeak for leet, as in elite, an expert, one of the best. Recognition of and supreme respect for some very serious cred, as my brother would say. And you earned it. The accolade has absolutely nothing to do with your father. You cut your own path."

As I watched her process the compliment, her shoulders straightened, and she stood a little taller. *That's it, Emma. You're all that and so much more. Don't ever forget it.*

"C'mon, rock star. Standing here isn't solving the problem." I bowed, extended my arm, and pointed to the door. Emma giggled and inclined her head as she passed me, opened the door, and waved me through. Just as I was about to move past her, she stood on tiptoe and kissed my cheek. "Let's do this, bossman."

Mind. Blown. Day made.

Chapter Thirty-Two

♥

Emma

After the briefing, Asher and I returned to our office just long enough to gather our notes and shut down our workstations.

We had been working in our office because there wouldn't be any need to work in the server room until the new servers arrived, were installed, and made ready for configuration.

Ben and Asher had decided it would be best to have everyone in one location, so we were moving down to IT. We stepped off the elevator, which was directly across from the main door. I giggled when I looked above the biometric lock. A nameplate no different than any other. Alpha numeric designation for the room, and below that in the standard company font:

BATCAVE

Asher smiled at my reaction. "There's a story there. Wait'll you see what's hanging on the wall behind the chair at Ben's desk."

The background hum and cold, not quite enough to chill beer, but close. Control center along one wall, on the opposite side the individual offices for the system, network, and security administrators, aka sysadmin, netadmin, and secadmin. Asher took the lead and knocked twice on Ben's door then opened it. As we walked in, of course the first thing I looked for was the mysterious hanging object. Ben stood, and I chuckled. Centered on his vanity wall among the degrees, certs, awards, and photos, a matted and framed sign printed on what at first glance looked like eleven by fourteen paper in one-twenty point Copperplate font:

BATCAVE

Ben came around the desk. "Like it? The first nameplate. Seemed appropriate since we're about thirty feet underground."

"I love it. So does that make you Bruce Wayne or Alfred?" I caught Asher folding his arms and covering his snort laugh with his hand.

"Nah. Makes me Lucius Fox to his"—he flicked his hand at Asher—"Bruce Wayne."

"That's perfect! Pleased to meet you, Mr. Fox."

"Lucius, please." Ben leaned on the front edge of his desk.

"Are you two finished?" Asher groused, then looked at me. "You know the Batman universe?"

I gave him my best 'of course, why would you even ask' expression. "I told you I haven't been living under a rock...or in a cave, Asher. My gamer group has analyzed and dissected the Justice League and the Avengers backward and forward."

Asher drew back and—no other word for it—assessed me from head to toe. "One surprise after another."

"Another subject for Friday night discussion at Whistle Spot. I know it's only been about a half hour since the briefing. Any more information? And are those fleeces on the rack by the door for everyone?" I prompted.

I could feel Asher's eyes on my back, the heat welcome in the cold.

"Yep. Feel free. It'll take a couple of days to get one with your name on it. The conference room is out the door to your right, in the back behind the glass wall. Let's go hunt down a hacker. You scored the first hit, so after you, Emma."

***

I stood and stretched. It was almost midnight. Asher had been called up to brief John Boyd, about an hour after we arrived on the server floor. Boyd authorized any resources we might need to find the intruder and repair any damage they'd caused. Food had been brought in, and we ate while we worked. At one point, someone Asher introduced as Jackie, the president's executive assistant, brought some paperwork that turned out to be a detailed addendum to my contract. It'd been electronically signed by Manning and by Boyd, and apparently it was my turn. This time, after a side-eye to Asher, I read every word before initialing each page and signing on the dotted line. An open-ended extension, and latitude limited only by FI tasking.

I was surprised at how quickly this modification happened. The back and forth to arrange for me to come to FI for the project had taken nearly three months. Were Greg and his gang trying to throw roadblocks to my promotion? It'd definitely be something he'd pull. Something to keep in the back of my mind.

Ben, Will, Tim, and Asher had divided up the activity logs and had been analyzing every line. I was put on examining code, line by line. By the ten-hour mark, I was nearly cross-eyed and my brain was turning to mush. Time for a reboot. Asher was bent over a printout. Margin notes in different colored ink framed the printed text. When I tapped his shoulder, he jerked, startled. He looked distracted but smiled at me and squeezed my hand.

"I'm going topside for some fresh air. I need to reboot. It's all running together. Want to join me?" I whispered.

"Excellent idea. Red Bull or water...or both?"

"Just water. I'm not sure how much longer I'm going to last. I'll see where my head's at after some fresh air and a walk."

"Another good idea. Let's meet in the atrium. I'll get the water."

I looked around to make sure no one was watching, then kissed my finger and tapped his cheek. "See you upstairs."

He stroked my cheek and headed for one door; I went out the other.

I stopped in the ladies room by the elevator. It looked like it had never been used. No surprise since there were no other women on IT staff. I let that marinate while I humored my body and gave in to its demands, and when finished, I washed my hands and splashed cold water on my face. While drying my face and hands, I took a long look at the woman in the mirror. Same as always, but different too. This time, I didn't look away.

When I first started working in the Batcave, I thought I was imagining some kind of change. I couldn't put my finger on it and attributed it to my imagination. Then, the longer I worked with Ben and his team, I realized I hadn't imagined it.

There was a mountain of data to go through. As we dug deeper, Will, Tim, and their technicians on the mid and night shifts weren't shy about asking me questions. Their interactions with me were no different than with their coworkers and Asher. They didn't talk over me or interrupt. When I answered their questions and made suggestions, their attention was fully focused on my answers and suggestions.

Tri-O-Tech's environment was the opposite and not in a good way. I was one of three women on the IT staff and the only female developer. I hadn't been on the staff a whole day before one of the network techs, Greg Webster, told me to refill his coffee. I didn't move, and he made the mistake of ordering—not asking—me and demanding to know why I hadn't moved. I wanted to leave smoldering ashes but decided to just lightly scorch him. He never made the coffee move again, but in meetings, he and his clique made it a point to interrupt and mansplain. On the floor, he'd make snide comments about my clothes and hair, always out of hearing of others. I refused to play his game. One day, he'd trip himself up. His kind always did. In the meantime, I'd keep my head down and wait for the inevitable.

Alex was a bit better. I suspected one of the reasons he—I heard later—reluctantly sent me on this job was because he knew it would probably be necessary to build unique software to facilitate the merging of FI's divisions, and my skillset made me perfect for the job. He also told me that I was on the short list for director of the department. First woman in that position with Tri-O-Tech, cracking the glass ceiling, more yada, yada, yada. I could see where that was going to end up.

Webster was also on that list, and when he found out I'd scored the Fantasies, Inc. project as well, he had to drop his two cents. "We don't have to wonder how Palmer got this assignment, do we?"

The elevator doors opened and interrupted my musings. As I drifted to the atrium doors, a mental lightbulb popped on.

Maybe going for that promotion wasn't such a good idea. It would mean having a team of men reporting to me, and the odds of gaining their respect weren't good, closer to the not gonna happen range. Why hadn't I thought about that before?

Probably because until I worked with Asher and his team, I hadn't experienced a different environment. They treated me like an asset, an equal. The level of respect Asher's entire staff had shown me was a little overwhelming,

but it was also eye-opening. What had Cassie said once...
"Sometimes you don't know how good or bad it is until
you experience the bad and the good." I understood what
she'd said at the time, but now I'd lived it. She was right.
I'd been existing in my own little world for too long.

"Are you okay?" Asher asked.

I was so wrapped up in my thoughts, I didn't see Asher
until I almost walked through him.

"I'm good. I got so caught up in my own head, I wasn't
paying attention. It's kind of cool tonight, but the air feels
great."

"I understand the head thing. You look wrung out."

"Yeah. I feel like it." But I knew we needed to push
through.

"I think that's enough for tonight."

I opened my mouth to argue, but he shook his head.
"We've secured everything as best we can for now. The
logs and code aren't going anywhere. It's not going to do
anyone any good if we don't have fresh minds to solve the
problem."

He was right.

"Okay. I don't relish the drive home."

"Good thing we don't have to."

"What?" Were we supposed to sleep on the floor? Ahh,
the heady university days and studying for finals.

"Knowing how critical this is, John's putting us up in the hotel down the street. On the executive floor, no less. This way, we can get some sleep and not worry about driving."

"I'm too tired to enjoy any of the perks. Good thing I restocked my overnight bag."

We walked side by side and linked pinkie fingers. What the security cameras couldn't discern wouldn't end up in the gossip pipeline. In the elevator, we leaned against the back wall, and Asher slipped his hand behind me and rested it at my waist. As soon as the car stopped, we were all business before the doors opened...just in case. At the door, a lifted eyebrow and a wink.

While Asher gave the rest of the team the news about the hotel, I shut down my laptop and shouldered my purse.

"Let's plan on getting back here by nine at the latest. John has to notify the feds, and he'll probably do that later this morning, depending on what we've found. In any case, when those guys get here, I want to make sure we've gathered as much information as possible. We definitely don't need the cyberspooks underfoot."

Ben and Asher exchanged a look that clearly telegraphed: *That's the last thing we need.*

Asher, Ben, and I brought up the rear, shut off the lights, and threw the locks.

The cool air brushed against my skin as we walked through the parking lot to our vehicles. I grabbed my bag out of the trunk, and Asher got one out of his.

"I should've asked if you wanted to drive?" Asher said as we walked into the hotel.

"The walk was nice. Drive for three blocks? Why? I've been sitting most of the day and night; I need the exercise. Besides, the fresh air felt good."

We strode to the reception desk. The minute Asher gave his name, we were given keys and told how to get to our rooms. Our connecting rooms.

Once we got to our rooms, I inserted my key into the lock and looked over at Asher.

"Sleep well," he whispered.

"You too." I slipped inside and closed the door. A second later, I heard his door close.

I slung my bag onto the entertainment center, yawned, unzipped it and pulled out a small cosmetic bag, nightshirt, toothbrush, toothpaste, and a hairbrush. Exhaustion weighed down every move. Everything was beginning to run together.

Once I finished in the bathroom, I changed into a nightshirt and climbed into bed. I glanced at the trail of my clothes from the bathroom to the bed. Nope. Later.

Thirty minutes later, I was still wide awake. My mind wouldn't settle down. Not unusual when I was working on something complex, but I needed sleep. Was Asher awake?

A knock on the door startled me. Climbing out of bed, I realized the knock was coming from the connecting door. I unlocked it and pulled it open.

"Asher." He looked as exhausted as I felt.

"Did I wake you?"

"No. My brain won't stop working."

"I know the feeling. May I?" He gestured to my room.

Stepping back, he walked in. Damn, I'd seen this man naked, but in a pair of pajama pants and no shirt, he was sexy as hell. He yawned. We both needed sleep. I hesitated.

"You're biting your lip."

"I'm not sure how to say this." I was just beginning to get comfortable with speaking my mind to Asher, but this was different. This was more intimate. *Get over yourself, Emma. You've had sex with the man.*

"Do you want me to go?"

"Hell, no." I winced at my loud voice. "Stay with me." There I said it, the ball was in his court now.

"Of course, sweetheart. Whatever you want." He reached down and held the covers open for me. I climbed back into bed, and Asher followed, his warm body cradling mine. "Close your eyes and sleep."

I instantly relaxed into his embrace, and my mind calmed.

I fell asleep before I'd taken two breaths.

Chapter Thirty-Three

♥

A sher

The ringing phone brought me out of my dreams. I reached for the noise and shoved the receiver between my head and the pillow. "Yeah, what?"

"Ms. Palmer, this is your wake-up call." Too cheerful for automation.

"Thanks." I dropped the receiver and didn't bother to raise my arm. I didn't remember ordering a wake-up call, but it was a good thing. I'd passed out.

"Who was that," Emma's sleepy voice penetrated my consciousness.

Oh yeah, we'd spent the night in each other's arms. In her room. "Wake up call."

"What time is it?"

I turned my head on the pillow and opened one eye. I couldn't miss the clock on the nightstand.

Eight o'clock.

"Shit!" I sprang out of bed. "It's eight."

How did that happen? I stared down at Emma. Her eyes drowsy and her hair mussed. That's how it happened. And I wanted to crawl right back into bed with her.

"Well, that sucks." Emma slid out of bed. "I guess we better get dressed."

I was reluctant to leave her, but this morning wasn't the time for bedroom antics. "Yeah. I'll go back into my room and come get you when I'm ready."

"Sounds like a plan." Emma padded over to me and brushed a kiss on my lips. "Thank you for last night."

It took everything in me not to pull her in my arms and really kiss her, but I wasn't going to start something I couldn't finish. I stepped through the connecting doors and shut mine behind me. No sense in tempting myself.

Seven minutes later, showered, dressed, and everything shoved back in the bag.

Was Emma ready? Maybe. Two more minutes and I'd shouldered my bag and was knocking on her door. *I never move this fast before coffee.*

"Good morning, again." The rush was worth every second to see that smile. "Who ordered the wakeup call?"

"I did." I turned to see Ben coming down the hall. "We said nine, but we all needed sleep. I figured eight would be enough time." Ben's gaze was assessing.

"Thanks, Ben." Emma grinned at him. "I'd probably still be asleep."

"You're welcome."

A quick look around. We were the only ones in the hall. "Where are Tim and Will? They stayed here last night, didn't they?"

"They're already at the office; they bugged out at seven."

"Then we should go."

"I'll get my bag."

I held Emma's door open as she grabbed her bag.

"You look well rested." I glanced at Ben who had a wide grin on his face. "You must have had a good night."

I stared at him. "I did thanks." Did Ben suspect I'd been with Emma? Did it really matter?

Emma appeared a second later with her bag. I took it from her, and the three of us made the short trek to the office.

We weren't even off the hotel property before Ben and Emma began debating Avengers versus Justice League, which concluded with a promise to resume later just as we stepped up the curb to enter the FI building.

A friendly debate on a mutually enjoyed subject. So why was I even the slightest bit jealous? I couldn't be *that* insecure. Could I?

"I need coffee," Emma remarked as we entered the building.

"Me too," Ben said.

"Someone is late today," Amelia observed as we lined up for coffee and muffins.

"Late night," Emma said.

"I heard." She pegged Ben and me. "Thank goodness you guys put my system on a separate whatever you called it thing from the company's."

I chuckled. "It's called a server. We did it because while you operate this fantastic coffee nirvana in our building, you aren't a corporate division of FI. Makes the IRS and Accounting happy too."

Ben and I gave Amelia our order. When we looked at Emma, she was barely moving, her gaze focused on something. I scanned the area, nothing unusual.

"Emma, you with us?" I prompted and waved my hand in front of her face.

She recited her order as if it was a second thought.

"Just something that popped into my head. I'll explain upstairs."

I'd seen this happen before. Distracted, deep in her head. The result was almost always a solution of some sort, be it to a problem or a better way to do something. The metamorphosis reminded me of cartoons I'd watched as a kid where a glowing lightbulb appeared over a character's head.

Amelia brought our coffee and muffins. Ben raised his card.

"I've got this. I'm headed downstairs." He looked a bit askance at Emma, shrugged, glanced at me and headed for the elevators, shaking his head.

Amelia watched us, her expression conveying a silent question. Emma's mind was definitely elsewhere as she picked up her coffee and muffin then began walking to the elevators. I looked at Amelia, shrugged, and whispered, "She gets this way sometimes, usually when she's cooking up some idea."

She tilted her head and smiled. "No need to explain. I've seen that expression a lot around here and labeled it 'coming attractions'. The idea vibe is strong with that one." And nodded toward Emma's departing back.

Emma said nothing in the elevator, and when the doors opened, she headed for the door to our office, definitely on the trail of something, and my curiosity quotient was rising fast.

Once inside, I watched as she set her coffee on the desk, dropped her purse and backpack, tapped her keyboard to wake the box, and turned on her monitor.

"Is keeping me in suspense deliberate, or is the plan to let me in on whatever's going on in your head?"

She took a bite of her muffin followed by careful sips of the hot coffee, then raised a finger in a clear *gimme a minute* signal. I stashed my stuff and tapped the keyboard to wake the box. I was about to take a bite of my muffin when Emma spoke. The reveal...maybe?

"How much do you know about coders, not code, but about coders?"

"Probably not enough. I've been trying to decode you since I first saw you at that party. Why?"

"Ha, ha, ha. I'm going to remain a mystery." Another bite of the muffin, the coffee chaser, a raised finger. I kept quiet. "Do you read a lot of fiction?"

Where's this going, Emma? "Sure. And in answer to your likely next question, most of the genres. I've even read paranormal romance, if you can believe that."

She giggled. "If you enjoy science fiction, why not PNR?" She switched gears in the blink of an eye, now all business. "Okay, just like people's signatures are unique and authors' styles—some call it voice—are unique, coders are the same. Work with them long enough, and you can recognize their coding style, signature, if you will."

Emma must have picked up the change in my expression. Code signing. Adding an encoded signature, kind of like a copyright. Ensured the work was genuine and hadn't been tampered with. Coders, developers, and ethical hackers signed their work, just like any other writer-slash-composer. The black hats prided themselves on their anonymity, but analyze their work often enough, and their style, as unique as any signature, could be described, cataloged, and used as a tool to expose them. Sure there were others who tried to duplicate original works, but there was always something 'off' about the duplicate, forgery, if you will, that set it apart from the original. And the cyberspooks, a kind of artist in their own right, were excellent at identifying and cataloging those patterns. Once the pattern was identified, it was only a matter of time before the cyberspooks matched the style to a username. No one could hide forever, but you had to give them credit, even respect, for trying.

"You know..." She licked the sugar from her muffin off her fingers, and my mind went places it had no business going right then, especially under the current circumstances. *Must ignore temptation.* "... like jewel thieves and the methods they use regularly. If you've watched the true crime shows, the serial killers always leave some repeating clue. In a lot of cases, that's how cops catch them."

The pieces were falling into place, but I wanted to see where Emma was going with this. "I understand that, but we haven't found the ghostware, and we haven't locked down the credentials yet."

"True." She waggled her eyebrows. "For now. I need some stuff from you."

"Anything. Fire away."

The wagging eyebrows and evil grin immediately gave way to business Emma. "Can you think of anyone who might have a grudge against you or anyone else in the IT department? And just because you might be thinking of someone but the circumstance would be unlikely, don't discount them. I also want the names of anyone who left FI and the reason or reasons why. Exit interviews, discipline documentation, whatever. Even if they started here and x amount of time later decided FI just wasn't a good fit."

"I'm ahead of you. I asked Ben to find the names of everyone who's left the technology department for *any* reason since day one. He sent the list to HR last night."

"Is that going to be a long list?"

"Not really. We've got excellent retention stats, remember?"

"I do. And Asher, I want their entire employment records including the findings on their background checks. *Everything*."

"In process if not already done."

"We need to meet with John and the guy from Legal, the one who wrote my contract, Nick Costanza. Is there any chance you can make that happen today?"

"Mind if I ask why?"

Emma turned in her chair to face me. "I'm going with my gut. Legit creds. What's weird is that we can't identify them, as in who they belong to...yet...but that will probably happen today. We also traced to a local ISP. My gut says this is definitely an inside job and the perp is a current employee."

"I agree with everything you've said. We're going to have to turn this over to the feds and soon. Once we're outside the FI firewalls and in the wild, we'll hit roadblocks only the feds can get past."

Emma twirled a pencil through her fingers. "Yep. If we put together as much information as we can gather *before* we go to the feds, that gives them a leg up. It also makes the cyber insurance guys happier. Shows we're not sitting on our butts wringing our hands. They like that."

As we were talking, I kept having this prickly feeling that something was right on the edge of my memory, but

I couldn't put my finger on it. A little like walking into a room but forgetting why you were there. Not surprising in a way because, at the same time, I was trying to remember everyone who'd left my department. Our turnover was extremely low. Maybe six people in the ten years since John started FI.

"Hey, Asher, are you with me?"

Blink. Blink. "Sorry. I didn't mean to check out on you. There's something in the back of my mind that's bugging me, and I..."

Emma tilted her head. "And you..." she prompted.

There it was. But was it even plausible? Maybe. My first impression of Emma was that she was extremely shy, even an introvert. But was she shy, or was she keeping her head down to get ahead. What was it like for her at Tri-O-Tech? She'd alluded to differences between FI and Tri-O-Tech, but she'd used pretty general language. She'd also told me about the stigma of being Roger Palmer's daughter and the assumptions and insinuations that came with it. I'd seen some pretty underhanded stuff women had to deal with in undergrad and postgrad. Even today, women still had to deal with the 'boys will be boys' attitudes.

Which brought me to the here and now.

"Hey, Asher..." Emma reached across the space between us and tapped my knee. "What's going on?"

Yeah, it was plausible, even probable, but I wouldn't know unless I asked. I turned my chair so I could face Emma full-on. She'd leaned back, watching me, her brow furrowed, expression confused.

"You asked me about disgruntled former employees and current employees that might have grudges..."

"Yes. We—you, Ben, Will, Tim, me—are going to turn over all the stones to see what's underneath. Did you come up with something else we should consider?"

If we were going to examine the probable, then the improbable was something we had to consider even if for no other reason than to explicitly rule it out.

"I have to ask you the same question: Is there anyone you've worked with in the past and/or currently who might have even the slightest grudge against you?"

The changes in her expression were subtle. If an observer didn't know her well, they would've missed the surprise, disbelief, cynicism, disbelief again, then full-on skepticism. And with that, Emma raising the emotional walls and armor.

The slightest squint, tilt of her head, first right then left, and pursed lips. "Me? You really are grabbing at straws. But for an instant, let's say that's a real possibility. Why would whoever they are come at me through a company that, until the last not quite a month, I've never been associated with?" She turned away and focused on her monitor, then lowered her head into her raised hands.

"Emma, as convoluted as it—"

Three raps on the door and I turned to see Ben poking his head in.

"What's up, Ben?" He looked at me then at Emma. I followed his gaze. Her head was up, watching Ben as he stepped into the office, his hand still on the doorknob.

"Need you both downstairs." Judging by his vibe, this wasn't going to be good news.

Chapter Thirty-Four

E mma

"Give us a minute and we'll be right there."

Ben turned with a curt nod and left, closing the door on his way out. As soon as I heard the latch click, Asher turned to me. I raised my hand.

"Look, Asher, I get it. What you don't seem to get is the list of grudges would include people my father messed with, people I went to school with, worked with, who think the only way I've made it this far was on my father's coattails. What can I say? Pick a name in tech. If it's not the person you pick, it's probably someone who knows some-one. You know how incestuous tech is in the stratosphere not to mention how cutthroat it can be in some circles all the way down to sea level."

I locked my box and turned off the monitor. What more was there to say? I tucked my laptop under my arm, intending to head for the elevators, when Asher gently grasped my upper arm. I glanced from his hand to his face and back to his hand. He released my arm.

"I realize the possibility is very likely zero, but I wouldn't be doing my job if I didn't ask the question. You said it yourself: The profession is interwoven and—your word, not mine even if true—cutthroat. Just think about it, okay?"

"If it'll make you happy…" I didn't look back to see if he was following me.

***

Ben, Will, and Tim were already seated on one side of the conference table. One guy, probably John Boyd, the president, was at the head of the table, and another guy—Nick Costanza from Legal?—sat to his left. Before we took our seats, Asher performed the introductions, confirming my assumptions.

John spoke first. "Miles is on his way. Nick has confirmed that access to the personnel records is permitted for the purposes of this internal investigation. Access by any outside entities will be by warrant only. Ben has brought us up to date with all of the latest information."

"We're making some progress on identifying who's behind the creds. They've covered their tracks pretty well, but at first glance, not a single person stands out." Ben slid what looked like a list across the table to Asher. He picked it up. "This is the list of those who've left and circumstances."

"All the signs are pointing to inside help. Access attempts indicate purpose. Are we any closer to figuring that out?"

Ben, Tim, and Will shook their heads.

Someone tapped on the door right then, and I heard Miles before he took the seat next to Asher. "Sorry I'm late." He passed a thumb drive to Asher and another to Nick. "Those drives have the HR information you requested, Asher. Nick, the drive I gave you is a duplicate." Nick nodded, but didn't speak.

Miles opened his laptop. "As you may be aware, Asher requested the records of anyone who had left IT for any reason since its inception. There were eight departures."

The information on the first five was benign. The employees had left for family or were poached. Not at all unusual, and Miles stressed that the exit interviews were positive on both sides.

While Miles briefed the group on the former employees, I was multitasking: listening to Miles and looking over the search results from the sniffer. After we'd
offloaded the preliminary findings, I reset the search
parameters and left it to run in the background. The
data collected overnight were interesting, particularly
in regard to the intruder's activity pattern, but I wasn't
ready to say anything just yet.

Then I realized there had been a very subtle change
in the room vibe as Miles dropped both shoes.

"Which brings us to Tate Riser, Baylor Moore, and
Hugo Wayne. All fired for cause."

Asher picked up the thread. Tate tried to hack into
the time tracking app. Baylor was fired for harassment.
Turns out Hugo had seriously mad skillz; Asher had
assessed them as outstanding, definitely high praise, but
the guy was eventually fired for insubordination.

"Do we still need to look internally?" Miles asked.

"The current employees in IT have the expertise, and
while I don't believe any of them would do this, we have
to be thorough."

"Asher's right," Tim said. "Due diligence."

"Yeah." Ben ran his fingers through his hair.

I raised my hand and felt seven pairs of eyes on me.
Chill, Emma.

"It sounds like any one of those three has the talent to hack the network, but your outprocessing regulations mandate that their access would've been shut down even before security had them off the campus."

"And it was. Timestamps from IT and Security documented the cred lockout and time removed from campus to the second," Ben confirmed.

"And to confirm, Hugo's skill level was assessed as excellent." I turned to Asher. "Good enough to hack in?"

Asher didn't hesitate. "Yes. But the intrusion was carried out using legit credentials. The profile we can't match up yet—"

"We're tracking that down," Ben noted. "I did pin down when the profile was created. Asher, Tim, Will, and I are the only employees authorized to create user profiles and set permissions." Ben raised his hand. "I know what you're thinking. No we didn't create the profile. Yes, I have a list of people who were working at the time, but between this building and campus B across the street, there were close to four hundred people active, and that's just on the domestic side."

"So right now, it looks like this: First: Someone has created a dummy profile, for lack of a better term. Second: All three ex-employees have the skills necessary to mess around the network once inside. In addition, they have the skills to build a ghostware program, right?" I alternately pinned Asher and Ben. Both confirmed with a nod. "Third: The intrusion alarm traced to a local ISP, meaning whoever was in at that time is local. So we're back to point one. Who created the user; who unlocked the door?"

Chapter Thirty-Five

♥

A sher

"We're going to find that out today." Before I could say anything more, John spoke up.

"Miles, I want all of the information we have on Riser, Moore, and especially Wayne. I've been in touch with a private investigation firm. Before they're done, we will know everything about those guys right down to what kind of cereal they eat."

Miles was typing before John finished speaking. "I just dropped the files directly into your box."

"Thank you." He turned to Ben, then me. "Asher, damage assessment?"

"As of now, minimal if any."

"It looks like all the intruder has done is jump around subnets, specifically HR, R&D, and Tri-O-Tech, the one specifically set up for the streamline project. We did confirm that the intrusion alarm triggered because of the way the intruder was doing quick in-and-outs. There were several over less than thirty minutes. That's one of the parameters we've set for suspicious behavior."

"Taking into account I'm no tech expert, I assume all of this is documented."

"Absolutely, John. We're going after all the information we can collect before we turn this over to the cyberspooks. Caveat here: We're going to try and use the access log info to find the origin, but to get the most current addresses from the origin's ISP"—Asher nodded in Nick's direction—"will require warrants. The ISP won't release directly to us."

"If there's nothing else..." John stood.

Everyone rose and headed for the doors. I held back and tapped Emma's hand, then motioned to John as he was passing us. "John, if we could have a couple of minutes..."

"Sure."

Will was the last to leave and nodded to Emma. "See you downstairs?"

"I won't be long. I have some more information. Would you please let Ben and Tim know?"

"Consider it done." Will touched his forehead in a two finger salute in my direction. "Later, boss."

I waited until I heard the latch. Emma stood next to me, closed laptop clutched to her chest. Her armor.

"Okay, Asher, you have me. What d'you need?"

"Not need so much as more to fill you in."

"Do we need to sit?"

I shook my head. "Emma brought up the possibility of disgruntled FI employees. We're on that, and we're checking into current IT personnel. I wanted to let you know that we're going to explore another possibility." I glanced at Emma. She spoke before I could continue.

"I'm going to get right to the point. In the context of the current issue, Asher asked me today if there was anyone who might have a grudge against me. I know you're aware that John Palmer is my father. I don't call attention to it, but it does come to light occasionally. As such, I cannot discount the fact that there are people who might want to cause him problems and wouldn't hesitate to attempt to do so by causing me problems. There are also those who believe what success I've achieved in my career is due to my father's influence. It would be naïve, even foolish to ignore these possibilities, and I wanted to make you aware of them even though I'm having a problem understanding what any of that would have to do with Fantasies, Inc. or why they would try to harm me through your company."

"I see. I will make the investigator aware of this information and, if necessary, pursue it accordingly. Is there anything else?"

Emma was clearly uncomfortable, and John must have recognized it, because he worked what the rest of us called his woo-woo. Hands in pockets, stance casual and loose. Voice a bit lower, tone what some would describe as smooth. I'd seen him use this technique many times, and it never failed to put the person facing him at ease. By the time he said the last word, Emma had moved the laptop and now held it under her arm, the other arm at her side, shoulders relaxed, and her hand so close to mine, I could feel the radiated warmth.

"There is one other thing, even though I'm not sure it's relevant, but in the context of what I've just told you..." Emma glanced at me and turned back to John. "Greg Webster, a colleague at Tri-O-Tech, is not happy that I'm up for a promotion. It's been inferred that this assignment will be the catalyst for the final decision. Based on some of his remarks and how those remarks could be interpreted, this is not the first time he's felt that I'm receiving some sort of preferential treatment. Asher felt, and I agreed, that you should have this information in the interest of full disclosure."

John's smile was actually friendly, and he extended his hand. Emma hesitated for a second, clearly not quite sure what to do, then shook his hand. "I appreciate the information, and I'll pass it on. I also want to thank you for your help last night and today. I've been apprised of the excellent work you've been doing on the project and your assistance with this intrusion. Again, thank you. Now, I have to get back to the investigator, and you both have to get back to work."

John switched the woo-woo off and pinned me, his gaze sharp. "Asher, take this bastard down…hard."

"You know I will." Once John was out of the room, I pulled Emma to my side. "This is one of those times I really like saying 'I told you so'." She rested her head on my shoulder.

"You win." She raised her head, expression open, her smile warm. "Let's get this guy."

Chapter Thirty-Six

♥

E mma

The atmosphere in the Batcave was pressured, intense, focused. Tim handed me a thumb drive before I sat down. Asher went looking for Ben.

"This contains copies of code written by Baylor Moore and Hugo Wayne. Tate Riser's a good kid with a lot of potential, but at the time, he wrote code by the book, didn't know how to improvise, you know, think outside the book or the box. I had to basically rewrite most of what he did, so there isn't enough in the archive to make a comparison."

"Thanks. I found signatures, but now I'll look specifically at Baylor's and Hugo's work so that when we find the ghostware, we can do a comparison. How's the search going?"

Using the captured information, they'd managed to eliminate FI workstations. They were now checking individual devices that had the same identifier.

We were close. Now I was going to bury myself in the samples on the thumb drive.

"When you see Asher, please tell him I've gone upstairs, and I'll see him later."

I left a note on Asher's chair in the conference room before I left. Once back in the office, I locked the door, woke the boxes, put on a pot of coffee, printed a *Do Not Disturb* sign, and taped it to the door. By the time I'd hung the sign, the coffee was finished. I filled my lucky mug, grabbed a power bar from my snack stash, pulled up my playlist, adjusted my headset, and got to work.

I had a hunch and free rein on the mainframe. My quarry had walked right in through the front door because someone had given them a key. The hubris shown by not using an offshore VPN was telling. We knew this wasn't the first time, but the pattern indicated they didn't know their way around. How could that be unless they'd never been in our house before? Or was what looked like lack of direction a distraction?

What would I find if I worked backward?

Chapter Thirty-Seven

♥

Asher

I opened my fourth Red Bull, took a bite of the cold pizza, then hoisted my feet up on the edge of the table and leaned back in my chair. After the meeting with John, Ben, Tim, Will, and I reconvened in the Batcave conference room. I found Emma's note, and Tim told me about the thumb drive he'd given to her. Code samples and more tracking information, which explained why Emma had gone back to the office rather than remaining downstairs.

It turned out Will and Tim had worked through the night and finally got to the hotel just before five in the morning, grabbed a couple hours sleep and headed back to work just after seven. They'd suggested they babysit the department so Ben and I could do whatever we needed to do. When the night shift logged in, we called a rideshare and sent them home. This time, they didn't bargain or argue.

Ben and I interviewed everyone on the day and mid shifts and turned up nothing new. No surprise. I didn't expect to turn up anything. My gut was telling me the malware had come in via a phishing scheme or links in a website. Ben was sure the upload was deliberate and had been accomplished with a personal device.

Once we finished the interviews with the night shift, we agreed we'd head home. John texted us before he left to tell us he'd scheduled a meeting with the feds at three the next afternoon, now today. That would give Ben, Emma and me time to sleep and organize whatever we'd found.

After checking my cell phone multiple times for some word from Emma, Ben cornered me in the break room just before the eleven p.m. shift change.

"It's not like she's booby trapped the entire floor. Go up and check on her. You're not going to settle down until you do, and we've got to get the last interviews done."

"I went up at four and again at seven. At four, there was just a *Do Not Disturb* sign. At seven, there was a sign below it, a skull and crossbones. I'm not sure what would've happened if I'd knocked."

Ben leaned against the sink and folded his arms across his chest. "The way I see it, you can keep checking your phone and be frustrated when there's no text, or you can take your life in your hands, go upstairs and just look through the glass, or be really brave and actually knock on the door." He finished off his coffee and set the empty mug in the sink. "Your choice."

I decided the risk was worth the reward and went upstairs. Peering around the signs, I couldn't read the screen she was looking at, but she was working from both boxes and all six screens were active, her back to the door, headset in place, at least three power bar wrappers and three empty cans of Red Bull on the desk.

When Emma was free of corporate chains, she really did look like the Hollywood version of a technogenius—headset in place, probably blasting the playlist she called her coding muse, the music from artists ranging from Swift to NIN, coffee or Red Bull and power bars her fuel.

After her clapback to me in the restaurant, I'd backed off. I'd also learned a lesson. To some people, their work really was their life. Interfering with that resulted in more harm than good. I also recognized Emma worked best when not limited by others' structure. She created her own, and the results validated her style. So, when I

found her note, I understood she was pursuing something worthwhile, and it was best to leave her alone.

I opened my hand and flattened it against the glass. I
hoped she'd notice the handprint the next time she took
a break.

***

I glanced at the clock. One thirty in the morning. Night
shift was settled in; I'd finished the pizza and tossed the
box, then texted Ben.

Me: Ready to get started again?

His response was almost instant.

Ben: Meet me in my office.

Riley's next, then Craig.

We'll catch Doug after the update.

I took a couple of minutes to collect the empty drink
cans, paper plates, and another pizza box. The trash was
overflowing, so I pulled the bag, tied it off and put a
fresh one in the can. The cleaners wouldn't be in before
four. Better not to risk overflow.

Do the mundane to organize the important.

By the time I'd made a pit stop, splashed cold water on
my face, and cleaned up, it was close to ten minutes after I'd

received Ben's text. Just as I opened the door to his office, I caught a last, "What the hell is she doing?"

"Hey, Ben, sorry I took so long. Who's doing what now?"

He didn't look up from the screens on his desk. "Yo, chief. Come take a look at this. You're the only one with a direct line to the way Em the ninja's mind works. Maybe you can tell me what she's up to. I have an idea, but I want to see if you're seeing what I'm seeing."

I moved around the desk so I could stand next to Ben's chair and watch the screen. It didn't take long to figure it out.

I zeroed in on another rolling chair and pulled it over beside Ben's chair.

"Don't you look smug."

"Got any beer and popcorn? Looks like the show's just starting."

Ben leaned back, folded his arms across his chest, and answered in his best spoiled kid voice, "I won't share unless you share your secret."

"If you're gonna be that way...Benny. Look here. I think Emma's hacked the hacker."

Chapter Thirty-Eight

♥

E^{mma}

It was right where Tim suspected it would be: The HR archive. The only reason I'd been able to take a peek was because Marcus had asked me to write an update for the reminder portion of the records app that notified department directors of upcoming individual reviews. No problem. I loved the occasional jailbreak, and in order to accomplish his request, I needed access to HR. Permissions for HR were extremely narrow. Tim didn't have access to the archive.

The read-me-first note on the thumb drive was short and to the point.

Emma,

We've looked everywhere. No joy. Thought it over. Where would someone put it to hide it in plain sight? Tate's not smart enough. Baylor's a total douche. Hugo is a devious SOB and probably wrote it. Posit: Someone had to let him in. He's been gone for two years, so who'd think he'd come back and drop malware into his HR archived file. I saw Marcus's closed support ticket and the notation that you had been granted access. What harm can it do to look? T

As soon as I read the note, the pieces fell into place. Tim had even included samples of some code Hugo had written. And miracle of miracles, Will had confirmed that the malware had been uploaded from a burner phone.

I wasn't going to jump to any conclusion yet, and I wasn't going to tell anyone until I had confirmed Hugo was the author of the malware, that he was using the creds, and who he'd used to create the dummy profile.

I'd work backward, but before I began my search, I set a shadow trap. If our intruder showed up again, the profile would be tagged at login and immediately shadowed. If the intruder was this guy Hugo, I'd have to make sure the trap was well hidden.

I'm gonna drop the hammer, you SOB. You're in my house now.

***

"Know your enemy." Sun Tzu was right. I didn't wait for the files I'd requested from Asher. I had access, so I used it. Hugo Wayne's file proved to be interesting reading.

Besides being an all-around bully, Hugo had all kinds of problems with authority. On the background, there'd been some hints, but no one came right out and said anything definitive. Same for university. He explained the gaps in his resume as freelancing, everything from classes on navigating computers, to repair, to basic software installs. However, the running thread was that he was a talented, excellent developer, coder. His first review wasn't exactly glowing, but Asher was impressed with the guy's expertise.

During his employment with FI, he'd been written up several times, each incident flouting or outright breaking company policy. At one point, he was referred for counseling. Result: No change. Asher finally laid down the law and put him on probation. One more infraction, Hugo was out. Didn't even take six weeks.

When Tate tried to hack the time tracking app, he confessed that Hugo was the mastermind. The final straw. When he was faced with the evidence, he actually hit Asher. I had to admit he had some big brass ones because even when faced with the possibility of assault charges, he'd demanded FI waive the noncompete. Asher and FI decided not to press charges—seems they didn't want to wreck the guy's life but made it clear if Hugo tried to break the noncompete, all bets were off. Nick's letter documenting FI's position made it abundantly clear he'd have no problem going after the guy.

***

I had no idea how much time had passed from when I started reading the file and finished building the trap. Where to hide it in plain sight? Oh wait, it couldn't be that simple, could it? Tate Riser. And voila! There was his archived record. I threw a chef's kiss into the air. Install was flawless, and it was running in the background. If you didn't know about it, you wouldn't see it.

Sometime after the third energy drink and another power bar, I got up to stretch my legs and make a pit stop. On my way back into the office, as I input the keycode, I noticed a faint handprint on the glass that wasn't there before. I flattened my hand over it. Asher, it had to be. Butterflies in my middle and warmth all over.

"When this is over, Asher, we will pick up where we left off, and I will rock your world. Count on it." As I'd done once before, I kissed my finger and instead of his cheek, I tapped the glass.

Now, playlist number four, fresh coffee, and time to figure out how to dissect the malware without triggering whatever it had been set to unleash.

Fun times.

Chapter Thirty-Nine

♥

Asher

"Damn! Why would we look there?"

"You're right. The guy's been gone for two years. But riddle me this: She's traced the access attempts. The intruder was never able to penetrate the subnets. I get why they tried HR, R&D, Finance, even email, but why the Tri-O-Tech subnet? People, products, money, communications. Makes sense if they're trying to take down FI. Still doesn't explain T-O-T. Are the attempts on T-O-T a distraction?"

I shook my head then mentally kicked my ass. The more I thought about what Emma had found, the more convinced I became that Hugo Wayne was our intruder. Sure, everything was circumstantial, but sometimes hoof-beats really did mean horses.

I should've pressed charges, but no, I didn't want to tack a criminal record onto lousy job performance. We'd received two inquiries. Yes, he'd been employed here. Resigned. No, we wouldn't rehire.

What was he planning now? I knew Emma was going to try and dissect the malware to see if she could figure out intent. For the moment, it looked like a cyber-attack and corporate espionage. But why try to access what was essentially Emma's subnet?

"Let's finish the interviews. Once that's done, you compile everything, and I'll write the summary. Once Emma has analyzed the malware, we may have a better idea of what his plan is."

Ben tilted his head and squinted at me. "You're thinking it's Hugo, aren't you?"

I nodded and ran my finger along the edge of the desk. "Still doesn't bring us any closer to finding out who created the profile. And why he's messing with Emma's subnet."

***

Two hours. Not wasted in the usual sense but definitely fruitless. Riley and Craig had nothing new to contribute. I wasn't expecting a Hollywood level confession, but I was interested in their insights into the problem and their observations and if they'd encountered anything they considered out of the ordinary.

Doug had finished the update, and I asked Craig to send him in. Twenty minutes ago. I was impatient to finish this and get back upstairs to see what Emma was working on.

I was so far inside my head, I didn't hear a knock on the door.

"That's probably Doug."

The kid looked unsure, even anxious. He froze when he saw me, then managed to recover.

"You wanted to see me?"

"Asher, you remember Doug Randall, support specialist?"

"Yes, I do. Good to see you again, Doug."

We shook hands. "Sorry to interrupt your shift. Ben and I wanted your input regarding the intrusion issue. Please… have a seat."

We were seated at the round table in Ben's office. Doug seemed like a fish out of water. I didn't blame him. He'd only been with the company for less than eighteen months. He'd come through the probationary period with flying colors, and his first performance review was unremarkable. Not unusual since he'd joined FI right after graduation from State.

Once settled, Ben and I began with general information to help Doug relax. He was more than a little nervous. As the questions became more specific, his answers began to become defensive. He couldn't sit still, and I noticed perspiration on his upper lip. Ben tried to reassure him.

"This isn't an inquisition, Doug. You haven't done anything wrong. I'm sorry if you got that impression. We're looking for your thoughts, insights."

"May I have some water?"

"Sure. I'll get it." Ben stopped at the door. "Do you want anything, Asher?"

"I'm good, thanks."

After Ben left, the silence was heavy. Doug wouldn't look at me, and his anxiety level had risen. I decided to try and shift gears.

"The new servers are scheduled for delivery in about a week. Have you met Emma Palmer yet? You're rotating to day shift right about that time, and you'll be working with her."

If he hadn't been sitting down, I'm sure he would've passed out. All the color drained from his face, leaving a greenish-gray pallor. With his color and the fact that he was sweating, I wasn't going to take chances.

My brother insisted our parents, my sister, and I take CPR classes. He was a total nag about keeping current. This kid was the textbook picture of an active heart attack. As I stood to check him out, I heard the door open, but I didn't take my eyes off Doug.

"I'd ask if you're okay, but it's clear you aren't. Are you in pain?" Doug was trying to pull in air.

Ben set the water bottle on his desk and grabbed his cell phone. "I'm calling 9-1-1. The emergency call button is right outside the door. Help's on the way, man."

"Don't...I can't...I...don't..."

"We're not taking any chances. Ben I've got Doug. You call—"

"*No.*" His color was starting to improve, but he still looked like the walking dead—or pretty damn close to it. "A minute...give...me...a...a...just a minute..."

I raised my hand. "Wait, Ben."

Then...

"I can't...do this."

Ben was kneeling beside the chair. I took hold of Doug's wrist and his pulse was racing but regular, and his color was improving. Air exchange was better. He wasn't in great shape, but I was confident that we probably didn't need the ambulance.

"Asher, what happened?"

Doug was trembling now, probably an adrenaline reaction, but his pulse was slowing a bit.

I glanced at Ben then resumed watching the kid. "I asked Doug if he'd met Emma yet and told him that he'd be working with her when he rotated to day shift. And this happened." I didn't let go of his wrist but leaned over to try and catch his gaze. "Hey, look at me. Ben, give Doug the water."

The water appeared and Doug accepted the bottle with his free hand and downed nearly half of the eleven ounce bottle. His pulse was almost in the normal range, so I let go of his wrist. He set the bottle on the table as Ben sat back down.

"Hey, Doug, look at me. What's going on?" I exchanged a look with Ben and then turned back to Doug. "What happened?"

Silence. I glanced at Ben and shook my head and raised a finger. *Give him a minute...*

When Doug looked up and pinned Ben and then me that lightbulb popped on followed by a sense of dread, followed by disappointment, then anger, but not at the person in the chair in front of me. I turned to Ben. He'd closed his eyes and slouched just a bit in his seat.

"I can't do this. No amount of money for any reason is worth this. I'll tell you anything you want to know."

And there it was. The final piece of the puzzle. "What can't you do, Doug?" Ben prompted.

Doug leaned forward and braced his elbows on his knees, hands folded between them. I leaned back in my seat. "Take whatever time you need," I said.

When he raised his head, he looked broken, deflated. "Do you need to get security in here, Legal, the police?"

We shook our heads. Ben deferred to me. "Not right now. Would you like us to contact anyone? Would you like to call an attorney?"

The full minute of silence that followed my questions was heavy, almost sad. Doug had lowered his head, then shook it once.

"You need to speak, Doug. Your answer has to be clear," Ben cautioned.

He shook his head again. "No, I don't need you to call anyone, and I don't want to talk with a lawyer. It is what it is."

The text tone on my phone sounded deafening in the silence after his statement. Emma. I picked up the phone.

Emma: It was a diversion.

The pattern matches. E.
Me: Can't come up now.
Big break. More later. A.

I put the phone back on the table, screen down. "Sorry for the interruption. Doug, we have all the time you need."

He finished the water. I didn't realize Ben had another bottle until he put the second bottle on the table.

"Do you want to record this?" *Oooookaaaaay.* A glance at Ben and a quick nod.

I picked up my phone again. "Yes, I think that's a good idea." I set up the voice memo app. "Do I have everyone's permission to record this meeting?"

"Yes."

"Yes."

Time to get the legalese out of the way. I gave the date, time, location, confirmed that Doug waived having an attorney present. Each of us repeated that permission had been granted to record.

"Start at the beginning, Doug. Whenever you're ready," I prompted.

And for the next hour, he told a story that was almost unbelievable. The confluence of circumstances had to be one in more than a million.

He was a member of an online gaming group; five lived in the local area, and they met occasionally at a bar south of Seattle. This had been going on for nearly three and a half years. The other four were Hugo Wayne, Baylor Moore, Greg Webster, and Lee Milligan. I knew that in the tech community, like other professions, especially in a local area, eventually, if you lived and worked in the same area long enough, everyone knew or knew of everyone else.

After we fired Baylor, he was hired at one of the big box electronics stores, hated the job, but couldn't get hired at the big tech firms. No surprise.

Hugo was a different story. Doug said he couldn't get a job, and his unemployment had run out. He'd lost his apartment and had moved in with Baylor. He definitely had a log on his shoulder toward FI because he thought we'd blackballed him. Doug's observation was spot on: Hugo insisted that everything that had ever happened to him was everyone else's fault, and why couldn't people see that he was an expert.

Greg Webster and Lee Milligan worked for Tri-O-Tech—the connection and the grudge. Doug explained that when I mentioned Emma, everything came together, and he knew it was only a matter of time. Greg made sure they all knew that Emma was the daughter of the guy that owned some big tech firm, Palmer Logistics or Technology or something, and she'd either slept her way up or daddy had somehow smoothed the way. Now Greg and Emma were up for the same promotion. Greg went ballistic when Emma was assigned to the project.

"I knew Tri-O-Tech was handling the expansion and streamlining, but I didn't make the connection until you asked if I knew her."

The plan was Hugo's idea. The malware was ransomware hidden in ghostware. Hugo stored it in plain sight. He would send Doug the trigger from a burner phone to a dummy FI email after Hugo duplicated the R&D project file that contained designs, drawings, and data on new products. He intended to sell it—Doug had no idea who the buyer was—had the buyer all lined up. Supposedly by the time the ransom money had been wired to an offshore account, Hugo, Baylor, Doug, and Lee would be out of the country, destination somewhere that had no extradition treaty with the US.

Greg intended to try and sabotage any work that Emma was doing on the expansion, tank the project, then somehow convince Tri-O-Tech management to let him come to the rescue. Greg wanted nothing to do with the ransomware attack. His only involvement was to ruin Emma.

"I know this all sounds like a B grade movie. All it's missing is the jilted lover. Turns out Lee wanted to get with Emma, said the idea was if he got with Emma, maybe she could put in a good word with her dad, but she ignored him. He said she acted like she was too good for everyone. Barely spoke to anyone.

"Anyway, I tried to tell them the plan wouldn't work because of how tight security is. Hugo said between him, Baylor and me, we'd figure something out. That was right before he got caught by the intrusion alarms. I was going to tell you; I swear, and then Craig told me you wanted to see me. I was sure it was because you found out."

Ben spoke for both of us. Doug seemed like he had his life together. "Why did you get involved in this? You're the last person I would've thought would have anything to do with something like this."

Doug scoffed on a bitter laugh. "The person you see today isn't the person I was as a kid. When I was fourteen, I stole a car. It belonged to a guy who lived at the other end of our street. Ever seen that movie about the old guy who restored an old car? He hated anyone that came around his place. They must've used old man Griffith as the inspiration. It was a black Vette. I got caught, charged with grand theft. If it hadn't been for old man Griffith, they probably would've put me in juvie until I was eighteen. The DA wanted at least three years. Mr. G tried to get them to drop the charges, but that wasn't happening, so Mr. G talked the DA into one year and got the record sealed.

Hugo found it. Said if I didn't help get them in, he'd send the record to HR.

"I fucked up again and here we are."

Chapter Forty

E mma

I watched the data scroll over my screen and pumped my arm in the air as I jumped from my chair and danced to an old rock song.

"*Emma*," a loud voice called. I turned to see Asher leaning against the wall next to the office door, arms folded across his chest, his expression a mix of curiosity and amusement.

I continued with random dance steps as I pulled my headset down, grinning in my triumph.

I punched my fist in the air. *V. I. C. T. O. R. Y.*

"I got the sucker." I hadn't felt a high like this since...well...*that* night. Who knew victory could feel almost as good as sex?

Elation filled me. I'd not only found the asshole who was trying to get into FI's system, but I'd figured out what that lowlife was trying to do.

"Who?"

"The hacker and what they were looking for."

"What?"

"I set a little trap, and he took the bait." I spun around and pointed to the right computer monitor. "It's all here. It was actually pretty genius. He hid his actions in plain sight."

Asher moved closer to look at the monitor. "That's the archive files."

"Yep. Probably the last place we'd ever look." Taking a deep breath, I continued. "I also found traces of Hugo." I wanted to dance some more, but a very subtle change in Asher's expression held me back. "You and Ben find something too?" My happiness dipped a little bit.

"We did. Sit."

I plopped down onto my chair and turned off the music still blaring from my headset. "How bad?" Damn, I was hoping this was the end of it, and we could turn everything over to law enforcement.

"Worse than we knew. Ben and I have been interviewing the night crew."

"Right. Someone knew something?" I wanted to be so wrong about this being an inside job, but all the evidence pointed there.

"Doug."

"I haven't met him."

"You would have next week when he rotated off the night shift to day shift."

I nodded. "What did he say?" Everything in me tensed up. How much damage had been done that we hadn't seen?

"Doug told us the file hidden in Hugo's folder is ransomware disguised as ghostware."

"I know. Hugo's the author. His signature was nearly impossible to find, but it's there." I grabbed my pencil and pointed to the lines of code on the screen. "Look. There's the proof."

"Fuck."

"The best part? It hasn't been triggered, and I've neutralized it and walled it off so they can't do any damage. Not only that, I've tagged the hacker with my own ghostware, so they'll be easy to find, but the tag is invisible on their device."

Asher rubbed his forehead. The lines of stress on his face hit me hard. I cupped his cheek, hoping to ease some of his concern. "Hey, we're about to hand the cyberspooks the entire case. Why do you look like you've lost your best friend?"

Asher took my hand, entwined our fingers and squeezed. "I'm afraid there's more."

His tone was so serious I suddenly felt like the floor had tilted, and whatever excitement I'd been feeling to that point dissipated like smoke in the wind.

"Ben and I didn't understand why Doug would help Hugo and his cohorts do this. Turns out, he's got a juvie record, and they threatened to expose him."

"You said cohorts, who else did Doug name?"

"There was Hugo, Baylor another former employee, Greg Webster, and Lee Milligan."

I could feel the blood drain out of my face. Good thing I was sitting down.

"Greg and Lee?" I knew Greg wasn't happy with me working on this project since we were both up for the same promotion, but Lee?

"Yes." Asher's fingers tightened around mine.

"But why?" Then it hit me. "Son of a..." I pulled my hand away from Asher and turned to the computer monitors. "This explains so much."

"What do you mean?"

"I'd noticed someone trying to access our subnet but couldn't figure out why." I tapped the monitor showing the access pattern.

"Greg was trying to sabotage your work," Asher said softly.

"To what end? If he wanted the promotion that bad he could have put in the work." I really didn't understand it. Was I that naïve?

"Emma." Asher cupped my chin and turned my face away from the monitor. "Greg was attempting to sabotage your work here at FI so he could ride in and fix everything." Asher's eyes darkened. "He was going to ruin your reputation and make sure you were fired."

Asher's words cut to the bone. Now I understood the origin of the phrase 'stabbed in the back'. Greg was prepared to have me blackballed in the profession I loved and excelled at, because he couldn't compete with me. "That doesn't explain why Lee is a part of this."

"From what Doug said, he wanted to date you, but you rebuffed him."

I shook my head. "Yes, I told Lee no when he asked me, every time. I had no interest in him." Well, this sealed the deal. I couldn't go back to Tri-O-Tech.

"And he took that as a personal insult."

Closing my eyes, I took a deep breath. Assholes.

Asher and his team treated me as an equal instead of the enemy. Time to take these misogynistic assholes down. "We have all the pieces now."

"We do."

"Let me get this all copied over with some information. Do you think a meeting with Legal is appropriate?"

"Yes, us, Legal, and John. This can all be turned over to law enforcement and let them take it from there." Asher dropped a kiss on my forehead. "Are you okay?"

Was I? I wasn't sure yet. I had to be strong for a little bit longer, then I could allow Asher to hold me while I processed everything. "I'll be fine."

"Emma."

I knew that tone. "Asher, this isn't the time or place. After we turn all of this over, then we can comfort each other."

"Promise?"

I bit my lip so I wouldn't smile. "Yes."

"All right." He dropped another kiss on my forehead. "I'll call the meeting."

Chapter Forty-One

Asher

I wanted to hold Emma's hand as we walked into the conference room where John and Nick waited. This was going to be hard on both of us, but I was worried about Emma.

"You have news?" Nick asked.

"Yes." I held Emma's chair out for her, once she was seated, I took the chair next to her.

"Earlier today," Emma started. "I put out a shadow tracker and the hacker took the bait. I found ransomware disguised as ghostware in the archived file for Hugo Wayne."

Nick sat forward.

"While Emma was doing that, Ben and I were interviewing the night crew," I said. "Doug Randall confessed to being the inside guy." I held up my hand when Nick went to speak. "Short version: Doug Randall was the inside guy. Hugo and Baylor, two former FI employees are involved and Greg Webster and Lee Milligan, two Tri-O-Tech employees, are working with them. Webster's motive was to sabotage Emma's work, get her fired, so he could swoop in and save the project. Milligan's motive is revenge, because Emma wasn't interested in dating him. Hugo was the mastermind; Baylor played along for revenge. Randall was essentially blackmailed to be the fall guy."

Nick let out a whistle. "Why would Tri-O-Tech employees want to come after us?"

"Like Asher said, they weren't interested in FI," Emma commented. "It was about professional jealousy and revenge. Trying to ruin me."

Emma was so matter of fact it worried me. Was she burying everything? I hoped not. She needed to let out her anger at what happened.

"Nick, next steps?" John prompted.

Nick looked at us. "I assume you've contacted the local FBI field office for the pickup?"

"Ben and I recorded Doug's confession after we covered all the legal bases. He declined legal counsel before and during the recording. Security has Doug in custody and will hold him until the feds pick him up. They're due here within the hour."

Emma slid two flash drives over to Nick. "These are exact duplicates, one for us and one for the feds. The drive contains all of the information the feds will need. Chain of custody is meticulously documented. The confession is included. I've made sure everything is readable across all platforms."

"Thank you both. I'll get on this." Nick stood and left the room.

The silence after Nick's departure lasted only seconds but felt like hours. The problem had been solved, but now we'd have to deal with the aftermath.

John leaned forward in his seat. "Asher, I'd like to take this opportunity to thank you and your team for the outstanding work you've all done here. I have no doubt the Board will want to meet with you in the immediate future."

He turned to Emma. "Thank you seems inadequate. I will be petitioning the Board for a written and monetary commendation for you. Your work has saved this company millions. You are an incredible asset to your employer and an outstanding member of your profession. Thank you, and I know I speak for my entire company when I say we are lucky to have you as project manager for the coming expansion."

Emma ducked her head, and her cheeks turned pink.

"Thank you. I look forward to our continued association."

"I couldn't agree more."

We stood as John rose from his seat. He shook our hands and left.

I turned Emma to face me, wrapped her in my arms, and wondered if she was as exhausted as I felt just then. "Let's go home, Emma."

She pulled away just enough that she could capture my gaze.

"Yes, let's go home. Now that the crisis is over, it's time to make good on my promise to rock your world."

Chapter Forty-Two

♥

E mma

I polished off my burger and fries quickly. Asher had picked up the food on our way to his house. Thank goodness, I'd totally forgotten about food with everything going on. One could only survive on Red Bull and protein bars for so long.

"You were hungry," Asher said.

"Like you weren't. I only ate one burger. You ate two."

He grinned. "I'll need my energy."

"Oh?" I picked up the wrappings and carried them to the trash.

"You do know you're staying here tonight."

I glanced at him. "I'd hoped you'd ask, but I don't have a change of clothes."

"I have a washer and dryer, and I'm sure I can find you something to wear."

The image of me in one of Asher's white shirts flashed in my mind. "I'd like that."

"Great." He sprang up and made a beeline for his bedroom.

I shook my head. Asher seemed to have rebounded quickly after what we learned today. I was still processing. I was aware Greg disliked me, but apparently, it went way deeper than that. I had no idea what I'd done to make him hate me so much that he would sabotage a project I was working on.

My breath caught. If I stayed in tech, would that ever change? Tears burned behind my eyes. I didn't want to leave tech; I loved it too much, but how could I continue?

Working with Asher and his team showed me what it felt like to be a valued member of a team. I needed to think about this, because there was no way I'd go work at my father's company. That would be worse than Tri-O-Tech.

Asher came back into the room with a pair of sweats and a t-shirt in his hands. "I think these will work."

Hiding a smile at his choice, I took them and went into the bathroom to change. Of course, they were a little big on me, but that was okay. I threw all my clothes in the washer, then met Asher in the kitchen.

"You're thinking about work," he said.

"How could you tell?"

"You stiffened and got a faraway look in your eyes."

"Sorry. I really feel like I've missed something else."

"Emma." He cupped my shoulders. "If you did, it was so tiny it shouldn't matter. I want you to relax now. We've all had a busy forty-eight hours." He pulled me into his arms.

"You're right." I leaned against his chest. Worrying wasn't going to help. Not right now, anyway.

"I'm always right."

I playfully hit his arm. "Not always."

"Always." He guided me to the sofa and gave me the two things I needed most.

Cuddled in his arms, we watched some disaster movie, and I finally fell asleep.

Chapter Forty-Three

♥

A sher

My steps were light when we walked into Fantasies, Inc. the next morning. Holding Emma in my arms all night did that to me. She'd fallen asleep in my arms on the sofa and barely stirred when I carried her to bed.

She'd been as exhausted as I was, but my body was wired this morning. "Coffee and food before we head up?"

"In a second." Emma pulled me off to the side. "What happens now?"

"What do you mean?"

"Someone from Tri-O-Tech tried to sabotage your systems and derail a multi-million dollar project. Do I still have a contract here?"

I blinked in shock. "Of course you do."

Emma shook her head. "There is no 'of course'."

The worry in her eyes made me draw her into my embrace, and she didn't resist. "Emma, you were instrumental in discovering the ransomware and chasing down all the evidence we needed."

"You and Ben got the confession."

"Which wouldn't have happened if you hadn't realized there was an insider component." Her forehead wrinkled with worry. "FI needs you."

"Just FI?" Her voice was soft.

"More than FI." I was being honest with her. I wanted...*needed* Emma in my life. "Now let's get something to eat and drink. We've got a project to finish up."

"Yes, boss." She slipped from my embrace and gave me a cheeky salute. For the moment, everything was right in our world.

Chapter Forty-Four

♥

Emma

I sat back in my chair with a sigh. The last three weeks had been busy ones. The new mainframe had been installed and configured without a hitch, and go-live was flawless. We finally got all the apps up and running, and on version ten, at my insistence. The international bridge still needed some minor tweaks, but we anticipated those would be completed in the next couple of weeks.

"We did it," Asher said.

"I can't believe it."

"I'm so glad we extended your contract. We can finish up the final clean-up in the next couple of weeks."

"Yes." I was glad we had extended it as well. Nick had let us know the FBI was pressing charges, and they were grateful for everything we sent. Plus Tri-O-Tech higher ups were cooperating and had been cleared of any wrongdoing.

None of that made any difference to me. I'd made some decisions about my future and wasn't about to change my mind.

I was honestly surprised at how fast the feds jumped on this until Nick mentioned John had an old friend at the Seattle FBI office, and the government took ransomware *very* seriously.

"I think we need to celebrate tonight."

I laughed. "You like to celebrate everything."

He grinned at me. "Since it's Friday, we can all meet up at Whistle Stop."

"As if we don't do that already." I was game. I really enjoyed our Friday night get-togethers.

I hadn't mentioned to Asher, yet, that I wasn't going back to Tri-O-Tech. The prospect of looking for a new job wasn't ideal either. John approached me about a job at FI, and I was still mulling that over. I enjoyed working with Asher and his team. They were great.

But how could I continue a relationship with Asher and still work with him? These past few weeks, we'd spent time at each other's homes. That was all fine because I knew my contract was coming to an end, but long term? I wondered how Cassie and Marcus handled it.

Was I ready to give Asher up? Hell, no. While I wasn't totally anti-social, certain situations still made me uncomfortable, and Asher understood. He grounded me in ways no one else had ever done. At times, it scared me, and at other times, it was pure comfort.

But I couldn't help wondering when the other shoe was going to drop, because it always did. I pushed the thought away. Asher and I were solid.

At four, we left the office and headed for the Whistle Stop. We grabbed a table for twelve as Asher asked Ben, Tim, and Will to join us. By six, everyone had arrived, and we were joking, laughing, and eating.

It made me happy to be a part of this family. Was I going to give this up? No. Decision made. Now all I had to do was execute it.

"I can hear you thinking," Asher whispered.

I smiled. "It's all good things." Tilting my head, I placed a kiss on his cheek.

"What until I get you home."

"And what do you plan to do to me?" Teasing him had become fun for me and something I enjoyed doing. Sometimes I could wind him up, and at other times, he'd just give me a look to let me know it wasn't the time. Tonight, his eyes darkened with desire.

"Just wait."

I squirmed in my seat. After we bid everyone good night, the drive to his house was silent, but I couldn't sit still. I was teeming with anticipation at what Asher had planned.

The second I stepped inside, he swept me into his arms, carried me to his bedroom. The anticipation was part of the foreplay, and once I was on my feet, he stripped my clothes off.

"You take my breath away." He dropped a kiss on my lips, and he took his clothes off.

"I could say the same of you." I ran my finger over his chest to his hard cock.

"Behave." He swept me into his arms and laid me on the bed before joining me. He cupped my cheek. "Rest." He pulled the covers over us.

"Don't you want me to take care of this?" I ran my fingers over his erection.

"No. I'm always hard for you. Tonight is for us to just be." He gave me a kiss and nudged me to turn over. I complied.

My back was against his chest, his arm over my waist, and the other above my head. Cherished. That was the feeling that went through me. But I couldn't resist wiggling against his cock.

"Behave, woman."

I grinned. This is where I wanted to be in Asher's arms and in his bed.

Chapter Forty-Five

♥

Asher

It was Friday, again. We'd both worked hard this week, finishing up the international bridge and making the last tweaks on the various departmental apps.

It was also technically Emma's last day. When she told me this morning that she was going to be late today, I was okay with it. But when I asked why, she wouldn't tell me.

I wasn't happy with her keeping secrets, but I let it go for now. Things between us were going smoothly, and I was ready to take our relationship to the next level. I was nervous about it mainly because I wasn't sure how Emma felt.

Yes, she seemed happy, and we were well matched in and out of bed. While I didn't have the best track record when it came to relationships, I really felt it was different with Emma.

Picking up the phone, I got Miles and John on a call. John had offered Emma a job if she wanted it; I was going to make sure that offer was still on the table. I was just hanging up when the object of my thoughts breezed into the office.

"I'm free." She twirled around with her arms in the air.

"What do you mean?" Was she happy our working together was coming to an end? My heart dropped to my toes.

"I quit Tri-O-Tech."

My mouth dropped open. "That's what you were doing?"

"Yes. After finding out Greg and Lee were trying to ruin my career, and with what I realized was the toxic environment at Tri-O-Tech, I decided I'd had enough."

"But your promotion?"

"Not important. I decided a while back it wasn't worth it, and I was going to decline."

"You're not upset you don't have a job?" This played right into my hands in convincing her to stay.

"No. I feel as if a weight has lifted."

"Good. Then I hope this will make you even happier?"
"What?"

"I want you to come to work with me here at Fantasies, Inc." I held my breath.

Her eyes grew wide. "Here? Permanently?"

"Yep." Standing, I encircled her waist and held her close. "John is on board. Remember the job offer? It's still on the table."

"I..." Tears filled her eyes.

"Hey..."

"I'm so overwhelmed. Asher, I can't believe you did this for me. Won't Ben and the others be upset?"

"Are you kidding? Ben, Tim, and Will adore you. Just as I love you."

"You love me?" The astonishment in her voice made me chuckle.

"I do. I think I fell in love with you when you walked into the building that fateful morning."

"Oh Asher." She rested her head against my chest. "I..."

"Hey." Cupping her chin, I lifted her head, dismayed to see tears in her eyes. "Baby, don't cry."

"I love you too."

I stared at her, taking in every curve of her face, the curl of her eyelashes, and the wispy curls at her temples before I grinned. "When did you realize you loved me?"

"I think during the whole hacking/ransomware issue. You let me do what I needed to and didn't try to interfere. You are such a special man."

"What did I do to deserve your loyalty?"

"You see me."

"I will always see you. Do you know how hard it's been decoding you?"

"Decoding me? Are you telling me..."

I chuckled. "Yes, I've been working hard at trying to figure out how you tick, and while I don't have it down pat, I do understand you better."

She laughed. "Now that we have that out of the way. When do I start becoming a permanent employee?"

"When you say yes."

"Yes, yes, yes." She threw her arms around my neck and hugged me.

"Good. Everything will be official Monday, but for to-day? I have plans for us."

"What type of plans?"

"Me." I pointed to myself. "You." I pointed to her. "And a beach house where we can be alone for the entire week-end, and I don't even care if I don't see the beach."

Emma laughed. "Sounds like a plan to me."

Epilogue

♥

Emma

I've never been happier in my life. My life has changed so much in the past two weeks. Asher and I spent the weekend at his beach house, then I started at Fantasies, Inc. as a permanent employee.

A week later, Asher asked me to move in with him, and I said yes. While I hated giving up the little house I'd been renting, my love for Asher has grown each and every day. I wanted to be with him.

I glanced over at him as he was talking with Marcus while we sat at Whistle Stop. Our normal Friday night hang out.

"I am so glad this FBI investigation is behind us, and all the culprits have been arrested," Miles said.

"Here, here," Marcus said as we all held up our beers and clinked our glasses and bottles.

"What happened with Doug?" Lucas asked.

"Ben and I advocated with the DA. Doug turned himself in and told them the same story. The DA agreed to help him as much as they could, but the final decision on any deal will rest with the courts."

In a way, I felt bad for Doug. He'd been blackmailed into helping Hugo and the others. I hoped it worked out for him because he was a nice guy. He'd called me to apologize for his participation in what had happened.

Asher placed his hand on my leg. Heat followed, as it always did. My body recognized his touch and reacted. As they continued to chat about Doug, I thought back to the call from my parents a week ago.

They'd heard about Tri-O-Tech's troubles from the news, and they were concerned. My father started pressuring me to make a statement, to come home and work from him. I couldn't hide how upset they were making me. Asher took my phone out of my hand and calmly explained that no, Emma didn't need to address the press. No, she wasn't going to testify because the FBI had confessions. No, she wasn't going to be homeless because she had him. Then he ended the call.

I'd stared at Asher before I burst out laughing as I pictured the outrage on my parents' faces when he told them off and hung up. He did what I'd intended to do.

Asher was so good for me. I placed my hand over his and squeezed. He glanced at me and winked.

"Hey, Miles," Lucas said. "Did you finish the paperwork for the forensic accountant?"

A more pleasant topic, in my opinion.

"Yeah. She's arriving Monday, right?"

"Yes. I'll meet her in the lobby and take her up to your office so you can get her all set up."

"Forensic accountant?" I asked. "Don't you have one on retainer?"

Lucas shook his head. "We don't need one full time. But in this case, we're buying one of our small supply companies, and something is fishy in their books, so I want a full forensic analysis before I agree to the purchase."

That made sense. I hoped the forensic accountant was a male because I could see a woman being overwhelmed by Lucas.

"Once an accountant, always an accountant," Josh commented.

"You got that right." Lucas grinned.

I loved this camaraderie. The group had folded me into their team, and I didn't mind it at all. No one here ever made me feel inferior.

"You okay?" Asher whispered in her ear.

"Fine. I'm just happy to be in such good company."

"I like to think of them as a found family."

My heart stuttered. "I like that. Found family."

"And you're a part of it."

"Yes, I am." My life had improved for the better, and I was no longer afraid of being social. I was happy to be a part of this found family and to have them in my life.

***

I hope you've enjoyed Emma and Asher's story. Please leave a review wherever you feel comfortable it does help with author visibility.

Bonus Material – I have two pieces of bonus material you can download for fun.

HR Handbook for Decoding Emma: https://BookHi p.com/CHGCJFJ

Fun Bookmarks for Decoding Emma: https://BookH ip.com/LJFNWAR

Next up will be Lucas the director of Finance and Valerie a forensic account who is hired and the woman Lucas never forgot. You can preorder here: https://books2read .com/AssessingTheRisks

About the author

M arie Tuhart lives in the beautiful Pacific Northwest with her two dogs, Tommy and Trina. Marie writes hot contemporary and mafia romances that deliver morally gray heroes, fearless heroines, and an intoxicating blend of passion, power, and play. Safe to read, impossible to resist. She provides a secure place to indulge your darkest cravings and most delicious fantasies. Embrace the temptation.

Check out Marie's website at: https://www.marietuhart.com

Other Books by Marie Tuhart

♥

Tempt (Wicked Sanctuary Series)

Entice (Wicked Sanctuary Series)

Seduce (Wicked Sanctuary Series)

Ravish (Wicked Sanctuary Series)

Possess (Wicked Sanctuary Series)

Tantalize (Wicked Sanctuary Series)

Edged (Wicked Sanctuary Series)

Unmasked (Wicked Sanctuary Series)

Too Hot (Wicked Sanctuary Series)

Wicked Sanctuary Novellas:

Untamed

Power Play

Claiming Rose

Standalone Books:

Embracing Desire

Broken Rules

Tangled Temptation

One Weekend in Seattle

One Wicked Weekend

www.ingramcontent.com/pod-product-compliance
Lightning Source LLC
Chambersburg PA
CBHW040513170726
48295CB00012B/187